Sta

MW01134259

. . . and Other

Writings

Tammy Marshall

1

A compilation of some of my sweetest writings in honor

of my dear friend

Amy Marie Vojtech Beran (1968—2018)

<u>Table of Contents</u>

Solitude

Solitude: a time for reflection.
During this quiet time,
We discover ourselves,
Inner ambitions and desires,
Whose whispers go unnoticed
Amidst the din of daily life,
Through tranquility are heard.
From solitude comes direction.
Shh . . . . Listen.

State of Georgia

A novel

Chapter One

The flowers were beginning to give her a headache. Not just the cloying smell of them, but the sight of them – too many of them – arranged neatly by the undertaker's assistant at the front of the church. The largest, a spray of lilies, carnations and daisies with its "husband," "father," and "grandfather" labelled ribbons prominently displayed, lay across the now-closed casket. *Why did people feel the need to send things that die to a funeral of all places, and why give them to a dead man who never appreciated the sight of a single flower his whole life?* Georgia almost chuckled at the ludicrousness of her thoughts, but fortunately she caught herself in time. She'd hate to emit a giggle, or worse, a guffaw, and ruin the widow-in-mourning image she was supposed to be exuding.

Georgia knew she shouldn't be ungrateful, especially since it was her own husband, or his body at least, lying in the casket only a few feet in front of her, but the past few days had been trying. She'd only begun to accept the fact that Donald was gone. He wouldn't be coming in the back door this evening and letting it slam behind him, a nightly ritual intended to catch the attention of his beloved semi-deaf beagle, Bowser, who would startle awake from his sleeping spot by the big front window, struggle to his feet and toddle to his master, tail wagging like mad.

She gave a small start in her pew as she realized that she hadn't thought about Bowser for the past few days. *Dear God, had anybody been feeding and watering the poor animal?* she wondered to herself before leaning toward her daughter and whispering, "Have you been taking care of Bowser?"

Sally, her middle child and devoted daddy's girl, glanced disapprovingly at her mother over the sodden tissue she held to her mouth. "Yes, he's fine. I fed him before we left the house."

Georgia nodded and patted her daughter's arm. "Thank you, honey." She felt Sally pull away from her in a gentle yet firm manner, as if to say 'how can you be thinking of the dog at a time like this!' Raising her eyes to the pulpit, Georgia attempted to focus on what the man up there was saying, but it seemed to be reaching her ears as nothing more than white noise.

Suddenly, she realized that those on either side of her were standing, and she began to rise also, but she felt her legs shake a bit, so she sat back down. Randy, her eldest son, bent down to assist her. "You all right, Mom?" he asked in a worried tone as he helped her stand. He kept her arm tucked into his while they waited for everyone to find the right page in the hymnal.

"Yes, dear. It's just a bit warmish in here, that's all." She smiled up at him and noticed how gray he'd become this last year. Where had her little boy gone? Tears began to well up as she saw him in her mind's eye bounding down the stairs and out into the freshly fallen snow – a ten-year-old full of joy at a day off from school.

Randy saw the tears form and said, "It'll be O.K., Mom."

She nodded and blinked back the tears. Of course it would be O.K. Why was everyone saying this to her? Did they really think that she was going to curl up into a ball and rock back and forth like some clichéd crazy person who didn't know what to do with herself now that her husband of forty-three years was dead?

Georgia looked at the casket as the pallbearers moved into place behind it. It was just a big shiny box. She knew that Donald was in it, but she didn't feel anything about that. She had to wonder why it was that she didn't seem to care that he was gone. That wasn't really fair to herself, though, because she did care; she cared very much. But there wasn't anything she could do about it.

She wasn't the one who had suddenly dropped dead at the table a few nights ago. One minute he was watching the evening news and grumbling about the weather report, and the next minute he was silent. She'd been at the sink rinsing off her plate to put it into the dishwasher because she always finished first and left him to watch the news while she got a jumpstart on grading papers or preparing something for the next day's lessons.

She'd had the garbage disposal running and hadn't quite heard what he'd said, so when she shut it off and leaned over to put things in the dishwasher, she'd asked, "What did you say?" He hadn't replied.

She'd stood up and looked at him to say something else, and that's when she'd noticed that he was slumped awkwardly in his chair with his arms hanging at his sides. In her haste to get to him, she'd tripped over the open dishwasher door and fallen hard, bruising her shin and her shoulder where she landed.

Rubbing that shoulder now, Georgia turned to follow Sally and her family down the church's main aisle. Randy took her arm, and she could feel his protectiveness coming through her skin.

He'd been the first person she'd called. "Did you call an ambulance?" he'd asked her and had been shocked to find out that she hadn't.

She did call one eventually, but there had been no reason to rush. It had been clear to her once she'd pulled herself off the floor and hurried to Donald that he was gone – gone to a place from which he wasn't coming back.

She remembered looking up at him from her crouched position next to his chair, really looking at him for the first time in years. Who was this man? She didn't even recognize the Donald she'd married. This man was an old man; he was no longer the Donald she'd fallen in love with.

She'd cried then, even though no tears had fallen yet today. Oh, how she'd cried. A part of her had secretly hoped the Donald of her dreams would return, but now that he was dead, she knew there was no hope of that happening. She'd pulled a chair close to his, picked up his limp arm and held his hand until Randy showed up.

Then Randy had joined her and sat on the other side of his father, holding his right hand. Finally, Randy had risen and made the other calls that had to be made –

the first to the hospital to make everything official, the second to his two siblings, Sally and Jerry.

Jerry had the furthest to travel as he was stationed in Honolulu, but he still managed to arrive only a few hours after Sally and her brood of five children and one hard-to-manage husband appeared. She, though, had been the most distraught, and Georgia had been secretly relieved that her daughter couldn't arrive sooner because she brought too much intensity with her.

However, she was glad to see her grandchildren. Sally's five were her only ones. Randy's wife had left him for another man shortly after their wedding, and despite a series of relationships, he hadn't been able to bring himself to permanently commit again. Jerry, she felt certain, was a bona fide bachelor for life, or at least as long as the Air Force kept him moving from place to place. She had a feeling he'd found a special someone in Hawaii, but that was just a mother's hunch – or her secret hope.

When Sally had arrived, her eldest, Willow, had rushed to her grandmother's side and hugged her hard. Georgia remembered wincing a bit from the pain she'd inflicted upon her still tender shoulder, but she'd been so happy to see Willow again. Of all her grandchildren, Willow was the most special to her, and the girl knew it, too.

Almost a teenager now, Willow had peered into her grandmother's eyes with adult compassion and said, "Don't worry, Grandma. You still have me."

Now as Georgia stepped out into the overcast day, she called lightly to Willow and watched the petite girl hurry toward her. "Walk with me, honey. I'm riding in your car to the cemetery."

As they headed toward the car, they were soon surrounded by Willow's brother and sisters who all piled into the back of the Suburban. Georgia waited outside the vehicle and watched as the pallbearers lifted the casket with Donald's body into the waiting hearse.

"Good-bye, dear," she whispered. "Your journey has come to an end, and mine, well, mine is starting anew I guess."

Chapter Two

Later that night after the last well-wisher had left her house, after she'd watched Jerry disappear in a taxi bound for the airport and his return flight to base, and after Georgia had rounded up enough sleeping bags for her grandchildren, she sat down at the table where she'd had her final words with Donald. Randy was now seated in the chair where his father had died.

They gazed at each other over the assortment of half-eaten pies and other saran-wrapped goodies left by neighbors and co-workers and people whose mail Donald had delivered for thirty years. Randy picked up a cookie and began to munch it, crumbs dropping to the floor where Bowser continued to wait patiently—it had been a good day for the dog who'd been pleasantly sidetracked all afternoon with fallen treats. Randy reached down and stroked the old dog's head.

"Do you think he knows?" Randy asked.

Georgia nodded. Then she had a sudden thought. "You should take Bowser home with you."

"With me? Why? This is his home." He shot a puzzled look at his mother before passing the rest of the cookie off to the beagle.

Georgia sighed. "Yes, it is, but I'm thinking of going away for a bit, and I don't want to kennel him; he's too old for that."

"Going away? Where to?" Her son furrowed his brow at her.

"I'm not really sure. Just away." She looked around the kitchen and its adjoining breakfast nook where she loved to sit early in the mornings and watch the sun come up, especially in the summers when she could linger over her coffee and not rush off to school. It was all so dear to her, but it was also so meaningless. "I need a change."

Randy scowled. "What about your job? Your students? You can't just leave them."

"Actually I can, at least at the end of this year. There's no saying that I have to accept my contract for next year."

Sensing a change in the atmosphere and that no more treats would be falling, Bowser trotted to his dog bed, circled twice and plopped down with a grunt. Georgia chuckled and then yawned.

"You need to go to bed, too, Mom. It's been a long day."

She nodded and rubbed her eyes. "Yes, it has, but I meant what I said." She looked long and hard at her eldest child. "I'm calling it quits at the end of this school year, and I plan to tender my resignation once I return to work next week."

"Don't you think you're being hasty?" Randy leaned back and crossed his arms over his ample belly. "Dad just passed away. You need to give yourself time to accept that. I don't want you doing something you'll regret."

Georgia smiled lightly. "If I don't quit, and if I don't go see some of this world I've only read about, then I certainly will regret it."

A silence hung in the air between them. Soft snores came to them from the living room where the grandchildren were all sleeping, and a louder one sounded from the guest bedroom down the hall where Sally and her husband were asleep.

"This is just between you and me for now, Randy. I don't want Sally or Jerry knowing my plans. Sally will only try to change my mind with daily phone calls and e-mails, and Jerry will worry and try to give me money. I don't need or want their concern or their money."

Randy smiled wryly. "Why am I always the secret keeper?"

"Because you are so good at it." She looked at her son and noticed the sunken spots under his eyes. "I shouldn't have told you this yet, either, but thinking about Bowser and wondering what to do with him made me bring it up."

"I don't understand, though. Just a few weeks ago, we were talking about throwing you and Dad a dual retirement party in a couple of years, and you never said a thing about retiring at the end of this year."

Georgia stood and began to cover the dishes of food. "A few weeks ago your father was still alive, and I was still planning on a retirement that included him." She moved toward the refrigerator, and Randy followed her with more platters.

He opened the door for her, and they made room for as many perishables as they could. As he closed the door, he caught sight of the numerous photos covering the top half of the refrigerator with magnets. None of the magnets were mementos of places visited, but they were all hand-made treasures from his and his siblings' younger

14

years along with a few newer ones from his nephew and nieces.

"Where will you go, Mom?" he asked as his eyes strayed over the pictures.

"Where won't I go?" she replied.

He turned and looked at his mother. Then he cocked his head enough to catch sight of Bowser asleep on his side with his legs splayed out across the tile floor. A small smile played at his mouth. "Funny. I'd been thinking of getting a dog."

Chapter Three

She hadn't expected the uproar that her resignation caused, both in her family and in the school system where she'd taught so long that many of her current students were grandchildren of a few of her first students. The school board had been counting on her for at least two more years, and while they wouldn't mind replacing her with a first year teacher and thus saving a lot of money in salary pay out, they were sorry to lose such a good teacher.

Many of her current third graders cried when she told them the news. Even reminding them that she wouldn't have been their teacher next year did nothing to quell the tears of a few of them. One girl said through her sobs, "Yes, . . . but . . . Mrs. . . Haines . . . I still . . . wanted to come . . . vi, vi, visit you . . . next year!"

Georgia hugged the sad girl and made a promise she doubted she would keep. "I'll come visit you instead. Will that be o.k.?" The girl considered it for a minute before wiping her face on her sleeve and nodding forlornly.

A slew of cards packed her mailbox at home once word got out that she was leaving. Many of the sentiments sent her in a frenzy of tears of despair as she wondered if she were indeed making the right decision. After all, what was two more years?

"It's two more years of my life that I don't want to waste," she reminded herself out loud when the doubt was at its strongest. And those two years would be years spent

16

alone in a house full of memories of Donald, and Donald was dead, but she wasn't.

Sally was the most contentious when she finally learned the news. Georgia had known she would be, and she was certain that part of Sally's ire came from the fact that she was the last of the children to find out rather than the first.

Georgia knew that Sally had always assumed she'd be there for her. They didn't live far apart, and Georgia and Donald had done their best to attend as many of their grandchildren's functions as possible. However, once when they hadn't been able to get to one of Matthew's recitals, Sally had said, "Don't worry, Mom. When you and Dad retire, you can move closer, so you don't miss anything."

She hadn't bothered to correct her daughter at that time, but Georgia had never had any desire to move to a retirement complex or a condo nearer her controlling daughter. She loved Sally dearly, but Sally was not her life.

When she'd finally broken the news to Sally, her daughter had scoffed. "Oh Mom, don't be silly. You've never travelled further than Iowa."

"That's why I'm doing this now, dear. Before it really is too late."

Sally looked with disbelief at her mother, concern etching her brow. "Are you ill?"

"No, honey, just bored with my life."

Another scoffing sound came from her daughter's throat. "You have a great life, Mom."

Georgia nodded. "I agree, but I've always wanted to see the world. Your father wouldn't go anywhere with me, though, and we usually had too many bills and too few dollars to justify me demanding we take a vacation somewhere more interesting than Des Moines."

"I don't get it, though, Mom. You only have a couple more years left until you can retire, so why do it now?"

"Actually, I could have retired years ago, but I kept doing it because I didn't know what else to do with myself. Now, I know what to do."

Sally shook her head as if denying it physically would make it not be true. "Where are you going, and how are you going to pay for it?"

Georgia smiled. "For starters, I'm heading to California. I've always wanted to see the ocean and those cable cars in San Francisco. I can start drawing my retirement benefits, and your father left a pretty hefty life insurance policy for me, so I'll be O.K. for a while. If I run out of money, I'll sell the house."

"You wouldn't!" A look of horror spread across Sally's freckled face.

"If I find a better place to live out my post-traveling days, then, yes, I will. After all, it is my house."

Sally looked crestfallen. "I know, Mom, but we all grew up here. It's home to me and to the boys."

At the sight of her daughter's tear-filled eyes, Georgia stepped toward her and wrapped her arms around her. "I know, dear, so I won't sell it unless I absolutely have to."

Sally hugged her mother, a rarity between the two of them. "Promise that you'll call me every night and e-mail me lots of photos of the things you see."

Georgia pulled away and smiled at her daughter. "I'll call you twice a week, and I'll send those photos only if you show me how to work that digital camera you got me for Christmas."

Chapter Four

Before Jerry returned to Honolulu he had asked her to come visit him during the summer. Perhaps a part of him suspected that his mother was unhappy stuck in Nebraska and craving some excitement. No matter his reason, Georgia fully intended to take him up on his offer after she was finished touring the West Coast.

Jerry had been the calmest of her three children when she'd sent him an e-mail advising him of her plans to retire early from the elementary school he and his siblings had all attended. He'd quickly written her a reply informing her that he already knew because Randy had beaten her to the punch.

He'd surprised her with a phone call later that evening. She'd known it was him without even looking at the display screen of her cell phone because he was the only person who ever called her on it. In fact, he was the reason she and Donald had a cell phone, or rather that *she* had a cell phone now. He'd bought it for them on his last visit home and insisted Donald start carrying it with him in his mail truck since his route took him out of town onto a few poorly maintained roads. Jerry had started to worry about his father after Donald turned sixty; he didn't want him getting stuck in the winter or slipping into a ditch on a rainy day without a way to contact somebody for help. She and Donald had laughed about it, though, because the roads their son worried about the most were the ones with the worst cell phone reception, so even if Donald had had an accident out there, he still would have had to walk to the nearest farmhouse to use a landline.

Without telling Jerry, they had simply left the cell phone at home where they would occasionally grab it if they were heading off somewhere together in case one of their children or grandchildren needed to reach them in an emergency. It had only happened once when Sally's youngest, Betsy, fell on the playground and broke her wrist and the school couldn't reach Sally or Clark, her husband, because they were out of state for a music convention for the radio station that Clark managed. Georgia had been listed as the emergency contact, and in addition to their home phone number, Sally had thought to include the cell number. She'd been lucky that Georgia had the phone with her that day and even luckier that it had been charged and turned on. In fact, Georgia had been puzzled by the ringing noise that suddenly interrupted her own classroom. Her students, amidst their giggles, had informed her that her phone was ringing. She'd initially asked "What phone?" before remembering that she had a cell phone and it was in her school bag.

Other than that one phone call from their granddaughter's school over a year ago, nobody called them on the cell phone except Jerry. When she told him that, he had asked her, "Well, Mom, have you ever given anybody else this number?"

She'd laughed and said, "No, I guess I haven't. Oh well, I prefer it that way. The last thing I want to become is one of those silly people addicted to their cell phones." At the quiet emanating from the other end, she'd added, "Not that you are one of those people, dear."

21

Jerry had chuckled. "Of course I am, Mom, but that's o.k. I'm more into technology than you are. I like you the way you are, and I know you prefer your big-ass phone that you can cradle against your shoulder so you can cook and talk at the same time."

She laughed again. Every time he called her on her cell phone, he joked that if she wanted to cook and talk, then she had to learn how to use the speaker capability, but she couldn't wrap her mind around the concept of being on a phone without actually holding it against her ear.

So, when Jerry called her after reading her e-mail, she'd quickly located it amongst the clutter on her desk and double-checked the caller I.D. just to be safe before answering it with her usual, "Hello, sweetie." Jerry was 'sweetie,' Sally was 'honey,' and Randy was her 'dearest.'

"Hi, Mom. So, are you all packed?"

"Not yet." She laughed. "It's been so long since I've gone anywhere for more than a couple days that I don't even know where to start."

"Well, let me give you some advice from somebody who has traveled all over the world. Pack light."

"How light?"

"If you even slightly question whether or not you'll need the item, then don't bring it."

"I'll keep that in mind. I mostly want to know what I may need if I get to Hawaii."

"You won't need much. Just a camera, some good walking shoes and beach wear."

Georgia sighed. "The beach. I've never been to one, and I don't have a swimming suit fit for public viewing."

"Well then, Mom, you'll need to do a little shopping when you get here because if there is one thing Hawaii has, it is swimming suits. And lots and lots of sunscreen and sandals."

Georgia glanced at the tropical beach calendar that she'd consistently bought every year when the calendar kiosk set up in the local mall during the holiday seasons. The May photo was of a beautiful white beach being kissed by a gentle wave. She leaned in closer to read the caption that informed her that the photo was shot in Tahiti. Another place she could only dream of visiting someday.

"Mom? You still there?" her son's voice sounded over the airwaves all the way from another tropical paradise.

"I'm here, sweetie. How long is the flight from California to Hawaii?"

"California? Let's see. About five hours, I think. I can double check for you."

"That would be great, and if you can help me book my flight I would really appreciate that. I've never flown, you know."

"That's right. It hardly seems possible that I can't count the number of planes I've ridden in, and you've yet to experience the thrill."

"I'm a bit frightened, I admit." She bit her lip, realizing that to get to her son, she'd have to fly over the Pacific Ocean. She'd be above it, far above it. The thought thrilled her, but it also scared her greatly. What if the plane went down? There were sharks in the ocean.

Before her mind wandered any further, Jerry interrupted her thoughts. "Remember what I've always told you and Da," his words caught in his throat and Georgia saved him from getting completely choked up.

"Yes, I remember. You always say that planes are far safer than cars. Your father may have never believed you, but I trust you, sweetie. After all, you are in the Air Force."

He chuckled. Then his voice became muffled, and Georgia was certain that she'd heard a woman's voice in the background before Jerry had covered the mouthpiece. She asked, "Do you need to go? Do you have company?"

"Uh, no, Mom. I am still at work. I was just talking to one of the staff sergeants."

Georgia glanced at the clock. Even with the time difference, she knew her son was lying. It was far too late for him to still be at work. His tone had betrayed him as well. She knew when her baby was lying to her. She chose to let him continue his little ruse. She'd be in Hawaii sometime in the next few months, and she'd see with her own eyes if he had a girlfriend he wasn't yet ready to tell her about over the phone.

"Then I'd better let you get back to work. You check on some flight details for me. I figure I'll want to fly out of San Francisco because I most want to visit that city."

"You want round trip tickets?"

She considered it for a moment. "No. I'll spend some time with you and see the sites of Hawaii for a while, and then I'll decide where I want to go from there."

He was silent for so long she thought she'd lost the connection. "Are you still there, Jerry?"

"Yes. But, Mom, I guess I hadn't thought past your trip here. You're really planning on traveling all over the world?"

"Well, at least all over the U.S for starters. Maybe I'll hit Alaska after Hawaii."

He laughed. "From one extreme to the next, huh, Mom?" Then he paused, and once again she thought she heard a woman's voice in the background. "Alaska, huh? Alaska would be nice. You know, I've never been there, and I've heard there are great cruises to see it."

She smiled. "As long as you are checking on those flights for me, look into one of those cruises, as well. I've never been on a ship either." She paused. "And you know, Jerry, you and anybody you would care to invite are totally welcome to come along."

He cleared his throat. "I'll look into things for you, Mom, and I'll be in touch."

"O.K., sweetie. Have a good night."

"You too, Mom."

They disconnected, and she turned to the photo of Donald and her taken on their fortieth anniversary. "Whoever she is, hon, I hope she realizes the gem she has in our son." She lightly brushed her fingers over Donald's smiling face, placed the cell phone back on the desk and went to bed.

Chapter Five

After Bowser was safely ensconced in his new home at Randy's, Georgia waited a few weeks more to be sure the dog adjusted to his new surroundings. They'd found the best substitute for his normal sleeping spot next to the patio sliding glass door, and with his bed in place there, Bowser had accepted it as his own, but Georgia learned a few days before she was due to leave for the first leg of her trip that Bowser's new nighttime sleeping spot was at the foot of Randy's bed.

She playfully scolded her son, "A dog doesn't belong on a person's bed. You're spoiling him."

Randy shrugged. "I don't have anybody else to spoil. Besides, he's old, and I can tell that he misses Dad."

Was that a pointed jab at her? Georgia wondered, but then she decided that if it was, she didn't really care. She couldn't bring Donald back, and if anyone thought that her decision to go exploring meant that she didn't miss and hadn't loved her husband, then that person was very wrong.

It wasn't her fault that most people assumed that when a woman's husband died, that woman should basically stop living for a bit and spend time being sad. What was she to do? Sit in the café with some of the other widowed women bemoaning her state and how there was nothing to do now that her husband was gone and all their social groups were comprised of couples who unwittingly made her feel like an outcast?

That wasn't her style. And she certainly wasn't ready to move into a retirement complex where she could spend her days playing cards with truly elderly widowed people.

No, she wanted to live. Despite being married for many years, having a wonderful career and raising three great children, Georgia felt like she'd never really lived her life. Not on her own terms at least.

She'd spent the better part of the past few years dreading retirement, actually, because she wasn't sure how she and Donald were going to pass their golden years. He always talked of traveling a bit, but only to the surrounding states and National Parks that were within a few days drive. Whenever she'd bring up wanting to go to Hawaii to see their son, he'd give a low whistle about the cost of the airline tickets and the tropical heat among other excuses he'd make for not wanting to go there. If she mentioned travel overseas, he'd laugh out loud and remind her that their ancestors fled the very countries she most wanted to see.

Once, after seeing her dejected look, he'd made a half-hearted promise to take her on a cruise around the world on one of the ships that cater to retired people because as he'd added, "I don't want to be stuck on a boat with a bunch of screaming kids. I might end up jumping overboard."

For a few days, she'd taken heart and even spent a little time researching such trips. They were pricey, but they sounded wonderful and they were geared especially for mature educated people. She'd shown him a few things, but when he'd barely taken notice, she'd known that his had been an empty promise. She'd tucked the printouts away in the hopes that after retirement, he'd actually decide that a cruise sounded like fun.

Now, he was gone, but the ache to go exploring had bloomed again within her after his death. She'd seen it as a whole new chapter in her life – perhaps the most exciting part of her life story, and she was about to turn the first page of that new chapter. Her bags were packed, stuffed actually, with all the things she couldn't imagine traveling without and a few things that Sally had insisted she take, and that she'd admitted were a good idea.

Sally had dragged her to the bookstore to load up on a few travel books for the places she knew she wanted to visit and a large travel journal in which she could record the sights and her impressions. She'd once kept a regular journal, but over the years, she'd stopped writing in it. She agreed that it would be wise to write down the places she visited at least.

She'd also made Sally give her a quick course on how to use her digital camera and then what she should do with the photos once she took them. Sally had attempted to convince her to buy a laptop where she could download the photos, but Georgia had balked at that. "I'll find places to develop the photos I take along the way, honey."

Sally looked at her mother under lowered brows. "Mom, I know you. You will either fill the memory card up completely without ever developing a single photo, or you will forget everything I've shown you and never take the camera out of your suitcase."

Georgia laughed. "I was thinking about the latter already." Her daughter sighed. "Honey, I promise that I will take photos, and I promise that I will get them developed from time to time, too. All right?"

"Fine, but when you get to Jerry's place, you have him help you download some onto his pages and then we can see your photos back here, or he can e-mail a few of them to us." She paused in helping her mother pack. "I still can't believe you are going to be gone so long. Months, you think?"

Georgia shrugged. "I don't know, really. Maybe longer even."

Sally sank onto her mother's bed. "Longer? Why? Wherever are you going?" Suddenly she gasped. "You're not running off with another man, are you, Mom?"

"Good God, no, Sally. Where would you ever get a notion like that?"

Sally looked down. "Sorry, Mom. I just can't understand why you are doing this. Clark says you are just running away from your grief." She looked up at her mother. "Are you? Because if you are, you don't need to. We're here for you. We miss Dad, too." The tears started to fall.

Georgia scooted the full suitcase a few inches and perched next to her daughter. She put an arm around her. "Honey, I'm not running away from anything. Maybe I'm running toward something instead."

Sally pulled away a bit and looked at her mother. "Toward what then? You said there wasn't anybody else."

"No, there isn't. Toward my future, I guess. Despite what you and your brothers may have thought, I haven't been happy in my job for years. I've just been biding my time until retirement, but I wasn't really sure what I was going to do with myself when I did. I had your father to consider as well." She stood and began folding the remaining clothes for the suitcase. "But now, I only have myself to worry about, and while I am sad that your father is gone, the fact that I can go do whatever I want is a very exciting prospect."

"But I worry about you. You've barely been anywhere in this world, and you are going alone."

Georgia nodded slightly. "I worry about me a little bit, too. You're right. I am going alone and it is a big world, but I'm only going alone to California because once I leave there, I will head to Hawaii, and I will be in Jerry's care for a bit out there. Then, well, we'll see what happens next. I'm just going to take a day at a time and a place at a time." She placed a hand on her daughter's shoulder. "Does that make you feel better about this?"

Sally shrugged but nodded. "Yeah, I guess so, but I wish you'd tell me when you plan to return."

"I'll tell you when I know. Until then, just come by once a week and check on the house for me. That's really all you have to do. I've paid most of the bills in advance for the next six months just to be safe, and I will turn off the water. You'll need to turn on the furnace if the weather gets too cold before I come back." Her eye fell on the empty plant stand by the window. "And, Sally, if at all possible, keep my house plants alive until I get back. I'm more worried about them in a house full of rowdy children than I am about myself walking the streets of San Francisco alone."

They both laughed, but Georgia knew that it wouldn't be the grandchildren who killed off her plants while she was gone – it would be Sally's black thumb. It had been hard to cart them over to her daughter's plant-free home, but Randy had drawn the line at caring for living green things. Bowser was enough for him.

Chapter Six

A few weeks after the close of the school year, Georgia stood at her hotel window looking out at the Golden Gate Bridge. Its magnitude and beauty continued to amaze her.

She'd originally had a room booked in a modest hotel, but on her first day of sightseeing around town, she'd seen a gorgeous high-end hotel with views of the bay. The cable car had stopped in front of the hotel, and she'd gone in on a whim. The receptionist had originally told her there were no rooms available as they'd all been reserved for a rich couple's daughter's wedding reception, but when he'd seen the disappointed look on her face, he'd leaned across the counter and beckoned her to come closer.

"Of course, I'm assuming you are one of the many out-of-town relatives they thought would be coming but who aren't." He paused to look knowingly at her. "I assume you simply forgot to call and reserve your special rate room, is that right?"

She smiled. "Yes, that's exactly right. I am a very forgetful person."

He turned toward his computer screen. "Would you prefer a room with a Jacuzzi or one with a fully massaging shower system?"

Georgia giggled. "I don't need either, but if I can get one that looks out over the water, that would be great." She bit her lip. "Just how special is the special rate? I'm sure this hotel is way over my budget."

"It's one hundred dollars off the normal rate, so the room will run you two-hundred eighty-nine dollars a night." He peered at her over his glasses. "Will that be all right with you?"

She swallowed and looked around the luxurious lobby atrium. "Yes, anything for my dear niece's wedding." They both laughed. "Can I get the room for a week?"

He paused and looked around him. "Well, the rate is only for the wedding this weekend. It is supposed to go up again after that, but we haven't filled even half of the rooms we were promised, so the girl's parents have to reimburse us for a percentage of those rooms. He winked at her. "I think I can make that work for you since you are helping us out by actually booking a room."

"That would be wonderful. I'll need to return to my other hotel and cancel my reservation and bring my belongings over here."

He handed her the room key. "You are on the eleventh floor. Your room has a Jacuzzi, so you can relax. The concierge will be happy to help you book any excursions during your stay in San Francisco. They can also arrange for our car service to drive you to your other hotel to retrieve your things."

She gasped slightly. "Oh, I don't want to be a bother."

"No bother, ma'am. It is part of our guest services. Just tell Beth at the concierge desk to your left what you need."

Georgia thanked him and walked toward the concierge, all the while looking around her in amazement at the lavishness of the hotel. She'd have to take some photos to show her daughter, or Sally would never believe that her unassuming mother would ever set foot, let alone stay, in a fancy hotel like this.

Beth told her they could have a car out front for her in twenty minutes. She made a call and then she asked Georgia what things she'd like to do in San Francisco. Georgia told her she'd already ridden on a couple of cable cars and she'd walked around Fisherman's Wharf, but she'd like to discover the real San Francisco while still seeing the sights.

Beth suggested a trip to Alcatraz and Angel Island along with a visit to Chinatown. She also said that if Georgia liked to read, then she should go to the famous City Lights Bookstore. Georgia nodded along with all of the suggestions and gathered the brochures the woman gave her. She knew that by the time she traveled to her other hotel, packed and returned to this hotel, it would be getting late, and she'd have time to simply sit in her room and study the information about the local sights.

A uniformed driver entered the lobby and approached the desk. Beth introduced him to Georgia. "This is Dave, one of our best drivers. He'll take you to get your belongings."

She stuck out her hand, and Dave shook it with his gloved hand. "Nice to meet you. If you'll just follow me."

When she stepped outside, she was surprised to see a stretch limousine pulled up at the curb and even more surprised when Dave opened the back door and waited patiently for her to overcome her shock and climb in the backseat.

After he got behind the wheel, she called up to him, "I've never been in a limo before, Dave."

He chuckled. "I got that impression, ma'am."

"Oh, please, call me Georgia."

"All right, Georgia." He pulled out into the traffic. "So, Georgia, are you from Georgia?"

She smiled. "No, but my mother's family was, so my mother stuck me with the name Georgia."

He turned a corner. "It's a pretty name, don't you think?"

She looked out at the people they were passing and noticed that most of them didn't even give a limousine a second glance. On the streets of her town in Nebraska, the car would have caused a sensation. "I guess it is. When it is your own name, it just becomes sort of ordinary."

"Have you ever been to Georgia?" Dave pulled up next to a bright red convertible at a stoplight.

She sighed. "No. I've always meant to, but I've never been there. At least, not yet, Dave." She rolled down her window to wave at a little boy who was waving at the car as it passed him. She laughed out loud at the odd look he gave her. "He was probably expecting a celebrity, not an old woman."

Before she knew it, the limousine pulled up in front of the quaint hotel she had originally booked based solely on its unique façade. Once she'd arrived, though, she hadn't been as impressed with its rooms or its views, so she was delighted that she was getting an opportunity to really enjoy the beauty of San Francisco's bay and its world-famous bridge.

She exited the limo and entered the lobby, a rather shabby affair next to the posh surroundings she'd just come from. The hotel manager greeted her politely, and Georgia felt a stab of guilt at leaving a place that clearly needed the business, but she didn't allow herself to dwell upon that. She walked over to the desk and told him she needed to check out.

He blinked in surprise. "Is there something wrong with the room?"

She assured him there wasn't, and she was honest with him and explained that she'd found a hotel nearer the water, and she wanted to stay there instead.

He squinted ever so slightly at her before informing her that she was still responsible for the remainder of her reservation as it would be impossible to fill the room now.

Georgia sighed. In her enthusiasm to stay at the nicer hotel, she hadn't really thought about canceling her existing reservation without still owing money. She couldn't afford to pay for two separate hotel rooms, so she excused herself and went out to talk to the driver.

After explaining her predicament, Dave suddenly got out of the car where he'd been sitting and reading the newspaper. He entered the hotel and strode over to the desk.

Georgia hung back by the door feeling a bit embarrassed, especially as Dave's voice rose and he pointed a finger in the face of the manager who had only been nice to her until this moment. She saw the manager raise his hands in surrender and start typing something on his keyboard. Dave motioned for her to come nearer.

Reluctantly, she approached the desk. "I didn't mean to cause any problems," she began, but then she stopped when Dave waved her apology away.

"This nice man is printing out your bill for one night's stay in his fine establishment, and I have promised to not speak ill of his hotel to any of the rich clients I meet every day."

She rushed forward. "Really. I need to apologize. I should just stay here like I originally planned to do."

The manager paused in his typing and looked up, but Dave motioned for him to continue, so he looked back at his screen as he said, "Mrs. Haines, it has been our honor to have you as a guest. I hope that if you ever return to San Francisco, you will come visit us again and stay longer." He pulled a sheet out of the printer. "If you will look this over and make sure everything is correct, I will bill the one night to your credit card."

She took the paper from him and scanned it quickly. "Yes, it is fine. I really am sorry. I promise to tell everyone I meet to come stay in your hotel, and I will definitely stay here if I ever come back to the city."

He gave her a pinched smile and then told her she could just leave the key in her room as there was no reason for her to return to the desk. Then he turned and exited through a door marked 'manager.'

Georgia looked at Dave in horror. "I am so embarrassed."

Dave said, "You don't need to be. You found a place more to your taste, and it's your dollar and your time, so you need to be sure you are satisfied."

She nodded. "You're right. I've spent far too much of my life worrying about other people's opinions and desires. This is my time."

Dave patted her shoulder and winked at her. "Atta girl. Do you need me to come help you carry your luggage down?"

"Oh, goodness no. That's not part of your job. Besides, I only have one large suitcase and a smaller one. I can manage. I will be right back."

"I'll wait for you in the car, then."

She hurried off and rushed up the one flight of stairs to the second floor. As she opened the door, she was immediately glad that she had decided to change hotels. It was mid-afternoon and her room still hadn't been straightened up. One of the main things she'd been looking forward to about staying in a hotel was having somebody else make the bed for a change.

Since she'd barely unpacked a thing before setting off to explore the city, it only took a few minutes to gather everything together. As she rolled her large bag out of the room, she took a quick look back at the small room. Through the window, she could see the tall modern buildings of the city jutting into the sky, and among them she spied the hotel where she was now headed.

She let the door swing shut behind her and rushed down the stairs to the waiting limousine.

Chapter Seven

Georgia stood on the Golden Gate Bridge's walkway and stared out over the water toward Alcatraz. Despite the chill of the wind rushing over her, she was warm from the exertion of walking so far to get only halfway across the long bridge.

Cars zipped by, but she didn't even hear them. She was attuned to the sensations of blue swirling around her as the sea and the sky combined, the island breaking the intensity with its starkness. She couldn't imagine being imprisoned out there, so near civilization and yet so far from it.

A thin layer of fog still floated above the water and hugged the island in a fleeting embrace. She'd considered buying a ticket to see the infamous prison on the inside, but then she had changed her mind. She wanted her trip to be full of joyful remembrances, and a stone fortress that had once housed some of the worst criminals was not the stuff of happy dreams but rather of frightening nightmares.

She knew Al Capone had spent over four years of his life in the island prison, and the thought of being locked away for that amount of time anywhere sent another shiver up her spine. She turned away from the gloomy view and cast her eyes upon the city spread out before her.

How had she spent her entire life shut up in the middle of the country when there were places like San Francisco to be seen? Unintentionally, she'd allowed the

Midwest to become her own prison, but now she was free, and she intended to make the most of this freedom.

She began walking back toward the city, looking upward and marveling at the engineering feat that was the bridge. She'd heard the bridge was especially built to withstand high winds, and she could feel a light sway beneath her feet as the wind rushed around her. It scared her a bit, so she began to walk faster to feel the solid ground beneath her feet again.

At the end of the bridge, she turned and looked back down it as far as her eye would reach. Funny how a manmade object could hold so much appeal not only for its sheer beauty but also for the morbid fascination it brought to those who knew of its history of jumpers. She shook her head and turned away. She'd admire it from afar from now on.

She caught a lift to Golden Gate Park, and once she arrived, she sought directions to the Japanese Tea Gardens she'd heard so much about. She doubted she'd get to the Far East, so she thought she'd take advantage of seeing anything resembling it on U.S. soil that she could.

She'd been told that she could enter for free if she arrived before 10:00 a.m., so she'd awoken extra early this morning for her jaunt out on the bridge and back. She was puffing a bit by the time she reached the gardens, but she made it just in time.

As she toured the immaculately kept grounds and marveled at the bridges and pagodas, she again was struck by the irony of its beauty. These gardens were tainted by a horrible moment in the country's history when the Japanese Americans were removed from their homes and forced into internment camps.

Imagine working to create all of this only to be forced out of it never to be allowed to return, she thought, sipping her tea and gazing into a koi pond. The large fish swam lazily in circles hoping for a treat, but she had nothing to toss to them. They, too, were prisoners of a sort.

Georgia shook her head to clear it of its morbid thoughts. She didn't know what had gotten into her today, but she seemed fixated upon seeing everything as some sort of jail – her home state, the magnificent bridge, the empty prison and now a simple pond full of fat fish.

She sat down upon a bench and watched the other visitors. Many were snapping photos, and she mentally slapped her head as she remembered that her camera was safely tucked away in her bag in her hotel room. Sally would be furious with her for missing such golden photo opportunities.

It just had never been her thing. Her three children's lives comprised a total of five photo albums at home, and there were gaps of years between some of the photos. Randy lost and grew in most of his teeth before she ever thought to snap gap-toothed photos of her younger children.

She simply wasn't accustomed to going places and carrying a camera with her. There wasn't much to see back home, and what there was she'd seen a million times, so there was no need to take pictures to remember them. Now, however, she was in a place she'd certainly never see again, and she did want to preserve those memories.

She vowed that before going anywhere else that day, she'd return to the hotel and grab her camera. Until then, she allowed her gaze to linger upon the plants and the buildings to firmly implant them in her own memory.

41

She wouldn't be able to share all the details with her children, but she'd be able to paint some pretty word pictures of what she'd seen.

She rose and headed out of the gardens. Realizing she was hungry, she stopped a lady who looked like she was a local to ask her where the best place to eat nearby would be. However, the woman didn't speak English, so Georgia continued on her way and decided to return to the hotel and eat there. That way, she'd actually remember to go to her room to get her camera for the afternoon's adventures.

As she walked, her mind wandered to the one time she had mentioned to Donald that she'd like to visit San Francisco someday.

"Why in the world would you want to go there? I hear it is full of freaks and homos." He'd then turned his attention back to the television and the auction show he was watching. "Can you believe somebody would pay 1500 dollars for that?" he asked as he pointed at the screen.

She hadn't even glanced at it to see what he was referring to; instead, she'd merely mumbled something noncommittal and left the room. Seeing a full moon peeking through the window, she'd opened the front door and stepped onto the porch. The sky had been clear and the stars swept the blackness as far as she could see.

Despite the chill, she'd stood on the porch gazing up at the night sky for a long time, long enough that Donald actually noticed her absence and called for her. When she didn't respond, she heard his chair squeak and sensed him approaching down the front entryway hall.

"What are you doing standing out there in the dark?" he called through the closed glass window.

"Just thinking," she called back over her shoulder. She kept her head turned slightly so she could see his silhouette out of the corner of her eye. He waited by the door for a minute, but he didn't come outside.

Finally, he grunted and then said, "Well, you should come in. You're going to catch a cold." Then he wandered back to the living room and sat back down in front of the TV.

Georgia took one last look at the moon, searching for answers to the longing in her heart. She wanted to escape, but to where? And she wanted to stay married, but with each passing day, she was dreading more and more a future she could no longer imagine with a person she felt she knew less and less.

She'd simply mentioned wanting to travel and see the sights with him, and he'd once again found a way to ruin things for her. Now, even if she could convince him to go to San Francisco, she'd know that he'd secretly be on the lookout for his so-called 'homos' and at the first sight of one, she feared he'd embarrass her with some sort of ignorant comment or an 'I told you this place was full of freaks' look directed at her.

How would she be able to enjoy herself when she knew he'd only be humoring her by accompanying her? It was bad enough when she had to tolerate that behavior from him on their infrequent trips together to the mall, but she wouldn't be able to stand a week or more of his glowering looks at things that displeased him or his sarcastic comments about the way they did things out in 'hippie California.'

The hotel loomed up before her, and she paused to admire it. No, this was certainly a place that Donald would not have approved of them staying – both for the cost and for the flow of dandified people through the lobby. If she'd come to San Francisco with Donald, they would have had to stay at a small motel on the outskirts of town, and they'd only have been able to accept rides in taxis from white people. She knew he would never have ridden in a limousine driven by a dark man like Dave, no matter how nice he was.

She'd tried to change his racist ways, but eventually she'd given up because she knew it was simply bred into him too deeply. Plus, he didn't think he was racist at all, and he constantly pointed out that he delivered mail to a black family and a bunch of Mexicans, and he didn't have any problem with them. When she asked him if he'd ever talked to any of those people, he'd shaken his head, shrugged and said, "I don't speak Spanish."

"Donald, those Mexicans as you call them are born and raised Americans just like you. I have one of their boys in my class and he doesn't speak a lick of Spanish either."

He'd snorted and looked away. "Well, I ain't racist."

She'd chosen not to argue with him despite all the racist jokes he'd shared over the years with his friend, Joe, when Joe and his wife, Arlene, would accompany them to the café for their weekly 'date night.' She had simply known that if they were to travel together somewhere, it would have to be somewhere in the Midwest where he would be surrounded by people like him, so that left out most of the places she wanted to see in the world.

Now, with him gone, she was seeing and enjoying San Francisco, the one city in the United States that had always appealed to her poetic and artistic and whimsical side. She admitted that she'd rather have somebody to enjoy the sights with, but she also preferred not having to listen to negative comments about the strange-looking people she'd seen. She also liked being able to rise in the morning and know that she could go anywhere she wanted to go without having to bow to the demands of another person who didn't like the same things she liked.

Donald would never have walked all that way out onto the bridge, and he wouldn't have set foot in the Japanese Tea Garden because, despite his claim of not being racist, he despised Asians no matter if they were from Japan, China or Korea. When Jerry had got stationed at Honolulu, Donald had said, "Let's just see those Japs try something there again. Not on Jerry's watch."

He'd been making a joke, she knew, but it was just another example of his warped sense of humor in which all non-Americans were fodder for insults, even if the 'non-Americans' were actually complete Americans in every sense of the word. To Donald, American meant white, or, at the very least, light-skinned. While she saw the Japanese Americans being forced into internment camps as an ugly stain on the country's history and one that should never be forgotten so as not to be repeated, he saw it as a necessary evil to protect the United States from enemies within its borders. They would never see eye-to-eye on matters like that, so she had stopped arguing them with him, and she knew it was better that she was seeing culturally diverse things without Donald there to irk her.

She would have loved to have been able to share the view with him, though. Her room had sweeping vistas of the bay, and she knew he would have loved seeing it. Despite being in a landlocked part of the country, Donald had always had an affinity for boats and ships, so he would have liked to look down upon the harbor activity, especially at night when everything was lit up.

It was at night in her room, looking out at the water, that she imagined Donald at her side, but he was the Donald of their early years – the handsome man who could still make her laugh at a joke. She'd imagine him slipping an arm around her waist and whispering how the beauty of the bay didn't even compare to the beauty of her blue eyes.

Then, alone in her room with a bay at her feet, she would feel the loss, and she had cried. Despite all his flaws, Donald had been hers, and she was still adjusting to the hole he'd left even though most of the time she didn't notice it. But when the sorrow hit, it was like the hole would just suddenly open in front of her and she'd fall in.

Chapter Eight

Georgia settled into her window seat for the morning flight to Honolulu. She still couldn't believe that her son had booked her first-class passage. After checking in at the desk, receiving her boarding pass and seeing that the seat was in the first few rows of the plane, she'd informed the agent that there must be a mistake. He'd assured her that the ticket was correct.

She'd stepped away from the desk and called her son in route to her gate. When he answered, she could hear the laughter in his voice. "You rascal," she scolded.

"Now, Mom, you're on vacation. You deserve a little pampering."

"You don't need to be wasting your money on silly things like putting me in first-class."

He chuckled. "Oh, just enjoy it. I never have to pay for my own flights, so I might as well pay for a decent one for you. You'll be a lot more comfortable than you would be in coach."

She nodded, and then said, "Well, I will have to make it up to you when I get there. I'll take you out to a nice restaurant." She bumped into other passengers in the crowded airport. "I'd better go for now, sweetie. I'll see you in a few hours."

"All right. I'll pick you up outside the baggage claim area. See you soon, Mom. Have a safe flight."

"Tell that to the pilot. Oh, and Jerry, did you find out how long this flight will take?"

"About five and a half hours."

"Oh, that will be perfect. We can have a late lunch when I get there."

"Actually, Mom, it will be a pretty normal time lunch. Remember, I am two hours behind you."

She looked at her watch and saw that it was almost eight o'clock, and her plane was due to depart in half an hour. With the time difference, she'd still arrive in Honolulu around noon. "That will be great, then. You can take me to someplace local."

"I already have reservations."

She frowned. "Reservations? Now, Jerry, I don't want you making a fuss over me. I just want to go to normal Hawaiian restaurants. Nothing fancy."

He laughed. "Don't worry, Mom. You'll understand when you get here. I need to go finish a few things before heading to the airport to get you. I'll talk to you when you arrive."

"O.K., sweetie. See you soon." She hung up and headed toward the security checkpoint. No matter how many times she'd have to go through one of these, she would always dread it and see it as a form of violation. She didn't know how to behave, fearing that being either too friendly or too aloof called attention to herself and made her seem suspicious, and the last thing she wanted was to suffer through an actual pat-down in one of those special rooms.

The officer on the other side of the scanner waved her through, and she entered it inwardly cringing in fear lest the machine should beep at her. When it didn't, she heaved a sigh of relief and managed a weak smile at the man who didn't even look at her; he was busy waving the next person through. She collected her carry-on bag from the conveyor belt and slipped on her shoes – the silliest security measure she'd ever encountered. What about all the foot disease germs that were being spread from passenger to passenger on the floor around the checkpoint? Wasn't that cause for concern?

Georgia headed for her gate and was dismayed to find that it was all the way at the end of a long walkway. She felt silly riding the moving sidewalks, but she assumed that they would get her to the end faster, so she stepped aboard. Then she laughed because the people on the outside of the short wall were actually going faster than she was on the moving sidewalk. Her attention was so focused on them, in fact, that she didn't see that her sidewalk was about to end, so when it did, she came to a sudden stop and fell over her bag.

A young man behind her helped her to her feet. She thanked him and looked around in embarrassment. Nobody else seemed to have noticed. She limped toward her gate, which was now in sight. As soon as she sat down to await her flight and rub her sore shin and wrist, the gate agent announced that first-class passengers could begin boarding.

Groaning, she rose and got in line. A man in front of her turned and smiled at her. She returned his with a swift smile of her own. She watched him give his boarding pass to the agent and pick up an oversized briefcase before heading down the jet way toward the plane. She followed, and, once on board the plane, she noticed that he was seated directly across from her.

After watching her mess with the seat and the controls a bit while the coach passengers were boarding, the man leaned across the aisle and asked, "First time on an airplane or first time in first-class?"

She squinted at him and noticed his nicely tailored suit and high-priced haircut. He was probably just trying to be polite. "The second," she replied, and then she pulled out the in-flight magazine from the seatback in front of her and began flipping through the pages.

Suddenly, he stuck his hand out toward her. "Name's Larry."

Hesitantly, she reached across and shook his hand. "Nice to meet you, Larry. I'm Georgia."

"That's a great name!" he boomed for everyone to hear. Then he laughed. "Aren't you heading in the wrong direction, Georgia?"

She looked at him perplexedly and then, as realization hit her, she smiled indulgently at his attempts at humor. "Yes, I guess I am." She tried to return to her magazine, but he apparently was a talker.

"I've been to Georgia a couple of times. How about you?"

She closed the magazine and placed it in her lap. "No, I've never been there."

"Are you from Hawaii?"

She laughed slightly. "No. Do I look like a local?"

He studied her. "Sort of. You have a bohemian look about you."

She blinked in surprise. "I do?"

"Yeah. Your big rings and your wild hair. And I like the beat-up denim jacket. You don't see many of those anymore."

Georgia smiled and touched her hair a bit self-consciously. She'd been letting it grow long ever since

50

Donald died, and it had been at least thirty years since she'd had hair past her shoulders. She'd forgotten what to do with so much hair, so it was rather unkempt. She tugged her jacket closed over the Hawaiian shirt she wore under it – a whimsical clothing purchase in a boutique near the hotel she'd just left.

She held out her left hand for him to see as she explained each of the rings she wore. Starting at her pinky, she said, "This gaudy old thing is a remembrance of my mother. It was her ring, but she didn't wear it much because it was large and purple as you can see. Then we have my wedding rings, and I insisted on the large diamond to replace the dinky engagement ring my husband had originally given me when we were young and penniless. He gave me this on our twenty-fifth anniversary." She paused to reflect upon the triviality of such a request on her part. It was really just a big rock, and the small one she'd worn for all those earlier years actually carried more sentimental value for her. She vowed to dig it out of the back of her jewelry case when she returned home.

Larry noticed her pensiveness. "Is your husband waiting for you in Honolulu."

She shook her head and looked out the window as the plane began to taxi down the runway. "No. He passed away a couple of months ago."

Her new friend coughed slightly to cover his embarrassment. "I'm sorry for bringing it up."

She turned back to him and for the first time really looked at him. He had an honest face, and he appeared to be in his mid-fifties. Perhaps he was a widower as well.

"Don't be. Our son is waiting for me in Honolulu. He's a first lieutenant in the Air Force stationed at Hickam."

His face lit up. "Really? I'm a retired airman myself. That's how I ended up in Hawaii. Hickam was the last place I was stationed, and I fell in love with the islands, so when I finished my twenty years of service, I set up shop nearby."

"What do you do for a living now?"

"I conduct chopper tours. Take people island-hopping."

"That sounds fascinating."

"It is." He whipped out a business card from the inside pocket of his suit coat. "I co-own a small tour company. As you probably know, tourism is big business in Hawaii."

She took the card. "Yes, I'm sure it is." She held the card up to the light coming in from the small window next to her. It read *Larry Wilcox, Professional helicopter pilot and tour guide.* The card also provided a phone number and website where he could be reached. "How much does a ride in one of the helicopters cost?"

"Depends on the tour you want. It can range from a hundred and fifty dollars to a four hundred dollar trip."

"Wow. That's a pricey tour. I hope you are worth the cost." She winked playfully at him and then looked down at the card again, shocked at her behavior.

He chuckled. "Well, if you want to see the islands from above, you just give me a call. I'll give you and your son a discount. Anything for another airman."

"My son doesn't fly, though. He's in charge of some area dealing with bookkeeping and correspondence.

He's explained it to me before, but when he got to the technical aspect, he lost me."

"No matter. A military man is a military man. All the jobs are important. You just call me if you two want to see the volcanoes up and personal without taking a long walk to the top."

She tucked his card into her jacket pocket. "I will. Thank you, Larry. That is very kind of you. So, what were you doing in San Francisco? You look like you must have been at a business conference or something."

"A baptism, actually. My godson's baby. The ceremony took place this morning, so I flew in last night, and now I'm headed back. I don't like being away from the islands for more than a day or two."

"My son really likes living there as well. In fact," she leaned toward him in a conspiratorial fashion, "I suspect he has a girlfriend there and that he's going to do the very thing you did and remain after retiring."

Larry chuckled. "If the islands don't seduce you, the local beauties will."

Georgia blushed and sat back, hating to think of her youngest son being seduced by any woman. "Did you marry a local girl, Larry?"

"Nope. I'm a lifelong bachelor. I like it that way." He paused. "Or it likes me that way maybe."

She raised an eyebrow at him. "But you seem like such a nice man." Then a thought hit her and she clammed up.

He saw the look on her face and reached across to pat her arm. "I'm not gay, if that is what you were thinking."

She tried to pass it off as if she hadn't been thinking that very thing. She felt silly for allowing her mind to even assume such a thing simply because he'd never been married and was well into middle age.

"I've had plenty of opportunities to marry, and I was even engaged once, but the bachelor life is a better fit for me. I don't like to be home much. When I'm not flying, I'm out on my boat fishing or just tooling around exploring all the coves."

Her interest was piqued again. "You have a boat as well? That must be nice."

"It is. It's old, but it gets me where I need to go, and keeping it afloat gives me something to do." He continued to tell her all about the islands, and she shared a few of her teaching experiences with him. Then he peered across her and out the window. "We're beginning to descend. You'll be able to see the islands soon."

She looked out the window at the large expanse of water below her, and immediately she was grateful that Larry had kept her busy talking the whole trip as the sight of so much water made her feel very nervous and a bit nauseous. She forced herself to take in the view, though, and she began to notice the boats which looked tiny from above but which were actually large cruise ships and ocean liners.

Suddenly an island came into view. "Is that Hawaii?"

"Yes. That is the big island. We'll fly over it and three others before we get to Oahu."

She admitted sheepishly. "I had completely forgotten that the state was comprised of different islands.

Here I'd been thinking of being able to drive all over to see the sights."

"Well, you can still drive, but you'll have to find alternate transportation to get you to the other islands if you want to see them." He paused to let his comment sink in, but she continued to stare out the window. "That was a hint, Georgia."

She turned toward him. "What? Oh, yes, of course. You just might get my business after all." She patted the pocket where she'd put his business card.

The pilot's voice came over the intercom to announce estimated arrival time and the local temperature of Honolulu. When she heard it, she said, "Looks like I'll need to shed this jacket."

"Yeah, but the evenings get cool, so you'll need it. I didn't mean to insult you earlier with the comments about your coat and your hair."

"Don't worry about it, Larry. I really should invest in a new jacket. I've had this for years, but it fits me like a second skin and it has all sorts of pockets for me to carry things since I don't care to take a purse with me when I go out."

The plane began to descend more noticeably. Larry suggested a few places for her to visit and some of his favorite restaurants. She made a mental note of them, yet secretly doubted she would go to any of them; she preferred to leave her time in Hawaii up to Jerry's discretion as he was the reason she'd come here.

The airplane touched down and before she knew it, they were at the gate. She said good-bye to Larry, and then she grabbed her carry-on bag and left the plane.

After collecting her large suitcase at baggage claim, she exited to find her son waiting for her wearing his military uniform and holding the hand of a tall blond woman who was holding the hand of a small dark-haired boy. She momentarily stopped in shock before she rushed forward to hug her son.

Chapter Nine

"Mom, this is my friend Ingrid and her son Evan." Jerry stepped back to motion them forward.

Georgia shook the woman's outstretched hand. "So nice to meet you, dear." Then she bent over to tousle the boy's hair a bit. "You, too, young man." She stood and looked her son in the eyes. "You should have warned me that I'd be meeting your young lady, Jerry. I would have dressed better."

Jerry coughed slightly, and Georgia saw a blush come into Ingrid's cheeks. "I know I should have, Mom. I'm sorry. I've been meaning to tell you for some time now, but Dad's death threw me for a loop."

Before she could reply, Ingrid spoke up. "I wanted to come to the funeral with Jerry, but he didn't think it would be the best time for the family to meet me, and I agreed. Who wants to be known as the 'gal Jerry brought to his father's funeral'?" She smiled weakly at Georgia.

She looked at the young woman closely and with new appreciation. This one was a keeper, she could tell that already, and she was proud of her son for not basing his choice solely on looks. Not that Ingrid was unattractive, but she certainly wasn't what most people would call a beauty either. Georgia wondered at the paleness of her skin while living in a place like Hawaii, and she noticed the scar above Ingrid's jaw line on the right side of her face and the fact that it looked like her nose had been broken a time or two.

"I suppose you were right about that, dear, but I still would have liked to have known before arriving here." She took her son's arm as they walked toward the car. Then she leaned closer to him as she said, "But I've had my suspicions for some time now."

He glanced at his mother. "I'm not surprised. You always manage to find out my secrets."

"That's a mother's gift, sweetie, isn't it, Ingrid?" The younger woman smiled at her and nodded.

They exited the airport and were hit by a wave of hot and humid air. Jerry hurried them toward a large navy blue SUV.

As they drove away, Georgia turned in her seat to talk to the two passengers in the back. "So, Ingrid, can I assume you are Swedish?"

Ingrid smiled and nodded. "Yes, I am, but I've lived in Honolulu since I was a child." Georgia's eyes flickered to her light skin. "I don't tan. I only burn, so I stay out of the sun as much as possible, and I invest in a lot of sunscreen. Evan likes the beach, though, so I take him, and I cover up with a big hat and a large towel."

"How did you two meet?" Georgia asked Ingrid and Jerry.

Before they could answer, though, Evan piped up, "We live next door to Jerry."

Georgia smiled. "Ah, I see. That must be nice."

Jerry smiled and looked at Ingrid in the rearview mirror. Georgia saw her blush again. Jerry interrupted before his mother could ask anything else. "It's a long story. I'll fill you in later, Mom. Now, it's time for you to experience some local cuisine."

He pulled into the parking lot of a small beat-up looking restaurant right next to an expansive beach covered with umbrellas and basking bodies.

"We're eating here?" she asked in surprise at the site of the weathered and warped walls which seemed to be leaning slightly away from the water.

Jerry and Ingrid both laughed. "Told you it was no place fancy," he reminded her.

They all climbed out of the vehicle and hurried to the shaded porch. Jerry pulled out a chair for his mother facing the ocean. She plopped down and peeled off her jacket. At the sight of her bright tropical shirt, her son burst out laughing.

"Nothing screams 'tourist' more than a Hawaiian shirt, Mom." They all sat down and grabbed menus.

"Now, don't be mean, Jerry," Ingrid scolded playfully. "It's a lovely shirt, Georgia."

"Thank you, but Jerry's right. I shouldn't have bought it. It's not really my style either."

Evan suddenly waved and shouted "Hi, Johnny!" to somebody behind Georgia. She turned to see a large Hawaiian man approaching their table carrying a tray of sweating glasses of water.

"Hi yourself, little man," the giant replied as he plopped the tray onto their table. A few drops of water sloshed onto Georgia's arm. "Sorry about that, ma'am," he said as he distributed the glasses around the table.

"Johnny, this is my mother," Jerry said.

The man peered down at her over his big belly and then stuck out a huge hand. "Nice to meet you, ma'am."

She took his outstretched hand and gingerly shook it, fearing that he would surely crush her fingers, but his grasp was intentionally gentle. "Nice to meet you, too, Johnny."

Pulling a greasy pad out of his apron and flipping it open, he said, "So, what'll it be, folks?"

Jerry looked at his mother. "Mind if I just order for all of us, Mom? We eat here all the time, and I know what's good."

"Sure, dear. I'm hungry, so I'll eat anything."

She watched her son order Kalua pig and an assortment of tropical fruit including coconuts, pineapple and papaya, a fruit she'd long enjoyed and looked forward to eating fresh. He also ordered them blended juice drinks. Suddenly Evan piped in with, "Don't forget the poi."

Jerry chuckled. "Of course not. And some ice cream for dessert, right?"

Evan cheered. Johnny waddled off to place their order and to greet some other locals who had just entered.

Georgia picked up her napkin and began to fan herself. "Would you rather eat inside?" Jerry asked. "There are fans, but it isn't a lot cooler in there."

"Oh, no. I just need to acclimate to the humidity, that's all."

"I told Jerry we should probably have picked a different restaurant for your first Hawaiian experience – one where we could eat inside in air conditioning." She gave Jerry a pointed look.

"No, really, dear, this is fine. It's wonderful, in fact. Just look at that view." She gestured to the surf rushing in upon the white beach. The sun glinted off the water and shimmered in the spray from the waves. "It's breathtaking. I can put up with a little heat for a view like that."

"I knew you'd like it," Jerry said as he looked with mock severity at Ingrid. They both smiled at each other.

Ingrid lifted the hair off the back of her neck and let the breeze dry the sweat that was beginning to form. "At least we have shade," she said.

Georgia gazed up at the shell covered porch roof and marveled at the sheer number of seashells glued to its façade. Jerry followed her gaze. "We've added a few ourselves over the years. Johnny invites patrons to find an interesting shell on the beach and then come find a spot to glue it."

"So, Johnny is the owner?" Georgia asked.

Jerry shrugged. "I guess so. It is called Johnny's Joint," he said as he winked at his mother and pointed to the crooked sign out front not far from their table.

She turned to see the sign and then playfully swatted at her son. Just then Johnny returned carrying a second tray of drinks. She was relieved to see him place them on a nearby table instead of in front of her this time. She didn't mind having a little bit of water spill on her, but she wasn't in the mood for sticky juice to attract any island insects her way.

"You bringing your clan to our luau this weekend?" he asked Jerry.

Jerry raised his eyebrows as he looked up at the tall man. "Have I ever missed one of your luaus, Johnny?"

Johnny slapped him on the back and tucked the drink tray under his beefy arm. Georgia frowned slightly and hoped it wouldn't be the same tray he'd use to serve the food. "Good to hear, man. Ever been to a luau?"

Georgia realized he was talking to her and quickly took the straw out of her mouth. "No, I've never been to

Hawaii let alone a luau. Sounds like fun, and by the way, this drink is absolutely divine."

"Thank you. It's my own concoction. It's got rum, Kahlua, white wine, . . ." he faded off as her eyes widened and then he laughed along with Jerry and Ingrid. "I'm just kidding you, ma'am. It's just a lot of different fruits blended with some natural teas. I'm glad you like it. Your food will be out soon."

"Does this really have wine in it, Jerry?" Evan asked with excitement from across the table.

"No, little man. Johnny was just giving my mom a hard time."

Evan's face fell and then suddenly broke into a grin as a large platter of fresh fruit was placed in front of them by a young waitress. "Mom, this is Johnny's daughter, Evelyn."

"Hello," the young girl said quietly before slipping away.

"Nice to meet you," Georgia called after the shy girl. "Pretty little thing," she added to Jerry.

He answered with his mouth full of mango. "She's the youngest of Johnny's brood. He has eight kids."

"Wow. That's a handful. Do they all work here?"

"They do and they did. Some have left home to have their own families, and one of them drowned a few years ago."

She carefully picked out one of each type of fruit to try and placed them on her own plate. "That's sad. You'd think growing up by the ocean, kids would be better swimmers."

"He was an excellent swimmer, actually, but a riptide caught him and washed him out to sea while he was surfing. They think his board hit him on the head and knocked him out, and before anyone could get to him, he was gone."

Ingrid joined in. "That's what the luau is for. He and his wife host it to remember their son. A lot of people come and then they do some night surfing right out here."

Georgia scowled. "Sounds a bit dangerous. Surfing at night to honor a man who died while surfing."

"I suppose it is, but they stay in groups and plan it when the moon is big and full and adding its light to help them see. It's really a beautiful experience."

"When is it, dear?"

"Saturday night."

"Do you surf?" she asked her son.

"No, but Ingrid does, and Evan is learning."

Georgia's eyebrows shot up. "Is that so? How exciting."

"I can teach you, if you want to learn," Evan told her.

Georgia giggled. "I think I'm too old to learn something like that, but I'd love to watch you sometime."

The boy nodded and then began bouncing in his chair. She felt the boards below her tremble a bit, so she knew Johnny was once again approaching their table. With one hand he reached down and removed the empty fruit platter and with the other he placed a large steaming mound of pulled pork surrounded by a variety of steamed vegetables.

"Oh dear," she exclaimed. "That is a lot of food."

"Yeah, but it's the best food on the island," Jerry assured her. "Dig in."

"Anything else?" Johnny asked them.

"Remember my ice cream," Evan said, his mouth full of meat.

"I will if you save some room for it, little man."

Evan nodded even as he continued to shovel in the tangy meat.

Georgia joined in and piled some on her plate. One bite told her that her son was probably right about the food. She'd never tasted anything so delicious in her entire life. Johnny knew how to cook a pig.

She told her son as much, and he said, "Just wait until the luau. He slow roasts an entire pig there, and it is the tenderest meat you could ever imagine."

As she dug into her food, she thought about Donald and knew that if he'd known how good the food was here, he'd have brought her to Hawaii a long time ago.

She raised her glass and said, "Indulge me, please, but I'd like to make a toast." They all stopped eating and raised their mostly empty glasses. "To my husband. He wouldn't go anywhere with me while he was living, so I will carry his spirit with me from here on out and imagine him at my side enjoying this fine food and even finer company with me."

Jerry clinked her glass. "To Dad," he said. Then they all touched glasses and took a sip before diving back into the best food to be found on the island.

Chapter Ten

The next morning, Georgia awoke to the smell of bacon frying. She rose, splashed some water on her face and donned the light robe she knew her son had bought special for her visit.

As she walked down the short hallway, she heard Jerry's voice. He seemed to be talking on the phone, so she hung back for a minute. "We'll leave here around one. I want to show Mom around the base." He paused to listen before continuing with, "Don't worry. We'll keep our distance."

She entered the kitchen and smiled at him. He returned the smile and handed her a coffee mug before finishing his conversation. "Mom's up now, so we'll talk later, o.k. Mmmhmm. I'll tell her. Bye." He hung up the phone and turned to his mother. "Did you sleep well?'

She added a spoonful of sugar to her coffee and stirred it. "Yes. I was more tired than I've been in a long time. That Evan really kept me on my toes."

Jerry chuckled as he flipped the bacon and added bread to the toaster. "He's a pistol, that's for sure, and he really took to you, didn't he?"

She nodded. "Yes, and now my knees are barking at me for all that time on the floor playing marbles with him. I'm surprised kids these days even know how to play marbles. I thought they were all into those handheld games." She sat down at the table and sipped her coffee.

"Evan's a unique kid. He's been tested, and he has an above average I.Q. Ingrid is looking into enrolling him in a special school even." He gathered together their breakfast and brought everything to the table. Then he poured himself a glass of grapefruit juice and sat down.

She eyed her son over her mug. Of the three children, he was the one who most took after their father, and she noticed that his close-cropped hair was receding at an alarming rate. Donald had been almost completely bald by the time he was forty, so she assumed Jerry would be as well.

He looked good, though. Hawaii suited him, and she suspected that Ingrid suited him well, too. She set her cup down and picked up a piece of bacon. "So, son, are you going to tell me how you and Ingrid got together? And where is Evan's father?" She bit into the bacon and realized it was turkey bacon.

He grimaced a bit, leaned back in his chair and squinted in the sunlight streaming through the curtainless window. "Evan's father works with me at the base."

She glanced up quickly and saw him avoiding her gaze. Immediately, she knew her son had been the cause for the breakup of Evan's parents. She sighed. "How did it happen, Jerry?"

"You want all the sordid details or the abbreviated version?" He gave her a wry smile.

"How about a little of both." She buttered her toast and added some jam on top of it.

"I bought this house because Chet – that's her husband, uh, her ex-husband – knew I was looking for something small and affordable. He knew I was wanting out of the apartment I'd been renting because it was overrun with college kids who made a lot of racket at all hours. Anyway, Chet came to me one day and said that the old lady who lived next door was moving back stateside to live with her daughter, and she was wanting to sell quickly.

"I came over, saw the place and made her an offer. It was a relatively low offer, but she accepted it. I think she liked knowing that a service man was going to live here as her husband had also been a military officer. He'd survived the Pearl Harbor attack even.

"Chet and Ingrid helped me move in. Until then, I'd never met her. She was nice, and at that time, Evan was just a baby, so she was home because she'd taken a long leave of absence from her job to take care of him. Chet's and my work times weren't always the same, and I'd run into her outside from time to time. One day, she invited me in for iced tea and to get my opinion about the best type of fencing for the backyard if she could convince Chet to get a dog.

"That afternoon tea led to other afternoon teas at both of our houses. Evan took long naps, and eventually we did more than have tea." He stopped talking and looked ashamedly at his mother.

"I see. Let me see if I can fill in the rest. Chet came home and found you two, and he filed for divorce and maybe even beat you up." She stood and refilled her coffee cup.

"Actually, not quite. Ingrid filed and took him by surprise. He had no idea what was going on between us. But yes, after he found out, he did take a few swings at me. Initially, he refused to leave or to grant her the divorce, but once he saw that his wife was in love with me, he gave in and moved out."

Georgia shook her head. This wasn't the way she had wanted her son to find love. "Jerry, how could you break up another marriage?"

He frowned at her. "I didn't set out to do that. Ingrid just suits me well, and Chet wasn't all that nice to her. Neither one of us ever intended to hurt him, though."

She sighed. Oldest story in the books. "No, I'm sure you didn't. So, where is Chet now?"

"Living in base housing until his transfer to Colorado finalizes."

She gasped slightly. "He's leaving?"

Jerry nodded. "He requested it, in fact. Wants to get as far away from Ingrid and me as possible."

"Yes, but what about Evan?"

Jerry shrugged. "Since their divorce, he's barely spent time with the boy. He came by drunk one night and started ranting about wanting a paternity test to prove he was his son. Then he broke some things and shoved Ingrid down the porch stairs. She broke her nose."

Georgia nodded. "I thought it looked like she'd broken her nose at some point. How horrible." She paused, hating to ask. "Is Evan his?"

Jerry scowled at his mother. "Of course he is. He looks just like him, too, so that makes it even stupider that Chet wanted a paternity test."

"So, why didn't you tell me about Ingrid sooner?"

"Well, considering the way we got together, I didn't really think you'd approve, and I was waiting for the divorce to be finalized, too."

"I see. Is it final now?"

"Yes, about a month ago, and then I knew you were coming to see me, so I figured it could just wait until you got here and met Ingrid for yourself. I knew once you met her, you'd like her."

Georgia smiled in spite of herself. "Yes, she is very nice, and that sweet son of hers certainly helps smooth things over with me, now doesn't he?" She stood. "I'm going to go shower now. I heard you say something on the phone about going somewhere. Where are we going?"

"Still eavesdropping on my phone calls, Mom?" he teased. "I'm going to show you around the base. I was telling Ingrid this and making plans to meet up with her and Evan later. She was reminding me to keep you away from Chet while we are there."

She patted her son's shoulder. "Jerry, Jerry, Jerry. Where did I go wrong raising you?" She mussed up his sparse hair and headed toward the bathroom.

"Hey, I think I turned out pretty well," he called after her.

Passing a photo of him fishing off a boardwalk with Evan, each of them sporting matching t-shirts and sunglasses, she could only agree that her son had turned out pretty well indeed.

Later, watching Jerry help Evan with his bowling ball, Georgia felt certain that Ingrid and Evan would become permanent members of her family. She laughed as Ingrid tried to take a photo of the two boys and almost got bowled over by their wayward ball.

Ingrid joined Georgia on the seats. "This was a great idea."

Georgia nodded. "As soon as Jerry told me there was a bowling alley on the base, I wanted to come here. I used to be part of a league, but I haven't bowled in years."

Jerry returned to the score table. "Don't believe her. She's kicking our butts."

Georgia rose and grabbed her ball, lined up and sent it roaring down the lane. All but one pin went flying. She picked it up with her second ball, and Jerry groaned. "Stop complaining, dear. It's not my fault you've let this great facility go to waste."

"I'm too busy to go bowling." He looked to Ingrid for support. "Plus, Ingrid's not much of a bowler."

She didn't back him up. "Actually, I like to bowl. You've never asked me to go before." She stepped onto the lane and threw a gutter ball. Turning, she playfully shook her finger at him. "Maybe if you'd brought me here before, your mother wouldn't be kicking our butts."

Georgia laughed and said, "Keep your wrist straight, Ingrid." She watched the young woman throw her second ball, which almost reached the pins before veering into the gutter. "That was better, but you still need to straighten it out a bit."

"Mom, can I have a soda?" Evan asked.

"Sure." She turned to the others. "Anybody else want something?"

Jerry and Georgia both shook their heads. They watched Ingrid and Evan walk toward the concession area. "She's a lovely girl, Jerry," Georgia said as she turned toward her son.

He smiled. "I know."

"But," she scowled at him, "you've put her and her son in a tough position, you know."

"Yes, Mom, I know. Don't worry. I love Ingrid. I'm not letting her go."

Amid the noise of pins crashing and bowlers cheering or groaning, Georgia scooted closer to her son. "So, are you planning to marry her?"

"I've asked her, but she's said 'no.'"

"Really? Why?"

"Well, actually she said 'not now.' She doesn't want to spring too much on Evan. He's still getting used to the divorce. I think she also wants to be one hundred percent certain that we'll be together forever before she subjects Evan to possible further disappointment. She doesn't want him getting too attached to me if I'm just going to leave."

Georgia sniffed. "That's idiotic, to be blunt."

Jerry looked past his mother to see if Ingrid was returning yet. "What's that supposed to mean?

"No marriage is disaster-proof. Nobody carries a crystal ball to show them that they will in fact live happily ever after. Disappointment is part of life and it is most definitely part of marriage."

"That's easy for you to say. You had Dad, and you guys had a great marriage."

"That's my point exactly. You are my son, so you had blinders on where it came to your father's and my marriage. It was far from perfect. Sometimes it was downright excruciating. If Ingrid loves you and wants to marry you, then you two should marry. Evan will see what he wants to see even if you two have problems down the road."

He shrugged. "I don't know, Mom. I would never want to let down Evan."

"What makes you think you will? And even if you do, so what? Are you telling me that I've never let you down? That your father never did?"

He thought for a moment. "I can't think of a time when you did."

She smiled indulgently. "See, there're those blinders at work. Believe me, we let you down plenty of times, but we did our best to not let any of you kids down where it truly matters. You'll do the same for Evan and for any children you and Ingrid have together."

He looked away and squinted. She knew that look – he was trying not to cry. She leaned toward him and placed a hand on his knee. "Ask her again and assure her that you'll always be there for her and for Evan. I think she'll say 'yes' if you do."

They heard Evan's voice and turned to watch him take a seat at a table nearby. Georgia laughed and walked toward the table. "I thought you were just getting a soda."

Ingrid rolled her eyes. "I thought so, too, but once we got over there, he saw somebody else carrying away a plate of onion rings, so he wanted some, too."

Jerry called to them, "I thought we were here to bowl?"

They all laughed. Georgia said to Ingrid, "You two go bowl. I'll sit here with Evan."

"Are you sure?"

"Absolutely. I insist. I'll coach you from here and help you kick Jerry's butt."

"I heard that," he called up to them. "No fair picking on me. I outrank you."

Georgia watched Ingrid walk to Jerry and give him a light peck on the lips. She could just barely hear Ingrid say, "Maybe here, dear, but you'll never outrank me in the bedroom." She quickly averted her gaze, so her son wouldn't know she'd heard. "So, tell me, Evan, what kind of soda are you drinking?"

"Root beer," he exclaimed. "It's the only kind Mom will let me have since it doesn't have caffeine."

"I see." She proceeded to engage him in conversation while keeping an eye on Ingrid's bowling technique and calling out advice and encouragement. By the end of the tenth frame, Ingrid was only a couple of pins behind Jerry.

They came up and sat beside Georgia and Evan. "So, how was the base tour, Georgia?" Ingrid asked.

"Wonderful. This is quite a place," Georgia said. "I couldn't quite get used to seeing some of the men salute my son, though."

Jerry chuckled. "Most of them were doing it to be smartasses since the word had spread that I was showing my mother around."

"Well, I'm sure you get saluted regularly without me being around. It was fun to see." Suddenly, she had a thought. "Ingrid, what do you do for a living? Jerry's mentioned a job, but he hasn't said what it is."

Ingrid blanched a bit. "I was a newspaper reporter, but I took a leave for a while when Evan was a baby, and when I wanted to go back to work, they said they couldn't afford to rehire me full-time because so many newspapers are struggling these days. You know, the online presence of so many news sources has really put a bite into the paper news."

Georgia nodded as if she really understood, but she rarely looked at anything online, so she wasn't aware of what was out there.

"So, I've been freelance writing for a few years now. Sometimes I make good money at it and other months, it's a real struggle. I never should have taken that leave when Evan was born. I'd probably be one of the editors by now if I hadn't."

Jerry patted her arm. "Stop kicking yourself about that. Your freelance work is wonderful, and I know you're bound to start getting more acceptances as the time goes on."

She smiled indulgently at him, but Georgia could see she'd hit a sore spot for Ingrid. "I didn't mean to make you sad," Georgia said.

"Oh, you didn't. I'm just a little frustrated at times."

"Yes, I'm sure you are. Teaching made me frustrated quite often as well. It's hard to invest so much time and effort into something that doesn't pay out the way you'd like it to."

"Exactly," Ingrid said as she nodded. "After Evan started in school full-time, I was hoping that my writing career would take off, but it hasn't yet."

"Well, don't give up." Suddenly, Evan let out a huge belch. They all looked at him in surprise before they burst out laughing.

"Excuse me," he said between giggles.

Georgia said, "The same thing happens to me when I drink root beer." Seeing that he'd eaten all his onion rings, she asked, "Are you ready to go bowl again? I can show you a few tricks if you'd like."

He slid off his chair. "O.K." He grabbed her hand and pulled her toward the lane.

Jerry called after them, "I'll order some more food for the rest of us. After we're done here, we can go catch a movie."

Evan jumped up and down. "Yay!" Then he looked at Georgia. "This is the best night ever." He picked up a ball and waddled toward the line.

Georgia followed him thinking *Yes, it is*.

Chapter Eleven

A few nights later, Georgia sat with Jerry and Ingrid at a long table enjoying the roasted pork from the luau. Lit torches scattered around the beach, a roaring fire and the full moon provided enough light by which to eat. Large waves crashed somewhere out in the ocean and then rushed to the shore for a short rest before being pulled out to deeper water to repeat the cycle. Small children joyously squealed and ran away from the little waves only to turn and run after them, giggling hysterically, as they returned to the sea.

Evan was not among the children as he was spending the evening with his father. Georgia wished he were here to enjoy the night with them, and she knew that Jerry and Ingrid wished the same, but Chet had insisted that Evan spend time with him since he was leaving for Colorado in a couple of days.

Johnny approached their picnic table and asked them if they needed anything else. They assured him that they'd had more than enough to eat, and he thanked them for coming to honor his dead son before turning his attention to the next table of spectators.

As she watched Johnny move on to another group, she noticed a man sitting at a nearby table looking her way. With a start, Georgia realized he was actually looking right at her. She averted her eyes and began to make small talk with Ingrid, but she could feel his eyes upon her, so she scooted over a few inches to directly face her son.

Sensing her discomfort, Jerry asked, "What's wrong, Mom?'

"Nothing, dear." Her eyes slid toward the man who nodded slightly at her before standing and moving off toward the water.

Jerry caught her line of sight and turned his head. Seeing the man rise, he grinned, "Uh oh, Manny has his eye on you."

She blushed and was grateful for the semi-darkness to hide her redness. "I don't know what you are talking about." She slid her plate in front of her and began to nibble on the pieces she'd abandoned a moment ago.

Ingrid prodded Jerry in the side with her elbow. "Don't tease your mother."

He laughed. "I'm not. Manny was looking at her, and you know Manny."

Ingrid nodded and rolled her eyes. She looked across at Georgia. "He's quite the ladies' man, or at least, he thinks he is."

"Then he certainly isn't interested in me." She gestured at their surroundings. "There are far younger and more attractive women here to interest a man like that."

Jerry smirked a bit. "Yeah, but they all know him, and he's tried his moves on most of them already. You're new."

She narrowed her eyes and huffed, "Well, he better not try any moves on me. I'll put him in his place right away."

Ingrid started to giggle. "I'd like to see that, actually." She quickly peeked over her shoulder where Manny was standing talking to Johnny by the fire. "But,

Manny's actually a nice guy. I feel sorry for him sometimes. I think he's just lonely."

Jerry nodded. "Yeah, he's a nice guy." Then he winked at his mother. "You should go talk to him, Mom."

She swatted his arm across the table. "Knock it off, you two. I have no desire to meet a man or have one try to pick me up." She rose. "If you'll excuse me, I need to use the restroom." She looked around. "Where is it?"

Jerry pointed behind him to the water and gave his mother a smug look. Ingrid nudged him again. "Don't believe him. The restaurant is open. You can use the one inside."

"Thank you, Ingrid," Georgia stressed her name while glaring at her son. She spun off the picnic table bench, stood and walked toward the restaurant, enjoying the feel of the cool sand squishing up between her barefoot toes. She slowed her walk to revel in the sensation a bit longer, even stopping once to wiggle her toes deep into the vestiges of an abandoned sand castle. When she reached the restaurant, she found it full of teenagers playing a game on a big screen TV set up for the occasion. A couple of them looked her way. "The bathroom?" she asked.

One of the boys pointed the way, and she thanked him. Their shouts followed her down the short hallway, and for a brief moment she found herself missing her young students and their unabashed joy at the simple things in life.

She took her time in the restroom and studied her newly tanned features. Her hair was in complete disarray from the salty breeze, and there was a noticeable blob of barbecue sauce over her left breast. Georgia wetted a paper towel and scrubbed at the dried spot. Then she ran her fingers through her hair to tame its wildness a bit. Taking one last look in the mirror, she said to her reflection, "Well, you're not bad for an old lady, but I doubt you'll be breaking any hearts."

As she left the bathroom, she noticed that the restaurant was now quiet. Thinking it was just a momentary lull in the action of the game, she stepped into the main room and was surprised to find it empty. Well, almost empty.

A large shadow stood against the opposite wall. *Shit*, she found herself thinking and was shocked at her internal profanity. She walked toward the door and pretended to be startled when a voice spoke to her from the dark.

"Hi there," the deep bass voice said.

She stopped. "Who's there?"

The shadow stepped into a lighted area. "Just me, Manny," he said.

She started to walk past him on the other side of some tables. "The bathroom is free if that is what you need," she offered.

He put out a hand as he came around the non-protective table, seemingly intent on cutting off her escape. "Truth be told, I wanted to meet you. I hear that you are Jerry's mother."

She stopped and peered up at him. "Yes, I am." She took his outstretched hand and watched her own age-freckled, newly tan hand disappear in the grip of his massive well-weathered mitt. "Nice to meet you." She shook his hand once, pulled her own hand free and started to move off.

He chuckled. "You know my name, but I don't know yours."

She kept walking. "It's Georgia." At the door, she turned slightly. "I need to get back to my family."

He sighed audibly and looked down at his own bare feet. "Of course. Nice to meet you, Georgia. Enjoy the rest of the luau."

She paused, wondering if Jerry hadn't told her about Manny's womanizing ways, would she be acting this rudely to him. She doubted she would, so, taking a deep breath and closing her eyes briefly to steel herself, she quickly blurted, "You're welcome to join us if you'd like."

His head shot up and he grinned at her. "Thank you. I'd like that." He followed her out the door and across the sand to their table.

Georgia could see Jerry's face lit up by the nearby torch and the look of wonder that passed over it as she approached followed by the towering Manny. She did her best to shoot him a motherly warning look, but she doubted he'd be able to see it, backlit as she was. To his credit, though, Jerry stood and shook the older man's hand. "Nice to see you again, Manny. How have you been?"

"Oh, I can't complain." Manny eased his bulk onto the table's bench seat. Georgia felt it sink beneath her and heard it groan in protest. For a moment she worried that it would break, sending both her and Manny tumbling onto the sand beneath them. As if sensing her concern, she noticed Manny shifting his weight so it fell over the x-shaped strut at the end of the bench.

Ingrid looked down to hide a grin, and Jerry took a sip of his rum and juice drink. An awkward silence fell over the small group until Manny asked, "You still in the service, Jerry?"

Jerry nodded. "Yep. This is my twelfth year."

Manny thumped the table and said, "Good for you, man." Then he turned to Ingrid. "Are you a service gal, too?"

"No," she replied. "I'm a writer."

"That's great. Anything I may have read?"

She shrugged. "I doubt it, but maybe. I sometimes write features for the paper, and I write a lot of travel pieces for the papers stateside about Hawaii."

"Sounds interesting." He shifted his focus to Georgia. "And how about you, Georgia?"

She shot her son a scolding look as she heard him lightly chuckle. "I am a retired teacher."

Manny leaned away from and looked at her with admiration. "Really? Little ones or big ones?"

"Excuse me?" she said.

"Did you teach the big kids or the little kids?" He gestured with his hand, first above his head and then at almost bench height.

She smiled. "Oh, I taught the little ones. Third grade."

Jerry piped in and said, "She was a great teacher, and she shouldn't have retired yet, but my dad died just a few months ago, Manny, and Mom didn't want to hang around without him."

Manny nodded slightly. "Yeah, Johnny told me about your loss. I'm sorry."

"Thank you. Jerry has simplified things a bit, of course, but I was ready to get out of there and into the world to see some of it before I'm too old to do so."

Manny scoffed at her. "Please. You're a young woman still."

Georgia waved his comment away and glared at Jerry who was biting his lip and avoiding her gaze. Just then, a loud pounding on a drum started up, and Manny clapped his hands together once. "The dancers are ready to start." He stood. "Georgia, would you care to accompany me to watch?" He held out a hand toward her.

Jerry waggled his eyebrows at her, and Ingrid elbowed him in the ribs again. Georgia stood and allowed Manny to help her keep her balance as she stepped over the bench. "I'd love to." She looked at Jerry and asked, "You two coming?"

"No, we're going to take a little stroll along the beach. You go and have fun. We'll find you when it's done."

Georgia hesitated and gave her son a withering look, but then she grinned in spite of herself and let Manny lead her to the bonfire and dance area. They sat on mats in front of a cleared area, and Manny proceeded to tell her the names and ages and relations of all the dancers lined up in front of them.

She was pleased to see that they weren't all buxom tropical beauties with lovely bodies. Some were, but most were older with noticeable and even pronounced love handles. However, they knew how to dance and they showed their love for the art of hula dancing in the synchronization of their moves and the smiles on their faces.

Manny explained what each dance move meant, and she was captivated with how a story could be told so beautifully without a single word. The mixture of the drum beats and other instruments and the tranquilizing, swaying movements of the dancers' hips along with the incessant whisper in her ear from Manny lulled Georgia into a state of total relaxation. Then suddenly the tempo of the music changed and the dancers started moving faster and faster. The small crowd joined in with enthusiastic clapping and cheering.

Georgia did her best to blend in with the natives, but she was the only person there for whom a luau was a new experience. Fortunately, nobody was paying much attention to the fact that Manny was pouring a constant commentary into her ear.

She had to admit that she was enjoying the attention. Manny might only be showering her with his usual "ladies' man" charm, but it was a novelty to her. Donald hadn't attempted to regale her with lively conversation or tried to woo her with charm since before the kids were born. She felt both silly and flattered by Manny's presence at her side. If he really were the don Juan she'd been told he was, then she hated to be the object of scorn by the people around her who were probably looking upon her as some naïve mainlander; however, if her son had exaggerated his womanizing ways, then he appeared to be a very nice man, and she was happy he'd taken a liking to her.

She couldn't imagine why he would want to spend the evening with her when there were many younger and far more attractive women to choose from all around them. She glanced up at his animated face and noticed that while he wasn't the best-looking man she'd seen since arriving in Hawaii, he did have native charm. Most of his tan was natural skin color, and she surmised that he was most likely of Samoan descent with a touch of European thrown in since his jaw line was very defined, and his eyes were a light shade of brown.

His voice was deep and resonant, and it reminded her of Donald's soothing baritone. Involuntarily, she smiled, and he noticed it. He paused in his story telling to ask, "Am I boring you?"

"Not at all!" she assured him. "In fact, I can't recall the last time I had such an enjoyable evening."

He grinned at her. "I'm so glad. Would you be willing to have dinner with me tomorrow?"

She frowned slightly, taken aback at the invitation. "Um, . . ." she mumbled because she didn't know what to say to him.

He patted her knee. "It's all right. I understand. Recently widowed, strange man in a strange land, that sort of thing." He winked.

She coughed and looked around to see if Jerry or Ingrid were nearby, but she saw that they were far down the beach sharing a romantic moment away from everybody else. "Manny, I am flattered. I just don't know what to say. I haven't been asked out for almost half a century." She laughed at the look on his face. "Must be a shocker to you, a man who goes out on dates regularly."

"Actually, Georgia, I was thinking that that must be nice – to have had somebody to share your life with for so long."

Tears welled up in her eyes, and she tried to surreptitiously brush them away, but he caught her hand before she could. "Careful. You'll get sand in your eyes. Here." He offered her the corner of his sleeve.

"Thanks." She used it to lightly wipe away the tears that had escaped her blinking. "You know, I would like to go out with you tomorrow, but I need to check with Jerry to see what he was planning before I commit to anything else."

He smiled. "All right. Let's go ask him, and then we can decide from there." He leapt to his feet much faster than she'd ever seen a man of his size or age do before. He extended a hand to help her up off the mat, and she gladly accepted it since her arthritic knee was throbbing from sitting cross-legged so long.

As they walked down the beach toward Jerry, she saw that he and Ingrid were hurrying their way and waving. She waved back. When they met, Jerry asked, "Did you like the hula show, Mom?"

"It was wonderful," she said. "Manny explained the whole story to me; otherwise, I never would have understood the significance of all those arm and hip moves."

"My mother was a hula dance instructor," Ingrid informed her.

"Really?" Georgia asked, puzzled even more by the young woman's light complexion.

"Yes." Ingrid smiled and filled in the blanks in Georgia's confusion. "But she wasn't a native either. She'd come here right out of school to learn how to surf from the pros, but she ended up being more adept at dancing than surfing, and when she met my father who was stationed here, they both ended up staying and working on the island."

"I see," Georgia said. "Do you know how to hula?"

Jerry interrupted. "Yes, she's fabulous at it."

"He exaggerates," Ingrid said as she nudged Jerry playfully.

Georgia thought they'd had enough small talk and that she should broach the subject. "Manny has invited me to dinner tomorrow."

Jerry's eyebrows shot straight up. "Really? That's great."

"But, uh, I told him I needed to see what you had planned before I committed to anything with him."

Jerry looked at Ingrid and winked. "We were just going to take you for a ride around the island in Ingrid's convertible."

Georgia looked at Manny who was hanging back a little. "Well, I don't want to miss that or ruin Jerry's plans."

Ingrid broke in before Manny could say anything. "Actually, Manny knows the island better than Jerry or I do. I'd be happy to loan you my car if you would like to use it to show Georgia around."

Georgia felt her face turn red. "Now, really, you know I am here to see Jerry, so I don't want to upset his plans."

Manny stepped forward. "I would love to show all of you around, if you'd like."

Jerry nodded and pulled Ingrid close. "Sure, I could drive and you could navigate. You probably know a lot of tucked away hidden treasures that I've never heard of."

"We could go up to Diamond Head."

Ingrid clapped her hands in glee. "Ooh, that would be great. Can you believe that I've never been up there?"

"What is Diamond Head?" Georgia asked.

"An extinct volcano. The symbol of Hawaii. You can see it from here in the daytime."

Georgia nodded. "Oh yes, I know what you are talking about. It is extinct, though, right?"

Manny laughed. "Yes, for a very long time. Would you like to see it?"

The group consulted and all agreed that it sounded like a fun thing to do. They decided that they'd better head home to rest up and get an early start to make the climb to the summit before the afternoon heat set in.

"We'll stop by the restaurant in the morning to pick you up, Manny," Jerry said.

"Sounds great. I'll see you then." He took Georgia's hand quickly and gave it a light squeeze. "See you tomorrow." He watched them walk away.

As they climbed into Jerry's small car, Georgia asked, "Is he really a notorious ladies' man or were you just yanking my chain?"

Jerry shrugged. "I don't really know. I've heard stories, but I've always known him to be a nice guy." He peered over his shoulder at his mother. "Why? Have you taken a liking to him, Mom?"

Ingrid chided him, "Don't tease her."

"It's o.k., Ingrid. He's always liked to pick on his mother. And, really, Jerry, I just met the man. Of course I haven't taken a liking to him." She looked out the window and watched the darkened road roll by. She said an internal apology to Donald because she knew that wherever he was he certainly knew what was in her mind, and her mind was saying that Manny was a sweet guy and that she was looking forward to the day with him tomorrow.

Chapter Twelve

The next morning, Georgia stood at the top of Diamond Head looking out upon the scene below. Honolulu stretched out before them, glittering in the sunlight.

Exhausted yet jubilant after the trek up the summit stairs, she looked to where Ingrid and Jerry were sharing binoculars and alternately pointing at places below them. Manny was conversing with his brother on his cell phone and urging him to step outside of the restaurant and look up to the top of the volcano and let him know if he could see them.

She laughed to herself at that crazy idea, and then thought back over the funny phone call she'd made this morning to her daughter, Sally.

When they'd arrived at Jerry's house the night before, he'd been surprised to find four messages on his answering machine. "Hmmm. Hardly anybody leaves me messages on this thing anymore. I usually get voice mail." Then he'd looked at her and grinned mischievously. "Ten to one they're all from Sally."

She had chuckled and said, "I'm not taking that wager because I'm sure you're right."

He'd played back the messages, and they both were right. The first ran, "Hello, or should I say Aloha! (giggles) You guys must be pretty busy as I haven't heard anything from Mom since she left San Francisco. I'll call her cell and see if she answers. Talk to you soon."

The second came in about a half hour later. "Hi, me again. I tried Mom's phone, but it went straight to voice mail, and I know she never checks that, so I just wanted to tell you guys to call me back when you get home. Bye."

On the third, a noticeably tired and peeved Sally said, "Well, it is pretty late here and I can't imagine what you guys are up to so late, but I guess there is a time difference to account for. I still want you to call me when you get in. Hope to hear from you soon. Bye."

Upon hearing the last message, Georgia and Jerry both burst out laughing. "(sigh) Well, I guess you either aren't home, and I know it is really late even at your time, or you haven't received my messages. Either way, I am going to bed now, so don't call me back until the morning. I expect to hear from you then. Good night."

Georgia had called her first thing upon waking this morning, and Sally had drilled her with questions until she'd finally admitted that she'd spent time with a man last night. There had been stony silence on the other end. "Are you still there, Sally?" she'd asked.

"Yes. I just can't believe you were on a date. Dad's only been gone a few months."

Georgia looked at the ceiling for support and took a deep breath. "It wasn't a date, honey. I just met him last night, and he explained all about the significance of the hula dance for me."

Suddenly, Jerry yelled from the kitchen, "Yeah, but they have a real date today!"

Georgia covered the mouthpiece but not before Sally heard her brother yelling something. "What did Jerry say?"

90

"Nothing." Before she could react, Jerry appeared at her side and pulled the phone toward him and repeated his initial comment. Then he gave her a rakish grin and winked at her.

Silence came from the other end. Georgia sighed. "It's not actually a date."

"Really? You're spending time with him today, is that so?"

Georgia said that she was.

Sally chided her, "Then, Mom, as I recall you once saying to me, 'If you're in the company of a male non-relative, then it's a date.' Am I misquoting you?"

Georgia shook her heard in consternation. "No, but you are misrepresenting the facts. He offered to show us around the island."

"Doesn't Jerry live there, and hasn't he lived there for years?"

"Yes, of course he has."

"Then why does he need a tour guide. I thought he was supposed to be your tour guide."

Georgia looked at Jerry who was still standing nearby reveling in her discomfort. Suddenly, she had a wicked idea. "Has your brother ever told you about Ingrid?" She saw Jerry's eyelids narrow, and he frowned at her.

"Ingrid? No. Who is she? Does Jerry finally have a girlfriend?" Sally emitted a tiny squeal of delight.

Georgia smiled impishly. "Oh, I think she's more than his girlfriend. Why don't I let Jerry tell you all about her? He's standing right here." She extended the phone to Jerry who gingerly took it from her and mouthed 'Thanks, Mom' before putting it to his ear.

"You're welcome, dear," she said as she patted his arm and walked to the kitchen to get some breakfast before their visit to the volcano. She could hear her son placating his sister and apologizing for not keeping her in the loop better about his life and their mother's visit.

Georgia sat and pretended to read the morning newspaper until Jerry joined her at the table. "Well played, Mother," he said as he plopped down across from her.

She lowered the paper. "Whatever do you mean, dear?" Then seeing his hangdog expression, she relented a bit. "I should have called her sooner and kept her abreast of what I've been doing here. She's angry at me, too, for not using that camera she gave me to send her photos of the places I've seen."

"Well, take it along today. You can get some great shots from the top of Diamond Head."

"The top?" she squeaked. "How are we going to get up there?"

"We're walking. How else do you think we could get up there?" He glanced at the clock. "We should get going, too. I said we'd pick up Manny at 9:00."

"Walk? Couldn't we fly up there instead?"

He started to walk away. "I don't have a plane, Mom, or a chopper for that matter."

She snapped her fingers. "I met a guy on the flight here."

Jerry turned and raised his eyebrows at her. "Another guy, Mom? Really, you've become quite the little flirt haven't you?"

She scoffed. "I don't mean it like that. Don't be vulgar. He's a tour guide operator, and he flies people to places all over the islands. He gave me his card." She stood up. "I'll go find it. Maybe he could take us up there."

Jerry laughed. "Even if he could, Mom, it's a little late to arrange a tour for this morning. Find his card later, and maybe we'll use him to go see some other places that are further away. Diamond Head isn't that bad of a climb. I've seen people way older than you make it to the top with ease."

"Really? How far of a climb is it?"

He thought for a moment. "Under a mile, I'm pretty sure."

"Well, that's nothing. I walk further than that on my treadmill every night while watching my shows."

He clapped his hands together. "Then get a move on, champ. We've got a mountain to climb." As she hurried off to change, he called after her, "And a mountain of a man to pick up."

Just then, the front door opened and Ingrid entered in time to hear Georgia yell back to Jerry, "Jerry LaMont Haines, you be nice to your mother, you hear?"

Ingrid cocked an eyebrow at Jerry, "LaMont?"

Jerry rolled his eyes and shook his head. "She's getting senile. Don't believe a word she says."

Ingrid laughed and pecked him on the cheek.

Now, Georgia watched Ingrid kiss her son again. Even though she'd only known the woman for a few days, she liked her and thought she was a good match for her youngest boy. She was both adventurous like him and well-grounded which he needed to be, so she was a good influence on him.

93

Lowering her camera, she attempted to review the photos she'd taken, but she forgot how to do that, so she had to ask Manny to show her. He ended his useless phone call and held out his hand for her camera. She watched it disappear in his giant hands.

"Let's see. This is a little like mine, so I think we hit this button, and, yep, there's the last one you took." He handed her the camera and showed her how to review them. Seeing that many of them didn't catch the light well since the sunlight was so strong, he showed her a different setting, and she then took a few more that way.

"Those are much better," she said after reviewing them. "Thanks, Manny."

"No problem. Here, let me take a few of you with the panorama view behind you. You look good in this light."

She blushed, but she handed him the camera and tried not to pose too noticeably. After he took a couple, she called out to Jerry and Ingrid to join her in the photos. They did. Standing between the two younger people at the top of a volcano in Hawaii made her feel like she was on top of the world.

Suddenly, Jerry said, "We have to take one of you with Manny." She wanted to protest, but she couldn't think of a polite way to do it. Then she remembered that she could always delete the photos since it was a digital camera, so she acquiesced.

Manny didn't appear to have any qualms about taking a photo with her. He hurried to her side and wrapped an arm around her shoulders and pulled her close to his side. She let out an involuntary yelp.

"Sorry," he said as he released her a little. "Did I hurt you?"

"No, just pulled me a bit off balance," she fibbed. She took a step closer to him and relaxed under his arm. "There, now I'm fine." She caught Jerry giving her a wicked grin before he snapped the photo.

As he handed the camera back to her, he said, "Here you go, Mom. That can be your Christmas card photo."

"Very funny," she mumbled as she passed him to get a different view from the crater top.

Behind her, she heard Ingrid once again telling her son to not pick on his mother so much. Suddenly, Manny appeared at her side and grabbed her elbow. "Don't want you to lose your balance again. The ground is a bit uneven up here."

She thanked him and together they walked around the area, and he regaled her with information about the myriad sites they could see in the distance. For most of the places she just pretended to know where he was pointing and nodded along, but she enjoyed hearing his stories nonetheless.

Finally, Jerry called out that it was time to go because he was hungry. Manny snapped his fingers and told them that he knew the perfect place just down the road from the volcano. He added that after lunch, he'd like to take them to Pearl Harbor.

Georgia looked at Jerry who didn't seem especially keen on the idea. "Don't you want to go, son?"

"I do, but Ingrid has to get back home. Evan is returning from his visit with his dad, and when he comes back from one of those, he's usually a bit wound up. She wants me to help her get him back in line."

"Oh, well, we don't have to go today," Manny began, but Ingrid interrupted him.

"Jerry, go with them. You love Pearl Harbor. I can manage until you get back this evening. You and your mother can come over for supper then."

"Are you sure?" he asked her.

"Definitely, but I am hungry now, and I have a couple of hours before Evan will be home, so let's go eat."

"All right, then. It's settled." Manny said. Then looking at Georgia with a gleam in his eye, he said, "I'll race you down."

Chapter Thirteen

Georgia studied with silent awe the wall full of the names of the people who died during the bombing of Pearl Harbor. She was struck with both gratitude for all the men and women who have served to protect the country and pride in her son for being one of those people. She couldn't imagine over 2300 people being wiped out in one fell swoop like what had happened here all those years ago.

Of course, until the Twin Towers fell in New York City, she couldn't have imagined an atrocity like that either. She shook her head with sadness as her eyes continued to scan the list of names. Suddenly her eyes lit upon the name Donald, and she paused to read the entire name. Then she continued to search the long list of names for additional Donalds. She found twenty-two, and for each of them she said a short silent prayer that they were resting in peace and that their descendants, if they had any, were remembering them with the honor they deserved.

Jerry appeared next to her. "Overwhelming, isn't it?" He nodded at the wall.

She nodded and then turned to look at her son. "I just hope I never have to read your name on a wall like this someday."

He squeezed her hand. "Me too, Mom, but if you do, then at least you'll know that I died trying to do the right thing."

"I don't know if that would be consolation enough, but I guess you're right." She turned to look around the floating room. "Where's Manny?"

"He's waiting on the ferry for the return trip. It's about time to go back."

"All right, but one more look." They stepped to the railing and peered down into the clear water at the wreckage of the USS Arizona. Here and there a few flowers floated upon the water in honor of those who had paid the ultimate sacrifice.

She shook her head. "Such a beautiful place and such an ugly event."

Jerry leaned against the railing. "Just like the 9-11 events, we were taken completely by surprise."

"And by air," Georgia added. "The irony, huh?"

"Yeah, I hadn't thought of that, but you're right." He sighed. "At least here most of the casualties were military people -- people who had signed on knowing that they might have to put their lives on the line someday."

"But both times we were attacked by cowards, weren't we?" she said with an edge to her voice.

"Of the worst kind, Mom." He gestured with his chin. "We should get going now. By the time we drop off Manny and get back to the house, Evan will be wondering where I am."

As they exited, she asked, "He means a lot to you, doesn't he?"

Jerry squinted into the sunlight as they left the small memorial building. He helped his mother on to the ferry. "He's a great kid, and Ingrid is trying hard to do right by him after the divorce. She hates that she's made him the product of a dysfunctional family."

Georgia scoffed at his choice of word. "There's really no such thing as a functional family. Every family has its problems, and sometimes the kids who are stuck in homes where the parents are together only for the sake of the kids are the ones who end up suffering the most."

Manny saw them and waved from his perch at the back of the boat. They returned his wave and weaved their way through the throng of visitors. As she squeezed in next to him, Manny draped an arm around the back of her chair. Involuntarily, she leaned forward a little to avoid too intimate of contact with him.

"So, what did you think of it?"

"It's a beautiful tribute to the people who perished here, that's for sure," she said. "Why didn't you stay in their longer?"

His mouth turned down slightly before he answered. "I come here once a month to pay my respects to my grandfather."

Both Jerry and Georgia looked at Manny in surprise. "Your grandfather died here?" Jerry asked.

Manny nodded. "Yes, he was one of the few civilians who were killed. He actually died at Hickam field where you work now, Jerry."

"I knew a few casualties came from the locals, but I had no idea that you and Johnny had lost somebody. I'm sorry to hear that."

"Why do you think my brother always treats you and the other servicemen so well at the restaurant?" Manny winked at him. "He's paying our debt."

Jerry said in the most solemn tone she'd ever heard her son use. "It's us that owe men like your grandfather a debt."

Manny shrugged. "He wasn't a hero. He just happened to be in the wrong place at the wrong time." He turned his gaze out over the water to the open sea. "I come here, and I try to imagine what this place must have looked like on the horrible day, but I just can't. It's too peaceful. I can't imagine people screaming and running and dying and fighting here. I can't imagine bombs falling on this harbor. I can't imagine such evil exists," he paused and looked up at the sky, "even though I know it does."

Georgia felt a tear threatening to escape, and she bit her lip to stop it. "We just have to do what we can to remember people like your grandfather and every other person who has died at the hands of terrorists or people trying to force their ways upon others."

The ferry began to move. The three sat quietly together watching the water and the other passengers and listening to the simple conversations taking place all around them. Georgia couldn't help but almost feel silly for sitting there between two wonderful men on a gorgeous day passing over the waters where so many had lost their lives.

After they got back to the dock, she remembered to grab her camera and take a couple pictures to send to Sally. She knew her daughter would lecture her if she didn't take some shots of the place her granddaughter had studied about in school just a few months ago. When they'd finally accepted that Georgia was going to go travel for a while, and they knew she would visit Honolulu, Willow had informed her all about Pearl Harbor. Georgia was certain that her granddaughter had enjoyed learning about it and imagined how excited she'd be to receive photos from her grandmother visiting the very place she'd studied and aced a test about in her history class.

A little while later they dropped Manny off at the restaurant. He appeared reluctant to say good-bye, so Jerry told him they'd call him and arrange another outing before Georgia left. He smiled and said that that would be great and that he would be looking forward to the call.

Georgia waved to him as they drove off, and then she turned to her son. "Now, why did you promise him that?"

Jerry laughed. "Aw, come on, Mom. You saw his face. He likes you."

Georgia blushed. "Don't be silly, Jerry. He's about ten years younger than I am, and you, yourself, told me that he is a player, as the young people say these days."

Jerry burst out laughing and almost lost control of the car rounding a bend in the road. "A player! Really, Mom, the things you say sometimes."

"You know what I mean, dear."

"Yes, but I also know the look on a man's face when he admires a woman. He has that look."

She chose to ignore him and peered out the window at the foliage as they passed through a less developed part of the city. Finally, she said, "Even so, you shouldn't encourage him. I'll be leaving soon, and I'm recently widowed. I'm not wanting or even ready to start seeing somebody else."

"I suppose you're right. We don't even have to call him. I can always tell him that you ended up leaving sooner than I had expected and that we didn't have time to call."

She shot him a look. "Or, you could have not promised him anything to begin with, and then you wouldn't have to lie to him."

They pulled into his driveway. "Uh oh," he said.

"What's wrong?"

"Chet's car is still out front."

She looked toward Ingrid's house and saw a shiny black sports car sitting by the curb. "Is that a problem?"

Jerry shut off the car. "Could be. He should have been gone by now." He glanced at his watch. "Actually, I thought he'd have been gone a couple of hours ago."

"Maybe he was late getting here," she proffered.

He shrugged. "Maybe. Let's go inside and we'll take a peek from the kitchen. We can see into her sitting room if her blinds are up."

She poked him in the back. "Window peeker," she teased.

He chuckled. "Sometimes, Mom, sometimes."

She clapped her hands over her ears. "I don't want to hear about it."

They entered the kitchen and took up positions to see without being seen. Ingrid's blinds were up, and they could see her chairs and couch, but nobody was present. Jerry poured them each a glass of lemonade, and they sat down to wait and watch.

Soon, they saw Evan rush past the entryway, and then they saw him enter the backyard and run to his swing set. A man who Georgia assumed was Chet appeared on the deck and watched him for a bit. Then he said something to Evan that they couldn't hear, and Evan waved. Chet moved back into the house where they saw

102

him walk past the entryway. A few seconds later, they heard a loud engine and the roar of a car as it rushed away.

Almost immediately, the phone rang, and they could see Ingrid standing at the window in the sitting room, a phone held to her ear. Jerry answered the phone. "Hi, is the coast clear?"

Georgia waited as her son continued his short conversation. She was watching Evan swing and remembering the days when Jerry and his older siblings were all small and at home playing and creating havoc in her house. She smiled to herself, missing those days.

Jerry hung up. "Ingrid has invited us to supper. I'm going to head over there now and play catch with Evan for a bit. If you'd like to rest for a while, go ahead. There's plenty of time before we eat."

At the mention of resting, Georgia realized how tired she was. The late night followed by a full day of sightseeing and climbing a volcano had worn her out. She yawned. "You know, I think I would like to take a nap. Tell her I'll be over later to help her with the supper."

Jerry shook his head. "Mom, you are the guest not the cook. Go take a nap and when you get up, come over and we'll eat. You can cook for us another night if it really bothers you."

She raised her hands in mock surrender. "All right." She yawned again. "Go play. I'll see you in an hour or so."

He opened the patio door. "Take your time, Mom." He stepped outside, and she heard him call to Evan. Looking out the window, she saw Evan's face light up and watched him leap off his swing and run toward her son.

She smiled and turned from the window. She walked to her room and pulled back the top quilt and lay down. Before she could even think to remove her shoes, she was asleep.

Chapter Fourteen

The ringing phone woke her, and she was surprised to find herself completely enveloped in darkness. She'd only meant to have a catnap, but she'd clearly slept longer than that. She sat up and rubbed her eyes. The phone rang again, and thinking it might be Jerry calling to ask what was keeping her for supper, she hurried to the kitchen to answer it.

Switching on the light as she entered the kitchen, she noticed that it was after nine. She couldn't imagine why Jerry hadn't waked her earlier. She grabbed the phone. "Hello," she said.

"Mom, is that you?" her eldest son asked from halfway across the country.

"Randy? What a pleasant surprise."

"I've been trying to reach you all day, but you haven't answered your cell phone. I figured you were out sightseeing and didn't have it with you, but when I couldn't reach you for the past few hours, I decided I'd better call Jerry's house and see if you were there."

She rubbed her neck to ease the crick in it from sleeping on Jerry's super soft pillows. "Well, you found me. Is something wrong?"

"Not really. I just haven't heard from you since you've been gone, and Sally told me that you met a man."

Georgia sighed. "Leave it to Sally to overreact and spread unnecessary alarm."

"So, you didn't meet a man?"

She could sense his smile coming across the line. "Technically, yes, I did meet a man. Ironically, his name is Manny even." She heard her son chuckle. "But, there's nothing to concern yourself with, and I certainly don't need the tongues wagging back home about me."

"Well, that may be a little late. Sally mentioned it to Louise."

Georgia groaned. "Oh, not Louise." Louise was her dear friend, but she had absolutely no filter when it came to knowing what items were fit for public knowledge and which things should be kept to herself. In the twenty plus years of their friendship, Georgia had never shared anything with Louise that she didn't want known across the town within a day or two. "Don't tell me, let me guess. I'm a horrible woman who has gone off to Hawaii to be with her secret lover and that is why I left town so soon after your father died. Am I close?"

Randy laughed. "Not bad, Mom. I may have heard you referred to as a tramp out picking up younger men because you can't accept that you are old and that dad's death pushed you over the edge."

She rolled her eyes. "Oh, sweet Jesus. I'm glad I'm not planning on returning anytime soon. I'd have some choice words for all those people who claim to be my friends but who only live to talk trash about anyone who dares to do anything for herself."

Her son was silent for a moment, and she could hear a muffled barking in the background. "Is that Bowser?"

"Yeah, he's outside barking at the neighbor's cat. He's lost some weight since he's been here?"

"He's not sick, is he?" She'd hate to lose Donald's dog so soon after losing Donald.

"No, Mom. You guys just didn't give him enough exercise, and you fed him too much."

"Well, I'm sure you are right about that. Your father was the guilty one, though, as he gave him table scraps all the time."

Randy yelled at the dog and covered the phone with his hand, but Georgia could still hear him trying to coax the dog back inside. "He definitely gets a lot of exercise now running up and down the fence line trying to get at the Coleman's cat. That cat loves to toy with him, too. It's sort of funny, really, but also sadistic."

She laughed. "He wouldn't even know what to do with the cat if he got ahold of it."

"I know." He paused and she heard him speaking to Bowser, good-naturedly chiding the dog. "So, Mom, how much longer will you be away?"

She shrugged and looked toward Ingrid's house. A lot of lights were on, but she didn't catch any movement. "I'll probably stay here another week, and then I'd like to go on an Alaskan cruise and maybe fly to New York City for a week."

"Wow, you weren't kidding when you set off to do this, were you?"

She shook her head. "No, Randy, I wasn't. I don't really have anything I want to return for back home except for you and Sally and the kids, of course."

"Isn't that enough?" She heard the hurt tone in his voice.

"It is, and it isn't. I could die tomorrow or live a long time yet. I don't want to teach anymore, and I'm not

107

ready to stop living and check into some sort of retirement home. Sally's kids could keep me very busy with all of their activities, but where am I in all of that?"

He didn't say anything for a minute. "I don't know, Mom. I'd never thought about it. I guess I always thought you and Dad would retire in a few years and spend some time gardening or, uh, I don't know."

"Exactly. We didn't even have much of a plan ourselves, but we also thought we had a few more years before we had to worry about it. We had briefly discussed spending part of the years down south where a lot of retired couples go to get away from the nasty Nebraska winters, but we didn't have any definite plans. When your father suddenly died on me, I realized that if I signed my next year's contract, I'd be tying myself to a year spent coming home to an empty house. I just couldn't do it."

"You could have moved in with me or even Sally."

She laughed but not with mirth. "Oh, don't be silly. I'd go crazy in Sally's boisterous household, and I know you; you'd spend your time trying to cater to me instead of living your own life. I want you out making your own friends and doing what makes you happy."

He sighed. "I don't even know what that is, Mom."

"Well, you don't need your old mother hanging around preventing you from ever figuring it out." She saw Jerry step out on the lit deck and come down the stairs heading toward his own house. "Jerry is supposed to help me send some photos to Sally in the next couple of days. Does he have your e-mail address, too?"

"Of course he does. That would be great. I'd love to see the places you've been. I've been wanting to get out to Hawaii myself to see him."

Jerry entered the kitchen just as she said, "You should definitely come out here. It is beautiful. With luck, maybe we'll all be coming here for Jerry's wedding soon." Jerry shot his mother a puzzled frown.

"Really? Wow, Hawaii must be the place to hook up with people. First, my mom and now my brother. I really need to get out there." He chuckled.

"Who are you talking to?" Jerry asked from across the room.

She covered the mouthpiece. "Randy." She saw him say 'oh' and asked him if he'd like to talk to his brother. He nodded. "Jerry wants to say hello."

She handed the phone to Jerry and listened as her son told his brother about Ingrid and Evan. Her stomach rumbled, and she thought again of how surprised she was that Jerry hadn't come to get her earlier. She got a drink of water to freshen her dry mouth from sleeping so long and talking to Randy.

After Jerry hung up, he said, "Are you hungry?"

"I'm starving. Did you eat without me?"

He shook his head. "Nope. Evan had had a very late lunch with his father, which Ingrid is still upset about, so we decided to postpone supper a bit. I came over earlier to tell you that, but you were really sawing logs, so I just let you sleep."

She blushed slightly because she'd been told many times by Donald that she was quite the snorer when she was exhausted. It didn't surprise her that she'd been snoring during her nap after her tiring day. "Well, you shouldn't have let me sleep so long. I could have come over for conversation."

"I know. I didn't mean to, actually, but Evan and I got wrapped up in his racing game, and I lost track of time. Ingrid was working on a story she's been assigned by the paper, and she lost track of time as well. I suddenly realized how hungry I was. I ordered a couple of pizzas. They should be arriving any minute."

She rubbed her hands together. "Mmmm, pizza. I haven't had pizza for some time now. Did you order pepperoni?"

"Sorry, no. I got a veggie one for Ingrid and a Hawaiian style one for you, me and Evan. He loves the pineapple on it."

"Sounds delicious. Let's go."

They exited into the sultry dark evening. Georgia looked up into an overcast sky and realized that that was why it had been so dark when she awoke. "Looks like a storm is coming," she said.

"Yeah." Jerry agreed. "The radio earlier said one was blowing in. We'll probably get a good soaking during the night."

"Have you had hurricanes here since you've lived here? I don't remember you ever saying anything about one."

"Not a hurricane, per se, but some pretty intense winds." He opened the patio door for her, and she stepped into Ingrid's tidy kitchen. She noticed the long shelf of cookbooks along one wall. "Is Ingrid a good cook?"

Jerry shook his head and put a finger to his lips. "You didn't hear it from me. Her meals are palatable, at best." He saw that her eyes were upon the cookbooks. "She collects them. She also collects books about Rome, but she's never been there." He shrugged his shoulders. "We all have our own idiosyncrasies."

She could hear Evan yelling in the next room before they entered it. This room was nowhere near to being tidy. It was the TV and game room, and Evan was clearly the main user of the room. His toys were scattered about, and he was currently in the middle of a high speed race against another car on the screen.

Looking over his shoulder, he called, "Good, you're back. Ready to get your butt kicked again?"

Jerry laughed. "Not right now, Evan. We're going to have some pizza, so finish your game and go wash your hands."

Ingrid appeared beside them. Jerry looked at her. "How's the story coming?"

"Just finished up. Of course, I could have been done sooner if it weren't for all the racket." She tousled Evan's hair. He sidestepped, telling her not to mess up his game. She reminded him that he needed to shut the game off and go wash up for supper.

He begged for a few more minutes, but she held strong and moved as if to shut it off for him. He said, "O.K., Mom. Let me save this game really quick, though." She stood over him and watched him do it.

As he trotted off to the bathroom to wash up, she made a slight face at Jerry and then told Georgia, "His father lets him play video games all night and stay up to all hours because he knows it annoys me, and then I'm the one who has to bring him back down to reality and his routine."

Georgia nodded, acknowledging her understanding of the situation. She was relieved that she and Donald had stood together in the raising of their children. They hadn't been perfect parents, but they'd been pretty darn good ones. Despite any differences between the two of them, the one thing they had always been proud of was the way they raised their kids. Where other parents seemed to play 'good parent, bad parent,' she and Donald stood together on issues and didn't allow their children to play them against one another.

She had a feeling that even when they were together, Ingrid probably had to play 'bad parent' to Chet's 'good parent,' which wasn't even good parenting, anyway, considering that he was the spoiler and she was the disciplinarian. Now that they were divorced, she could see that Chet was using Evan to punish Ingrid for falling in love with Jerry. She hated to see her son in the middle of this, and even more, she hated to see Evan in the middle of it. She could only hope that Jerry would fill the void and step up to be the father figure Evan really needed.

Seeing that they'd been playing games all evening while she'd been napping, she knew that her son had a ways to go still, but she also knew that he wasn't officially in the position of stepfather, yet, either. She could see the writing on the wall, though, and she knew it was just a matter of time before the three people before her became their own family unit.

She hoped that he and Ingrid would have children of their own, but even if they did, she'd do everything possible to make Evan feel like one of her own grandchildren. She was so glad that she'd come to Hawaii and met him and Ingrid before they became a part of the family. It would make the transition so much easier.

The doorbell rang, and Evan raced down the hall to answer the door. Jerry followed closely behind him, reminding him to not mindlessly open the door at night just because someone rang the bell. Evan said, "But you told me you had ordered pizzas."

Jerry said, "I know. You're right, but it still could be somebody else at the door, so let your mother or I answer it at night, o.k.?"

"O.K., Jerry." He waited patiently beside Jerry as Jerry opened the door and admitted a young pizza delivery girl. He paid her and added a tip, and then he let Evan carry one of the pizzas to the kitchen.

They all sat down and dug into the warm pizzas. The crust was thin yet still a little chewy, just the way Georgia liked it. "This is delicious," she said, and everyone agreed with her.

"So, Georgia, how do you like Oahu?" Ingrid asked.

"It's beautiful. I could see myself living here and spending my remaining years simply exploring the islands."

Jerry raised his eyebrows at her. "Manny made an impression on you, eh?"

"Now, Jerry, quit teasing her," Ingrid chided.

"Who's Manny?" Evan asked, his mouth full of pizza.

"Don't talk with your mouth full. Here, use this." Ingrid handed her son a napkin.

"Manny is Georgia's boyfriend," Jerry said.

"Oh, stop it. He's not my boyfriend." She turned her attention to Evan. "He's just a friend. Do you remember Johnny from the restaurant?" Evan nodded. "Manny is his brother."

"Ohh. Does he work at the restaurant, too?"

"Sometimes, I think," Jerry answered. He turned to his mother. "So, you think you'd like to stay in Hawaii?"

She shrugged. "I don't know. I'm not ready to go home, and I like it here, but I do want to go see some other places before I make any decision concerning my future." She took a big bite of pizza.

Ingrid asked, "What else would you like to do before you leave?"

Georgia thought for a moment, and then she said, "I'd like to see the waterfalls I've heard so much about."

Jerry frowned slightly. "Most of the waterfalls require long walks to reach them, or you have to see them from the air."

She smiled. "I realize that. I still have that card from the guy I met on the plane. I'd like to give him a call and see if I can take him up on his offer to show me the sights."

"It's not like he'd fly you around for free, Mom. Those trips cost a lot of money."

She nodded. "I know. He told me. I could afford it, though, and I think it would be fun."

Ingrid agreed. "It would be fun. I went on a chopper tour to see the active volcanoes many years ago." Jerry shot her a puzzled look. "With Chet, on our honeymoon." She looked at him apologetically. "Anyway, it was a neat experience. Seeing the islands from the air gives you a whole new perspective, and I bet the falls would be impressive from above."

"Would you care to go with me?" she asked Ingrid.

Evan about jumped out of his seat. "Can we, Mom? Can we, can we, huh?" He tugged on her arm.

Georgia was immediately sorry she had asked in front of the boy. Seeing the uncertain look pass over Ingrid's face and the quick glance Jerry shot her, she said, "I'm sorry. I shouldn't have said anything."

Jerry shared a look with Ingrid over Evan's head. "If you'd like to go, I could arrange a day off, and we could find the money."

Georgia protested. "No, I insist. It was my idea. I will pay if you go with me."

Ingrid shook her head. "Oh, no, I couldn't accept. That is much too generous of you."

Jerry interrupted. "First things first." He looked at his mother. "You'll have to call that guy tomorrow and see if and when he could even get us in. Before that, though, I want to check him out online and make sure his business is legitimate."

Georgia wanted to object, but then she realized that her son had a point. Maybe Larry from the plane was some sort of scam artist. "Good idea. You check him out tonight, and I will call in the morning and see about tours for all of us."

Evan jumped up and down. "Goodie! I can't wait."

"All right. Sit down and finish your supper," Ingrid admonished her son. "Then it's time to go to bed."

"Aw, Mom. I don't want to go to bed yet."

"Too bad. It's late already."

Jerry added, "I'll come read you a story if you'd like."

Evan thought for a moment and then nodded in agreement. He finished his pizza and slid off his chair to go get ready for bed. His mother called after him, "What do you have to say to our guest?"

Evan turned and looked at Georgia. "Good night, Jerry's mom. I hope we can go on the helicopter together."

"Good night, Evan," she replied. "I hope so, too."

As Evan disappeared down the hall, Georgia apologized again for bringing up the tour in front of Evan. Ingrid waved her apology away and said, "It will be fun, actually. He'll never forget you, that's for sure, if we do go on the ride."

Georgia considered that for a moment. She liked the thought of that. It had been a while since she'd made a lasting impression on a child despite her years of teaching them. She felt a warmth spread through her chest that she hadn't felt since the early years of her teaching.

Jerry walked off to tuck Evan into bed, and Ingrid stood to clear off the table. Georgia started to help her, but then she suddenly asked, "Ingrid, are you going to marry my son?"

Ingrid stopped in mid-stride, turned and looked at Georgia. She pondered the question for a minute. "I take it he's told you that he's proposed?" Georgia nodded. "And that I refused?" Georgia nodded again. Ingrid placed the plates on the counter and leaned against the sink. "I don't know if he'll ask again," she said quietly.

Georgia smiled. "I think he will."

Ingrid looked from under her lashes at the older woman. "You do?"

Georgia nodded. "I do."

Ingrid shrugged and smiled. "I'd probably accept." She shot a glance toward the hallway, and then added, "But don't tell Jerry that. The proposal needs to come completely from him."

Georgia nodded. "Of course." She walked to the young woman and said in a low voice, "and when that moment happens, I want to say 'welcome to the family.' I may not be here for the actual event, so just know that Jerry will have my full blessing."

Tears welled up in Ingrid's eyes. "Thank you, Georgia." She stepped forward and gave her a hug.

Chapter Fifteen

"That's Makapu'u Lighthouse," yelled Larry over the noise of the helicopter. He pointed to the right, and Georgia looked down to see a red-capped small white lighthouse perched precariously on the top of a craggy cliff.

"It's lovely," she said, and she heard similar comments coming from the back where Jerry, Evan and Ingrid were seated. All wore headsets to drown out the noise of the chopper blades and to aide their ability to converse, but it was still a little difficult for her to hear everything they said without them raising their voices some.

"Look, Evan," she said as she pointed into the distance, "there is another island out there."

"That's Molokai," Larry said. "When we get to the other side of the island, you'll be able to see Kauai also."

"I can never remember the names of the different islands. To me, they are all just Hawaii."

Larry nodded. "Most visitors are the same way, but Hawaii is actually the big island at the end of the chain."

"I know that, but I forget." She smiled at him and clutched the grab bar as he made a sudden turn inland. "Where are we headed now?"

"To see some falls and just look at the island from above."

From the back, Evan squirmed a bit. "I can't see very well, Mom," he complained.

"Feel free to switch seats with him," Larry said. "He probably can't see all that much from the middle since he's so small."

Georgia turned in her seat a little and watched Jerry unstrap Evan and remove his own safety belt. Then he quickly lifted the boy over him and slid to the middle. Jerry strapped Evan in before he fastened his own belt, and Georgia smiled at the natural ease in which her son had done that.

"Is that better, little man?" Larry asked into his headset.

Evan looked out the side window onto the splendor of Oahu, and declared, "Yeah!"

Everybody laughed. Georgia enjoyed the view of the back seat more than the view outside the window despite its breathtaking quality because looking out at the world passing closely beneath them was making her a little ill. She hoped she wouldn't have to resort to using the vomit bag Larry had pointed out for each of them.

When she'd called him yesterday morning, he'd been noticeably thrilled to get her call. Of course he remembered her, he'd said, and then he'd told her his prices and tours. She'd balked a little bit at the cost of some of the ones designed to see the volcanoes and waterfalls on all the islands. She really just wanted to fly around Oahu and see it better with no set agenda.

He'd pondered for a moment and quoted her a price she could live with for the four of them since she was determined to pay for the trip. She still felt guilty for blurting it out in front of Evan and putting Ingrid in a no-win situation. Larry had said he could make time for them the following day as it was a Sunday, and he normally didn't schedule any tours for himself on that day. She had thanked him but said that he didn't have to deviate from his normal routine for her and that they could wait another day or two even. When he'd told her that he was pretty backed up for the following weeks, she'd agreed to his original plan and thanked him profusely for taking them out on his day off.

"That's why I leave it open – just in case a special person wants a tour," he had told her.

Now she listened to him tell them all about the island of Oahu and its history of royalty and subsequent take-over by the United States. He suggested she visit the royal palace in Honolulu and Chinatown.

Shocked, she asked, "There is a Chinatown here? I thought that was just in San Francisco."

Larry chuckled. "Another mainlander misconception." He pointed down to the right. "There is Sacred Falls."

Everyone oohed as the helicopter flew into the lush valley and approached the falls low only to rise straight up in front of the thin waterfall. Georgia remembered to grab her camera just in time to snap a few shots before they rose above it and continued on their way to North Shore.

Ingrid breathed, "That was beautiful. I haven't been this far north for a long time."

Jerry added, "I've never been up here."

"Really?" Georgia was surprised. This part of the island was really pretty, and she would have thought that anybody living on the island would have come to see it at some point. However, she'd lived in Nebraska her whole life, and there were many parts of it she'd never seen, so it was probably the same for people everywhere.

Soon the helicopter came in sight of the ocean, and Georgia marveled at the intense beauty of a vast blue spread out before them.

"I'm going to drop you at the beach, and then I'm going to hop over to my buddy's hangar and get some extra fuel for the trip home," Larry told them.

"You're not joining us for lunch?" Georgia asked. She had planned to treat him to a nice meal as a tip for taking them out on a Sunday.

"Nah, I'll leave you all to enjoy the beach for a few hours, and then I'll meet back at the drop-off point later. I haven't seen my friend for a month or so, and I'd like to catch up with he, uh, him."

Georgia looked over her shoulder and exchanged a small smile with Jerry. They'd both heard Larry's slip-up and were now certain that he was meeting a woman friend, so of course he'd like some time alone with her.

Larry landed on an open clear spot on the expansive sandy beach. He pointed out a long row of shops and restaurants nearby and told them that he'd return in two hours. Georgia removed her headset and told him to go ahead and make it three hours if that wasn't too much of a problem for him as she'd like to shop a bit, and she knew Evan would like to play on the beach a while. Larry smiled and gave her a thumbs-up.

They exited the helicopter and moved quickly away from its rotating blades. Larry looked to be sure they were all clear before he took off and flew away.

Jerry watched the helicopter disappear and said, "Well, I hope he's actually coming back for us. It's a long walk home from here."

Ingrid laughed. "I'm sure he is. He's a nice guy." She turned to Georgia. "Thanks for bringing us along."

"No problem. I wouldn't have enjoyed any of it without all of you with me." She clapped her hands together. "Now, who's hungry?"

Evan yelled, "Me, me," as he jumped up and down.

"Then, let's eat," Jerry said as he grabbed the boy's hand.

They walked across the warm sand toward the restaurants on display and saw that most of them nearer the beach were crowded, so they continued down the line a ways until they found one with a few empty tables outside. "This place reminds me of Johnny's restaurant," Georgia said as they took their seats.

When a large man appeared at their side to take their order, they couldn't contain themselves and burst out laughing. He looked at them perplexedly and asked if they needed a few more minutes to decide.

They said that they did but that they'd all like some iced tea first. He moved off to get it for them, and they again started laughing.

"It's like an alternate universe where Johnny exists in two places," Jerry said. He winked at his mother, "Maybe Manny has a double also."

"Oh, Jerry," Ingrid said and patted Georgia's hand. "Don't pay any attention to him."

"I never do," Georgia kidded in return, but inside she found herself thinking about the large friendly man who seemed to have taken a liking to her. He'd called yesterday when she'd been spending a relaxing day at Jerry's teaching Evan how to play simple card games like Kings' Corners and Rummy. She'd felt the boy needed to learn the joy of non-noisy mental games as well as the loud video games he'd already mastered.

When Jerry had handed her the phone, he'd done it with a noticeable glint in his eye. "It's for you," he'd said, and she'd taken it assuming it was probably Sally calling to chide her for not sending any photos yet.

After saying hello, she'd been startled to hear Manny's deep baritone in her ear. She'd shot her son a nasty glance before excusing herself from the game with Evan and exiting the room for a little privacy.

Manny had asked her about her plans for the remainder of her visit, and when she'd told him about the helicopter trip, she'd heard the hopefulness in his voice. She couldn't invite him along, though, as the helicopter only held four passengers, and she knew there would be an extra cost for Manny simply due to his size, but she didn't want to explain that to him.

She'd told him that she wasn't sure how much longer she'd be on the island, but that it wouldn't be more than a week as she'd like to go see Alaska next on one of their cruises. He'd whistled at that idea and said it sounded like a great time.

Then he'd asked her to have dinner with him before she left, and despite her inner voice telling her she shouldn't, she had accepted and promised to have dinner with him on Monday evening. "Will we eat at Johnny's?" she had asked him.

He'd laughed. "No, I'm taking you to a much nicer place."

They'd agreed on the time and that he could pick her up at Jerry's. After hanging up, she'd gone back into the kitchen to find both Jerry and Ingrid looking at her expectantly.

She'd simply handed Jerry the phone and sat back down at the table to reengage Evan in the game. Jerry had continued to make silly speculations about what Manny wanted including things like he wanted to run away with her to Africa and other such nonsense that she'd finally told him about the date just to shut him up.

He'd said, "I can't wait to tell Sally about this."

She'd shot him a look and then ignored him for the rest of the afternoon. Later, she'd felt silly for accepting the date and confided as much to Ingrid. The younger woman had told her that she wasn't the one who had died and that she should enjoy herself. "Besides," she had reminded her, "it's just a date, and you will be leaving soon after it, so it's not like you have to see Manny ever again. Plus, it's far from home, and the people back there don't have to know about it."

She'd scoffed at that. "The minute Sally knows about it, the whole town will know about it. They all already think I'm a horrible person for coming on this trip so soon after Donald's death."

Ingrid shook her head. "Let them talk. By the time you return home, they'll have forgotten all about it and have found other things to gossip about."

Georgia nodded. "You're probably right." To herself, she'd thought that it didn't really matter what they chose to say about her back home because she might not ever return to live there. She was giving herself a few more months to figure that out.

After they ate their lunch of shrimp and French fries, Jerry took Evan to the beach while Ingrid and Georgia perused the offerings of the many boutiques nearby. Most sold similar beach-related clothing, but in one store Georgia found a collection of handmade hammocks. She decided to get one for Jerry since she knew he had the perfect spot in his backyard to put it, and his birthday was coming up.

She asked Ingrid for advice in choosing the perfect one, and they both decided on a bright red one to match his enthusiasm for his home state's Husker football team color. He had a special corner of his den that was full of Husker memorabilia, and when they were playing, he'd either watch it on TV or listen to a broadcast of it on the radio. The hammock would be a great place to lie while listening to the games on the radio.

The clerk wrapped the hammock into a manageable bundle, and Georgia asked him the time. Hearing it, she said, "We'd better head back. Larry should be returning soon."

The women headed across the sand toward the small specks that they knew were Jerry and Evan. As they approached, they started to laugh. Evan was proceeding to bury Jerry in the sand but had only managed to cover his legs so far. Jerry was a bit oblivious to it all as his attention was fixated on two striking young women wearing the skimpiest of bikinis and frolicking in the waves directly in front of him.

As the shadows of his mother and girlfriend descended upon him, he snapped out of his daze and

125

looked up at them in chagrin. Then realizing he was half-buried in sand, he quickly stood and shook the sand from his pant legs, but he had to remove his shoes and socks to dump out the sand that had encroached upon him there.

"How was the shopping?" he asked as he purposely turned himself away from the sight of the buxom and barely clad women.

"Not as fun as it seems things were here," Ingrid said as she gave him a slightly withering look.

Jerry continued to look down and brush sand from his legs. Suddenly, Evan yelled, "I see the helicopter."

They all turned their attention away from the sea toward the approaching chopper. Simultaneously, they all began to wave with both arms to attract Larry's attention, but they mostly just attracted the attention of the other beachgoers at their odd behavior.

Grabbing Evan's hand, Jerry hurried toward the landing chopper and assisted Evan inside. The women followed, and Georgia saw Ingrid glance back once at the now staring young women. She heard her sniff in disgust before the sound of the chopper drowned out any other noises.

After they climbed aboard, Larry asked, "Did you have a good lunch?"

"Yes," they all said. "How about you?" Georgia asked.

Larry maneuvered the helicopter up and away from the beach. "It was great," he said, and Georgia and Jerry exchanged meaningful glances once again.

"I'm just going to fly along the coastline all the way back to Honolulu if that is all right with you," Larry said.

They all agreed that that was a great idea and sat back to enjoy the ride. Georgia noticed a stony silence emanating from the back between Ingrid and Jerry, so she engaged Evan in conversation by pointing out various ships at sea and volcanoes in the distance.

She also remembered to snap a lot of photos on the return trip and even managed to turn around to get one of the three passengers in the back. Before she took it, though, she forced a smile out of each of them, including Ingrid who she could tell was still smarting from Jerry's infatuation with the semi-naked bathers.

"Say Hawaii," she coaxed before taking the photo.

"Hawaii!" Evan yelled and then gave her a big grin. Jerry snaked an arm around Ingrid and one around Evan and pulled them both close for the shot.

Georgia took it and watched it appear on her screen. "Now, there's a keeper," she said pointedly as she looked at both her son and Ingrid.

Chapter Sixteen

Basking in the glow emanating from the covered candle between them, Georgia sat across from Manny at a cozy table. Only yesterday she'd learned that Honolulu had a thriving Chinatown, and tonight she was smack in the middle of it at one of its more storied restaurants.

When Manny had picked her up, he rather sheepishly said, "I hope you like Chinese food. I should have asked you before making the reservations, but I was excited about taking you there."

She assured him that she was open to any dining experience even though, if she had been honest with him, she would have told him that her one and only prior experience with Chinese food had left her vomiting in the toilet the next morning. Her husband had assured her that it was just morning sickness since they'd been out celebrating the discovery of her first pregnancy, but she hadn't been convinced and had refused to eat Chinese food after that.

However, she was now starting a new journey in her life, and she reminded herself that that doing so meant trying new things and being open-minded about old prejudices. So far, she was thoroughly enjoying the ambiance and Manny's funny stories.

He appeared to know every person in the restaurant and maybe even in all of Chinatown, and he was regaling her with humorous tidbits about every one of them.

"See the guy over there at the corner table with the nice suit on?" He pointed with a jerk of his chin, and Georgia casually glanced in that direction. She nodded. "Well, that's not his granddaughter across from him like you might think."

She had to admit that she would have assumed it based on the man's age compared to the very young and very pretty woman sitting across from him talking animatedly into a cell phone. "His mistress?" she asked in a whisper, feeling like they were having a clandestine conversation about all the patrons.

Manny smiled. "Nope. She's wife number eight."

Georgia's eyes flew open. "You're kidding me. They must be at least fifty years apart in age."

"You're close. He's seventy-eight, and she's twenty-two."

"That's horrible. Why in the world," she began but stopped herself. "He's filthy rich, I suppose," she guessed.

He tapped his nose to indicate she was right. "Owns all the dry-cleaning businesses in town and is suspected to be a big-time drug kingpin."

She glanced once more at the man who sat looking bored out of his mind while his nubile wife continued to jabber away on the phone. "He looks like a college professor." She shook her head. "What some people will do for money."

Just then a large plate of steaming rice appeared before her with a set of chopsticks. She looked around the table in vain for a fork, and Manny seemed to sense her distress as he quietly asked the waiter to bring the lady some Western silverware. She detected a look of scorn cross the waiter's face before he politely bowed and hurried off to comply with the request.

"Thanks. I've never used these before." She attempted to hold them the way she'd seen the other guests do, but they slipped out of her hand.

"Here, let me show you." Manny reached across the table and took her hand in his large one. She felt a jolt rush through her, so she kept her eyes fixed on what he was trying to show her and avoided looking at him.

She tried to use the chopsticks to pick up the rice and did manage to get a few grains to her mouth, but most of the rice fell back to the plate, so she was relieved when the waiter reappeared with a wrapped set of silverware for her. He then asked if they needed anything else, so Manny requested some sake and more tea.

She shook a playful finger at him. "You're not going to try to get me drunk, I hope."

He smiled. "No, I just want you to try it. They have really good sake here." His grin widened. "Unless getting you drunk and convincing you to go back to my place is an option."

She choked slightly on some rice and had to take a sip of her tea. He quickly apologized for being so forward, and she waved his apology away.

They spent a couple awkward moments staring down at their plates before she got up the nerve to quietly ask, "Manny, why are you wasting your time on me?"

He looked at her. "What do you mean?"

She chewed on her lip a moment. "I'm older than you, recently widowed, and I don't live here." Then realization hit her, and she leaned back in her chair. "Ah, I see. That's exactly why you like me. I'm an easy

130

conquest you never have to see again." Her stare hardened.

He stared back at her in shock. "Georgia, is it so hard for you to believe that I enjoy your company and that I like you?"

She thought for a moment. She'd like to believe what he was saying was the truth and that she could still get a man's attention. It had simply been too long since anybody had shown any interest in getting to know her as a person and not just as "so-and-so's teacher" or "Sally's mother" or "Donald's wife," etc. that she didn't know how to read if a person was actually interested in her, Georgia.

She shrugged. "Yes, it is hard for me to believe. You are a well-known bachelor and ladies' man, and I am a lonely widow passing through your field of play."

He looked up and paused in their conversation to thank the waiter who had just set the sake and tea down in front of them. He waited for the man to leave before he leaned across the table and said, "I like you, Georgia. Plain and simple. Something about you caught my eye at the luau, and I couldn't take my eyes off you from that moment. You've invaded my mind since then and my dreams every night." He covered her hand with his. "I don't want you to leave because I'd love to spend every single day getting to know you better."

She blinked back tears and looked intently into his eyes. If he was a liar, he was a good one. She smiled weakly at him and apologized for her suspicions.

He leaned back and smiled at her. Then he poured a small amount of the sake into a cup for her. "Try this. If nothing else, it will take the edge off, so we can enjoy the rest of our evening."

She took a sip and then a larger gulp. It wasn't bad. Setting the cup down, she let the warmth of the wine spread through her body, relaxing a bit. "I'll take a smidge more," she told him.

He raised his eyebrows and gave her a comical look. As he poured the drink for her, she gazed around the room and saw that most of the patrons were couples like them. She commented on that, and he chuckled. "That's why I picked this restaurant. I wanted to woo you a bit, and I didn't want to do it surrounded by a bunch of screaming kids."

She smiled and allowed a touch of flirtatiousness to enter her look. "Woo me? We're really showing our age with that word choice."

He laughed. "True, but I've always liked the word." Then he winked. "And since this is Mr. Wu's restaurant, it is a fitting one, don't you think?"

She was still laughing when the Kung Pao chicken appeared in front of her. She'd allowed Manny to order for her since her experience with Chinese food was so limited. Taking a bite, she gave him an appreciative look to indicate that he had chosen well.

As the meal progressed, Manny told her about the woman who had broken his heart many years ago and about his resistance at letting any other woman get too close ever since then. "Eventually, I simply let too many years go by, and before I knew it, I'd become one of those confirmed bachelors you hear about. It was never really my intention, though. I always had planned to end up like Johnny with a fat wife and a huge brood of children."

She smiled at him and felt a bit sorry that he'd never experienced the joy of being a father. She knew he was close to all of his nieces and nephews, but she couldn't imagine that was anything like the experience of having your own child. "What happened to the woman who broke your heart?"

He chuckled. "She became the fat wife of some other man and moved to the big island to raise their brood."

"Well," she said, trying to be polite, "it's never too late for a man, you know."

He propped his chin onto his open hand. "It is for me. I have no desire to start a family at my age." His eyes twinkled. "I'd rather meet some hot grandmother and help her spoil her own brood of grandkids."

She grinned maliciously at him and leaned closer to him. "You're wasting your time with me, then. I haven't been hot since I went through menopause."

He burst out laughing so loudly that all conversation around them ceased. She felt her cheeks burning red and mentally chided herself for going too far.

"Georgia, you're a hoot!" he exclaimed. Then quieter, he said, "As to your hotness factor, leave that for me to decide." He looked her up and down. "I'd say it's even more sizzling than the platter being served at that table over there."

She looked to the side and saw a waiter lowering a platter on to a trivet in the middle of the neighboring table. The waiter was using a hot pad and advising the diners to not touch the edges because they would get burned.

She smiled and rolled her eyes at him. "You're impossible, I'm afraid, but for now, I will simply accept your compliment." She paused before adding, "But you simply must get your eyes checked."

Again his booming laugh echoed through the establishment, and she was glad that their meal was over. He indicated that they could leave, so she stood to go. He reached for her hand, and she hesitated only a fraction of a moment before she extended her own and let him guide her through the crowded restaurant and out to the sidewalk.

They paused there, and he asked if she would like to take a walk around the streets of Chinatown. She said that she certainly would, so they set off down the road still holding hands.

They walked around admiring the interesting architecture until they found themselves in front of a majestic looking theater. She noticed the lit marquee and the singer's name on it. "I know him," she said with a hint of enthusiasm in her voice.

Suddenly Manny released her hand and stepped up to the box office. He asked something and then turned to her. "The show has already begun, but we can still see most of the show if you'd like."

She appreciated his gesture, but she declined upon seeing the prices displayed behind him. She knew the meal he'd just bought her had been pricey enough. "I'd really just prefer to walk and talk some more if you don't mind."

"Not at all," he replied as he rejoined her. This time he slipped an arm around her shoulders instead of taking her hand. For a moment she allowed herself the comfort of snuggling up against him, but suddenly an image of Donald popped into her head, and she pulled away. Manny quickly apologized, and they continued down the sidewalk in silence a ways.

Sensing that he'd felt rebuffed by her, she took the initiative and grabbed his hand. He smiled down at her and gave her hand a squeeze. They continued walking up and down the darkened streets with their strategically placed well-lit pockets for about an hour talking about her children and grandchildren the whole time.

A sudden ache of longing to see or talk to her grandchildren overwhelmed her, so she promised herself that she would spend tomorrow learning how to send photos to Sally and how to web chat with her grandchildren. She knew Jerry had the capabilities to do so because he'd told her as much already, but she hadn't been interested enough to learn until this moment of missing her family back home. While she wasn't yet missing her actual home or the town, she did miss Randy and Sally and all the rest.

When they arrived at Manny's car, he looked down at her. "I don't suppose I can convince you to come to my place?"

She swallowed and licked her lips. A part of her was dying to go, but the composed and still-married part of her was telling her not to go. Finally she said, "Not tonight, Manny."

He nodded his understanding and opened the door for her. On the drive back to Jerry's, he pointed out other places of interest to her and openly invited her to return to Hawaii someday to see all those sights and many others with him.

She smiled at him, but inside she doubted she would ever see him again after tonight. She'd be leaving in a few days, and he would find some other lonely tourist to flatter and wine and dine – probably with more success than he'd had with her. Secretly, she was certain that he'd be chasing the next woman in his life within a week.

At Jerry's house, Manny jumped out and hurried around to open her door. She stepped out of the car and right into an embrace. She returned it, feeling a little like a young girl hugging her much taller father as her face only hit him in the chest, but suddenly he leaned down and planted a kiss on her lips which erased all paternal images from her mind.

The kiss lasted a while and became quite intense before she managed to pull away for air. As she looked up into his eyes, she almost regretted not taking him up on the offer of spending the night at his place. Instead, she reached up a hand and gently stroked his face. "I had a great time. Thank you so much."

She started to move away, and he said to her, "If you're ever in Hawaii again, you know where to find me." She looked back at him and nodded. Then she stepped onto the porch and gave him a light wave before she entered the house.

She waited by the closed door until she heard him drive away, and then she turned only to find her son waiting for her in the hallway, a big grin plastered across his face. "A little late coming home, don't you think, young lady?"

She playfully swatted at him and brushed past him to the kitchen where she poured herself a glass of water and drank it, attempting to quench the fire that had suddenly been lit inside her.

Chapter Seventeen

A month later, Georgia sat on a ship deck chair gazing at the small Alaskan town of Sitka. She'd opted not to go ashore because she was feeling a bit lonely. The snowcapped mountains behind the town added to her melancholy feeling.

She'd regretted coming on the cruise ever since the ship left Seattle. Not that the trip hadn't been enjoyable. Far from it, in fact. She'd viewed more natural beauty in the past five days than in her entire life before, and she had a full memory card on her digital camera to prove it.

She smiled a little imagining Sally's dismay when her mother sent her over a thousand photos. She'd probably never hear her daughter complain again about her mother not using her camera.

Once she'd boarded the boat, though, she'd realized that she was just about the only solo traveler on board. Seeing the happy couples and families had made her miss Jerry, Ingrid and Evan immensely, and she wished she'd been able to convince them to come along. However, she knew that they had to work, and they didn't have the luxury of being able to take off whenever they wanted. Jerry had given up enough of his vacation time for her during her stay at his home, so she couldn't ask him to use more when he might have plans of his own.

She'd hated to say good-bye to them, but Jerry had reminded her that they would see her again before the year was out as they were planning to come to Nebraska for

Christmas because Evan had never seen snow. She'd nodded and bit her tongue to prevent herself from telling him that she didn't know if she'd be in Nebraska for Christmas.

Despite her loneliness of the moment, she still wasn't ready to return to the town where she'd spent all her married life with Donald. Even though it was full of memories, it didn't feel like home to her. Most likely that was due to Donald being gone, but she also knew that deep down she'd never felt truly at home there.

Maybe she wouldn't feel at home anywhere, she feared, but she had connected to Hawaii, or Oahu, more in a short span of time than she'd ever connected to any place before. She definitely wanted to return there someday, maybe permanently.

There were three other widows traveling together on this cruise, and they had tried to include Georgia in their activities. She had joined them at meals and even for the trek across the glacier, but most of their conversations were about people and events she had no association with, so she felt silly trying to fit in with them. She understood they were simply being nice, so when they asked her to come along today, she had politely declined saying she wasn't feeling well, and she'd noticed a slight wave of relief wash over their faces.

They were pleasant ladies, and she was sure they were enjoying themselves without her. They would surely fill her in on all the sights and shopping experiences when they gathered for supper later. Until then, she was content to sit on the deck and let the peacefulness of the surroundings wash over her.

She picked up her book. It was the third she'd read so far on the short cruise. She was happy that the ship had a fully stocked library available for passengers; she had passed a lot of her time in there due both to her solitary traveling and to the fact that she'd neglected her love of reading far too often over the past forty years while raising three kids, being a devoted wife and teaching full-time. It was good to have the luxury of uninterrupted reading. The library sported a massive window with comfortable reading chairs in front of it. She'd spent many hours sitting in there reading and taking frequent breaks to look out at the water. From there, she'd seen whales spouting in the distance, and for that sight alone she was glad she'd come on the trip despite her overall loneliness.

Her current bookmark was a ship's brochure about Juneau, a town she actually was looking forward to visiting. She opened the pamphlet and reread the information about the tram that led from the dock to the 1800 foot level of Mount Roberts. She'd never ridden a tram before, and she was looking forward to the experience despite her extreme fear of heights.

Apparently, she might see a lot of local animals including bald eagles and even bears. She swallowed in trepidation at the thought of seeing an actual bear, but the idea thrilled her as well. She'd see if the widows wanted to accompany her as she didn't relish the thought of going on the tram or walking on a trail in the wilderness alone.

A presence appeared at her side, and she glanced quickly, without appearing to do so, to see who it was. She immediately became more immersed in her book in the hope that the man standing near her would get the hint and leave.

Sadly, she wasn't the only ship passenger traveling completely alone. Roger Jameson, a rancher from Montana, was also alone, and once he'd learned that they were roughly the same age and both newly widowed, he'd been attempting to spend every conceivable moment with her. She had hoped he'd gone ashore with the rest of the passengers.

"Georgia," he boomed as he pulled a deck chair alongside her, "whatcha doin' out here, darlin'?"

She raised the book slightly and continued to pretend to read, but when she saw that he wasn't going to leave, she lowered it and slipped the brochure between the pages to mark her spot. "Why didn't you go in to Sitka?" she asked him, barely able to hide the annoyance in her voice.

He sucked on the yellowed strands of his moustache that hung over his top lip, and she cringed in disgust. "I was planning to, and then I ran into them other three widders, and they tole me you was still aboard, so I thought I'd keep ya company."

"That was kind of you to think of me," she said attempting to be polite, "but you shouldn't have skipped the town on my account."

"Why didn't you go ashore?" He turned to look intently at her over his small glasses.

"I just wanted to be alone for a while," she said pointedly.

He pursed his lips. "Seems to me that you and I got nothin' but alone time for the rest of our lives. Why waste this time bein' alone when you can be with someone else?" He raised his eyebrows meaningfully at her.

She swallowed her distaste as she looked at his scarred and craggy face, overly wrinkled and deeply lined from working and squinting in the sun and wind all his life. She imagined that once he might have been attractive, but even if he still were, his reptilian personality was too much for her to stand.

"Roger, I've told you before that I did not come on this cruise to meet a man. I'm not interested, so please stop bothering me."

He raised his hands in surrender, but she knew it was only a temporary reprieve. She tucked the pamphlet further down in her book, so he wouldn't see that it contained information about the tram. She didn't want him appearing on the trail high up on a mountain in Alaska asking her for a quickie in the woods. If there were truly bears up there, he might just become their next meal, she thought and smiled slightly.

Unfortunately, he mistook the smile for encouragement and reached across to lightly stroke her forearm. "You know where to find me, Georgia, if you change your mind. I can be real nice to a lady, if you know what I mean."

She pulled away from him. "I think I do, Roger, and like I said, I am not interested. Go use your charms on the other widows."

He smirked. "Those old biddies? They're too old for me."

She laughed unintentionally. "I highly doubt it, Roger."

"They are," he insisted. "I'm only sixty-two."

She was surprised to learn that because he looked closer to eighty. Secretly, she suspected he was lying about his age, but she didn't really care because she just wanted him to go away. Certain men her whole life had simply made her hackles rise at the mere sight of them. Roger was one of those types of men. She could tell he was a man who didn't respect women, and she was surprised he'd even been married, but he might have lied about that as well.

A certain part of her chastised the other part saying that she was dwelling too much on Manny and not letting Roger even have a chance to impress her, but she also knew that without ever having met Manny, a man like Roger would never make a good impression upon her.

Her current predicament centered on how to get rid of Roger, so she could enjoy the rest of her afternoon before the other passengers started returning from their shore time. She'd had the lesson of being polite firmly ingrained in her by her mother, and she'd spent the majority of her adult years trying to instill the same decent quality in her own children and those she taught; she'd rarely ever had the occasion or the desire to be rude to somebody.

She hated to change her ways now, but what better time and place to start than on a ship far away from those who would judge her and at a time in her life when she was starting a new journey alone. She considered the best way to get him to leave her alone, but she couldn't come up with anything that might sway him to abandon ship and leave her in peace.

Finally, she stood and simply said, "If you won't go away, I will." She looked down into his shocked upturned face and stifled a smirk. She nodded and walked away.

142

Unbelievably, he called after her, "I'll see you at supper. Until then, I'll be in the gym if you change your mind."

She shook her head and continued walking, unsure where she was going. She didn't feel like returning to her cabin even with a book to read as the cabin made her feel slightly claustrophobic and enhanced the seasickness she'd felt off and on the whole trip. It was a spacious cabin, but the ceilings were low, so she felt uncomfortable there during the daytime.

Since he said he was going to the gym, Georgia decided to head to the library and see if one of its comfortable reading chairs were available. It really was her favorite place on the ship, and as long as Roger was elsewhere, she could enjoy it. After all, the library would be the last place he would show up since he didn't strike Georgia as the reading type.

She came at the room from a different direction than the gym and peeked inside. No sign of Roger. She sighed in relief and returned to the chair she had vacated before going out to the deck. She settled down into the comfortable wingback, kicked her sandals off, placed her bare feet on the ottoman and tried to read her book, but something outside the large window caught her eye.

There was Roger hobbling down the pier waving at the three widowed ladies who were standing outside of a shop they'd apparently just exited by the looks of the bags they were toting. He certainly didn't waste any time, she thought, nor was he picky about his women like he had claimed to be only a few moments ago.

She watched the other ladies attempt to ignore him and move off quickly in the opposite direction. She started to laugh because she was pretty certain they'd been on their way back to the ship since they were well laden with full bags. She imagined them cussing under their breath and urging each other to walk faster. However, the weight of their purchases along with their substantial combined girth prevented them from making a hasty retreat, so Roger quickly caught up with them.

Unfortunately, a delivery truck blocked her view of their reunion, but she could well imagine it, and she was even happier that she was safely onboard away from a weasel like Roger. She shook her head and returned to her book.

Once again, though, she couldn't get drawn into the story like she would have liked because she kept thinking about Donald and what he would think if he could see her now only a few months after his death and already pursued by two men. For starters, he probably wouldn't believe it, she was certain of that. While Donald had once considered her beautiful, it had been years since he'd voiced that opinion, and more than once she'd caught him eyeing her with a strange expression on his face.

He'd probably been thinking the same thing that she used to think: *Who is this old person I'm married to and what happened to the good-looking, sexy one I used to know?*

Or maybe his expression just meant that he had gas. Who knew? She could only speculate now since Donald was gone. She wished she'd asked him what those looks meant because she was prone to assign negative meanings to things that often didn't merit such a classification.

More than once early in their marriage, her unintentional negativity had led to horrible arguments as Donald's feelings were easily offended, so she'd learned to quell her inner critic for the sake of peace between them. She sighed in relief and in sorrow as she realized that she no longer had to worry about riling up her partner, and she could think whatever she wanted about somebody else even though she still might want to censor herself before sharing her opinions with others. Donald could be a harsh critic, though, too, and they'd often shared some good old bitch sessions together about people they found mutually offensive.

She wondered what he would have thought of Roger. He certainly would not have had the same opinion as she had of the rancher who exuded such an ick factor that she couldn't see past it to any redeeming qualities he might possess. She tried to see him the way she imagined Donald would have – as a hard-working man who clearly had a lot of self-confidence and had lived a long, interesting life in the great outdoors. Yes, Donald would probably have enjoyed meeting and talking with Roger, and if Donald had been at her side, Roger wouldn't be hitting on her, and then maybe she would be able to see him in a different light as well and enjoy his company and stories.

Sadly though, Donald wasn't with her, and she was left to deal with men like Roger on her own. Here she was on a small ship sailing in her own personal unchartered waters. She'd met and married Donald at a young age, and her experience with other men in a romantic light was extremely limited and very much in her past. That was why she hadn't recognized Manny's flirtatious behavior and why she hadn't believed that it was legitimate or that she was deserving of it.

She realized she was smiling, and quickly looked down at her open book before somebody saw her staring off into space with a silly grin on her face and decided she was experiencing a moment of senility. Why couldn't she stop thinking of Manny? She barely knew him, and she doubted she would ever see him again even though he had given her his phone number and his e-mail address and urged her to send him photos and messages about her further travels.

She decided that she would stop waiting to send Sally a message and take care of it right now. The library had a number of laptops available for passenger use, so she asked the attendant to show her how to log on and find her e-mail provider. Once he did that, Georgia spent a few minutes digging in her bag to find the paper where she had recorded her own e-mail information and the addresses of her children and of Manny.

She opened a new message window and began to write about her cruise, painting the trip in a more positive light by dwelling on the interesting sights she had witnessed and some of the more colorful passengers she'd met. She also included a detailed description of her stateroom and the great meals she'd had on board. Then she told them of her plans to ride the tram in Juneau and her hopes of spotting some bears and other wildlife.

Rather than sending a few individual messages, she simply added all the addresses and then hit 'send.' She hoped that when Manny saw that she had sent the same message to him and to all her children, too, he would realize that she wasn't trying to establish a romantic connection with him; she was just writing to him as he had asked her to do.

While she was online, she began researching some of the other places in the United States and abroad that she'd like to see. After about twenty minutes of reading about New York City, she was startled by the sudden sound of a 'ping' from the computer. She looked at the screen completely puzzled and realized that she'd left her e-mail open on the taskbar.

Clicking on it, she was stunned to find a message from Manny. Foolishly, she looked around to see if anyone else was watching her before she opened the mail.

It read, "*I'm glad you are enjoying your cruise. I've been thinking about you every day since you left. Be careful if you see a bear – I'm not there to scare it off. ☺ I wanted you to know that I had a great time with you, and if you ever come see Jerry again, please let me take you out on some more dates. You're different than any other woman I've known, and I love that about you. Enjoy the rest of your cruise, and keep me posted. Manny.*"

She reread 'you're different than any other woman I've known,' and immediately her inner grump assumed the difference he meant involved her age as she was certain that she was the oldest woman he'd ever taken on a date; however, he had also said that he loved her differences, so she doubted it had to do with age after all. Thinking back over their time together, Georgia couldn't recall him saying anything about what was different about her, so she could only speculate.

"Or," she said quietly to herself, "I could e-mail him and ask him what he means." She hit 'reply' and then sat staring at the screen for a long time. She didn't know how to ask him what he liked about her, and once again, she didn't want to unintentionally lead him to think she liked him as more than a friend. However, she was beginning to doubt herself on that subject as she found herself thinking about him every day.

Then she internally chided herself for the umpteenth time and reminded herself that she wasn't interested in a man ten years younger than herself, a man who had been a lifelong bachelor, a man so unlike her recently deceased husband who she should be grieving over every day instead of fantasizing about the first man to come along and show an interest in her. Frankly, she was a little embarrassed for having these teenage daydreams about another man while her own dear Donald was slowly rotting away in a mahogany casket their children had lovingly picked out while encouraging her to put a deposit on a matching one. She hadn't, though. She'd been appalled at the idea of it, and currently she was appalled at the direction in which her late afternoon wool-gathering had taken her. She shook her head to clear her mind of its silly meanderings and looked down at the empty message page. At the moment, there was nothing for her to say.

Finally, she simply closed out of her e-mail and logged off. She could see that the sky had darkened much while she'd been using the computer, and when she checked her watch she realized that it was about time for supper.

As she walked toward her room to freshen up before heading to the dining salon, she ran into the three widow friends. "Did you safely elude Roger?" she asked them, a devilish grin on her face.

They all groaned and made faces and then asked her how she knew he had accosted them. She told them about seeing the action from the safety of the library and how he had started in with her before leaving the ship to seek them out.

"You naughty thing," Melinda, the clear leader of the trio said as she shook her finger at Georgia. "The least you could have done was to warn us somehow."

"How was I to do that?" Georgia asked as she suppressed a laugh. The others looked at Melinda for an answer as well.

The elder lady shrugged and then grinned. "You could have blown the ship's horn in distress." They all laughed at the thought.

Kathy, the youngest, asked, "Are you heading to supper now?" When Georgia replied that she was after she cleaned up, they all insisted that she eat with them and that they grab a table that only sat four to be sure that Roger couldn't squeeze his way into their group.

After agreeing to it, she hurried off to wash up and prepare for supper. Once she was in her room, she changed into a light cardigan and added a bit of color to her cheeks and lips. Then she slipped on the matching bracelet and necklace that Donald and the kids had given her many years ago and that had always been her favorite.

She looked at herself in the mirror and felt a bit silly to be dressing up to impress people she barely knew and would never be with again. She put a hand to her throat and covered the tiny heart at the end of the necklace. "What am I doing here?" she asked her reflection, but the woman in the glass did not have an answer for her.

She thought about just going to bed and reading some more, but her stomach reminded her that she was very hungry, so she left her room and headed toward the dining salon to meet the other ladies.

When she entered the room, she immediately noticed Shantelle, the more robust of the widowed ladies, waving frantically at her. Seeing Roger ensconced in what was supposed to be her chair, Georgia looked around the dining room for a different table with a vacant seat, but she didn't see any free seat at a table that also didn't contain families with children, and she was in no mood to sit and listen to whining or exaggerated bragging. So, with a sigh, she walked across the room, winding her way among the crowded tables.

"Hello, Georgia," the three women all called. She returned their greeting and stood patiently beside Roger, hoping he would get the hint. True to his nature, he didn't. Instead, he scooted closer to Kathy and told her to pull up a chair.

The three ladies shot her a pleading look, but she shrugged. A ship steward appeared at her side and asked them if they needed another chair, or if she'd like to sit at another table. For a moment, she considered leaving the women at the mercy of Roger, but then she decided that, if nothing else, it might be fun to torment the guy a little.

When the steward brought the chair, she placed it between Melinda and Shantelle instead of next to Roger. He gave her a puzzled look, but she ignored it and sat down. She could tell that Melinda wasn't happy about having to pull her chair closer to Roger, but she didn't really feel sorry for the woman. After all, the three ladies had only invited her to join them as a buffer against Roger, and they had failed to save the fourth chair for her, so he was their problem and not hers.

"I was just telling these ladies about the blizzard we had in Montana last winter and how I lost ten head and one of my best horses."

Kathy rolled her eyes and took a sip of water. Georgia noticed her surreptitiously slide her chair a few inches away from Roger who was still sitting close to her. After moving to make room for Georgia, he hadn't bothered to put his chair back in its original location.

Deciding to at least attempt to enjoy herself and do whatever she could to both ignore and exclude Roger from the conversation, she asked Melinda how long they'd all known each other.

Melinda's response surprised her. "Well, we've been doing our yearly cruise for about five years now – a couple years after we first met in a widow support group in Phoenix."

Georgia's eyebrows shot up. "I thought you ladies had been friends forever."

"Goodness no," Shantelle said as she wiped her mouth with a napkin. "Melinda and Kathy already knew each other from the group, and my daughter insisted I join a support group after my Kenny passed." Tears immediately sprang into her heavily shadowed eyes. "I asked around at church, and somebody told me about the group that met each week at the library branch not too far from my house, so I went once to appease my daughter, and I never looked back." She smiled at the other two ladies. "Without Mel and Kat, I don't think I would have survived this long."

"You've done just as much for us, dear," Kathy said.

Roger started to interrupt, but Kathy cut him off. "After Shantelle joined the group, the three of us just hit it off so well that we started doing things together outside of group meetings."

Melinda jumped in, "We went sightseeing all over Arizona and California and Nevada, and one day we even got up the courage to cross the border into Tijuana." That sent the three of them into a paroxysm of giggles. "I'll never forget us trying to get back across the border laden with about twenty bottles of tequila and completely drunk." She paused to think and then almost yelled, "Borrrrrrrachas!"

Kathy was wiping at her streaming eyes and gasping for breath. "I don't know how we escaped a night in jail that night."

"Most likely because we reminded that senior guard of his own dear *abuela*, if you recall," Melinda said.

Georgia grinned in delight at the three women's joy and at Roger's obvious discomfort. He was once again chewing on his overhanging moustache and picking at his food. "So, then you ladies started doing more traveling together?" she asked.

They all nodded. "Yes," Shantelle said, "we enjoyed our little escapades so much and kept saying how we'd always wanted to travel abroad but our husbands would never go with us."

"Yeah, so one day, I said 'what the hell are we waiting for, gals, we're not getting any younger' and off we went to the Caribbean." Melinda winked at her friends. "We haven't looked back, have we gals?"

The other two shook their heads. "Next, we plan to cruise around the Mediterranean and see Greece. I can't wait," Kathy said, sounding like a little girl.

"I've always wanted to go to the Mediterranean," Roger said as he leaned closer to Kathy and looked at her lecherously.

Georgia heard Melinda sigh loudly before she said, "Then you should go sometime – alone."

Roger looked in surprise at Melinda who just glared back at him. He paused and looked at each woman in turn. All of them looked back at him in contempt. Finally, he rose and said, "If you ladies will excuse me, I believe I'll retire to the bar."

They all politely told him good night and waited until he was a safe distance away before bursting out in simultaneous laughter. "We're horrid," Shantelle said, "but I'm so glad he left.

"Me too," Georgia said as she stood and walked around to reposition and sit in Roger's vacant chair. "The man is a walking snake. I can't believe he was married for all those years to the same woman."

"Don't you believe a word of it," Melinda told her. "He's been married at least five times, and that might be on the low side."

Georgia gasped. "How do you know that?"

"I didn't buy a word of his story when he first made his moves on me, so I checked him out online. He's got profiles on every imaginable dating site, and he has a web site for his ranch. I learned a lot about him, and by piecing together parts of all his stories, I can bet he's been married multiple times. He may be rich, but that's the only thing he has going for him. With luck, he'll leave us alone now."

"I hope so," Georgia said, remembering still the way he'd made her skin crawl simply by entering the room.

"So, tell us about yourself," Kathy said to her.

Georgia shrugged. "What's to tell? I was married for over forty years to Donald. He died a few months ago. I have three grown children – two sons and a daughter. My youngest, Jerry, is stationed in Hawaii and I just came from a visit to him. My first time to Hawaii, actually."

Kathy squealed. "Oh, we loved Hawaii, didn't we girls?"

The others nodded, and as they all ate, the ladies proceeded to tell her all about their cruise to see the islands and their visit to Pearl Harbor. Georgia told them that she had recently been there, too, and then since she was feeling adventurous and close to these women that only earlier today she had considered to be silly, she told them about Manny.

A hush settled upon the table. Finally, Shantelle asked, "What's he like?"

Georgia shrugged. "He's a real Hawaiian. Big guy but very nice. A lifelong bachelor."

Melinda's drawn-on eyebrows shot up. "Wow, and he took a liking to you, you say? That's impressive."

Georgia waved her comment away. "I'm too old for all that dating nonsense, and I'm only recently widowed."

"So what," Kathy said. "Remember what Melinda said to us before we started to travel together. You're not getting any younger, dear."

Georgia looked away for a moment. She pursed her lips. "I know, but I'm not ready to start another relationship."

Kathy patted her hand. "But you like him, don't you?"

Georgia looked at her and saw a benevolent face looking back at her. Finally, she nodded. "Yes, I like him. I had a great time spending time with him, and," she paused, uncertain if she should tell them this, "I even got an e-mail from him today."

The other women oohed and ahhed at her and teased her. She blushed and scolded herself for telling them and then brushed it aside knowing she would never see them again after this trip, so it didn't matter.

Suddenly, Kathy blurted out, "You should join us on one of our upcoming cruises, Georgia." Surprisingly, the other two echoed her sentiments.

To be polite, Georgia said, "You are too kind. I wouldn't want to cut in on your time together."

Shantelle said, "You wouldn't be cutting in on anything. We would love to have another woman join our group. Not only is their safety in numbers, but it would be nice to have a fourth, so we could break into twos from time to time."

Melinda joined in, "Yeah, Shantelle often doesn't care to do the museums like Kathy and I like. She just wants to shop."

"Oh, that's not true, but I do get sick of the museums," Shantelle said with a wry smile at Georgia. "I wouldn't mind having somebody to go see other sights with me."

Georgia looked at her and smiled apologetically, "Actually, I kind of like museums myself."

Shantelle shrugged. "No matter. We'd still love a fourth for our trio."

"I'll think about it. I've never been to the Mediterranean."

Melinda said, "We'll get you our contact information, and we can talk more about it later. I'm a bit tired now, so I'm going to turn in."

The rest of them added that they were ready to retire as well. Before they all parted, though, Georgia invited them to go ashore with her at Juneau and go on the tram with her. The other ladies all agreed that they wanted to go ashore, but only Shantelle was willing to commit to the tram ride with her. The other two said they couldn't handle heights and tight spaces.

"See," Shantelle said with a twinkle in her eye, "I need you, and you need me. You think about the Mediterranean. We would have a lot of fun."

Georgia smiled at her and promised to think about it. They all wended their way through the now nearly deserted dining hall and parted ways at the door. Georgia passed the doorway to the bar and glanced inside. She saw Roger sitting alone at the bar.

For a brief moment, she felt sorry for him and considered joining him for a nightcap, but she knew he would misconstrue her motivation and attempt to talk her into his bed, so she continued on down the passageway toward her stateroom.

Chapter Eighteen

"Oh, dear me," Shantelle squealed as she looked down upon the rapidly shrinking cruise ship, "I don't think I was quite prepared for how high we'd be going."

Georgia patted her friend's bony shoulder. "Don't look down, then, silly. Look up." She turned Shantelle so she was facing the other direction and the two of them watched the trees passing beneath them and the mountain rising to meet them.

At the upper landing, they exited the tram and decided to attempt one of the easier hiking trails in the hopes of spotting some wildlife. Georgia had inserted a new memory card into her camera, so she was ready to capture any glimpse of a bear or eagle.

As they walked, Shantelle told her all about her long and devoted marriage to her one and only love, Kenny, and their only child, a daughter. "Sadly, my daughter hasn't been as blessed in love as I was, and she hasn't found the right guy yet."

"Maybe I should set her up with my oldest son, Randy," Georgia kidded and then was embarrassed when Shantelle seemed to the love the idea. She mentally smacked herself, knowing that Randy would not be at all happy with her for making such a suggestion as he still clung to the hope that he could win back his ex-wife.

She quickly explained that she was just kidding and apologized by explaining Randy's predicament. Shantelle said she understood perfectly, and if Randy's heart still belonged to another woman, then she wouldn't want her daughter getting her hopes up over nothing.

Suddenly, Shantelle squealed again and grabbed Georgia's arm. Pointing below them among the trees, she whispered, "Look."

Georgia prepared her camera as she followed the line of sight from Shantelle's finger. "Goodness me," she exclaimed in disbelief, "it's a bear."

"No," Shantelle shook her head, "it's three bears."

"What?" Georgia shuffled closer to the railing and aimed her camera. She used the zoom and peered at the screen on the back of the camera. Sure enough she saw three bears ambling through the thick foliage. "It's a mama and two cubs," she whispered.

The two women both looked around, hoping that no other tourists would notice and scare the animals away. "Dear me," Shantelle asked, "should we be worried?"

Georgia was still shooting photo after photo, but she stopped to consider the question. She scanned the area and noticed that very few other people were on the trail with them, and she realized how foolish it was for two elderly women to be out here alone in an area where wild bears and other creatures roamed freely. "We should head back to the tram," she suggested to Shantelle who immediately nodded and took her arm in a steely grip.

They began to walk toward the tram when suddenly, behind them, they heard loud voices raised to alert others that a bear was in the vicinity and to be cautious. They looked at each other in fright and hurried toward the landing. Once they were there, they sat down on a bench to catch their breath.

Shantelle giggled. "If my Kenny could see me here, he'd have a fit." She peered at Georgia out of the corner of her eyes. "He was always overprotective of me." She leaned back and looked up into the Alaskan sky. "During our marriage, I thought of it as sweet because I always thought he'd be with me, but when he died and I was all alone, I realized how few things I knew how to do. I remember one day just getting so angry at him that I even drove out to the cemetery to scold him."

Georgia couldn't suppress a snort at the image that sprang to her mind. "I'm sorry," she said. "I don't mean to laugh at your pain."

"Don't be silly, dear. I was really mad at him. I mean, I didn't even know how to change the bulb in our entryway light because you have to use a ladder to get to it, and Kenny would never let me get on a ladder for fear I would fall and break something."

"He sounds like a very sweet man," Georgia said as she patted her new friend's knobby knee.

"Oh, the sweetest, don't get me wrong. I adored that man." She dabbed at her eyes with the edge of her jacket sleeve. Then she started to giggle. "But if he could see me here at the top of a mountain in Alaska, he'd have another stroke and die all over again."

Georgia nodded in understanding. "Donald wouldn't have believed I could do this, either. Not because he was overprotective at all – not in the least, even – but because he just wouldn't have believed that I'd be willing to try something new." She took a deep breath of the fresh mountain air. "He never understood that he was the only thing preventing me from trying new things. His idea of a new thing was trying a different item from the café we went to every Thursday night. Every time I'd suggest a trip or even a new place to visit in Omaha the few times we went there, he'd immediately have some lame excuse for not doing the thing. Finally, I just gave up trying."

They sat in silence for a bit, each lost in her own memories, the good and the bad. A sudden movement above them caught their attention and they both simultaneously pointed for the other one's benefit at a large eagle soaring past. They watched it until it disappeared.

The next tram arrived at the platform, and the two ladies decided they'd better take it down so they could find Kathy and Melinda. "Most likely, there aren't too many museums in this town for them to spend all their time in," Shantelle said as they boarded the tram.

Watching the ship grow in size as the tram returned to the dock area wasn't as frightening as watching it shrink, so Shantelle was able to face downward as the tram descended. As they got nearer and people's faces became discernible, Georgia pointed to where they could see the other two ladies waiting for them, laden with bags.

"You ladies aren't going to be able to fit all the stuff you've bought in your suitcases for your return flights home," Georgia said.

"Oh, we always pack super light and leave a lot of extra room when we first come because we know that we will be buying a lot of goodies during the trip," Shantelle assured her.

Georgia laughed. "I never thought of such a thing. That is a good idea."

"Yeah, we learned the hard way on our first trip to the Caribbean. We each had to buy a second suitcase for the return trip. Plus, we've learned that we don't really need to bring much of our own stuff on these ships. They come fully equipped with most of the amenities we need, so it's silly to bring shampoos and things like that."

The tram reached its docking spot, and the ladies stepped off. They hurried over to Kathy and Melinda and showed them the photos of the bears they had seen. Melinda clutched at her chest and exclaimed that she was happy she didn't go because seeing that bear in person would have given her a heart attack.

They told Georgia and Shantelle that they had been heading back to the ship to get rid of some of their packages when they'd seen the tram descending and decided to wait to see if the other two ladies were on it. They wanted to return to a store they'd seen but hadn't entered. "Want to come with us?" Kathy asked Shantelle and Georgia.

They nodded and said they'd wait on the dock for the other two to return. While they waited, they bought steaming coffees and sipped them as they looked out at the harbor. Suddenly, a whale jumped out of the water and startled Georgia so much that she spilled her coffee onto her boots. Not even noticing that, she grabbed her camera and waited in anticipation for another appearance of a whale.

Only moments later, one reappeared on the surface of the water in the middle of the harbor. She zoomed in on it and snapped away. Suddenly, another whale appeared on her screen and another and another.

"It's a pod," Shantelle said with a squeal. "Ooh, Melinda and Kathy are going to be so jealous that they missed this."

The two women watched the whales frolic in the deep water not far from their ship before they all submerged beneath the waves caused by their flukes and disappeared. Suddenly, Georgia realized that her feet were wet, and when she looked at her boots, she saw that she had spilled her coffee.

She shrugged as Shantelle too looked at her feet and expressed concern. "They'll dry," Georgia said and dismissed the dampness from her mind. "Here they come," she nodded in the direction of Melinda and Kathy.

"Did we miss something?" Kathy asked. "We heard some commotion and something about whales."

Georgia showed them her photos once again. Kathy groaned, and Melinda cussed which surprised the other three. "I've always wanted to see a whale up close in its natural environment," she explained.

"There's still time. We have a couple more days at sea, so maybe we'll get lucky," Kathy said, trying to cheer her friend.

The four women headed into town to do some more shopping. Georgia mentally calculated how much space she might have in her suitcases to put any purchases and knew that it was very limited. She also knew that her funds for unnecessary purchases were limited as well, but she was happy to be included in a group where she was truly enjoying herself in the company of others for the first time since the beginning of the cruise.

Only two days ago she had been seriously regretting her decision to come on the cruise alone, but she was now glad she had. If the rest of the day went well, she might even give some serious consideration to joining the ladies next summer in the Mediterranean.

Chapter Nineteen

Georgia looked out the window at the city of Omaha coming into view below her. The airplane was descending rapidly and soon would touch down. She mentally prepared herself for not only the landing but for what was to come once she returned to her home in a few hours.

She'd finally caved to Sally's insistence that she come home for a bit before setting off on more adventures. Some of her daughter's argument had made sense while other parts had simply been justifiable in Sally's mind.

She agreed that she hadn't seen her grandchildren in months and that they probably did miss her, and she would like to spend a little time with them before their summer vacations ended and they returned to another busy school year. She didn't believe that Bowser was dying because Randy would have told her if that were true, and even it were true, what was she to do about it? He was basically Randy's dog now, so any decision to put him down would have to come from Randy, not her.

Secretly, she knew that her daughter didn't approve of her widowed mother out gallivanting around, having fun, and, worst of all, actually meeting another man. Sally had adored her father, and Georgia knew that even if she ever wanted to remarry someday, Sally would vehemently object to it with no concern for her mother's happiness.

Sally was a great daughter, but she'd been seriously spoiled by Donald who always refused to see any faults in his 'little angel.' Georgia would punish Sally for being disobedient, and Donald would slip her a few dollars later to go buy herself something sweet. Georgia had always known this went on, but she ignored it. Now, she was the one left to deal with Sally's manipulative and demanding ways.

Georgia was certain that once she was home, Sally would attempt to talk her into staying and find all sorts of reasons for her not to leave. Most would involve her grandchildren, but she knew her daughter could be quite creative when she wanted something done her way. Georgia often felt sorry for Chet, who Sally kept eternally busy with chores and charity work.

The plane touched down, and Georgia toyed with the idea of simply buying a ticket to someplace else and leaving on the next flight out of town, but she did miss Sally and the kids, despite Sally's annoying habits, and she wanted to see Randy and Bowser. She figured that she could handle Sally for a few weeks, and then she'd leave for New York City. She'd already made her reservations from the computer aboard the cruise ship before disembarking in Seattle to catch her flight home.

She'd also received and responded to e-mails from Jerry and from Manny. She'd hesitated a long time before replying to his message because she didn't want to lead him astray, but since Jerry's message had mentioned that Manny kept contacting him to find out if he had any news from his mother, she thought it best to let Manny know how she was doing.

She hoped she'd been both vague and polite in her message to him. While one side of her didn't want him holding out hope, the other side of her liked the idea that there was a man in Hawaii thinking about her. She knew she had to decide if it was just the 'thought' of Manny that she liked or if it was Manny himself that had crept into her heart and burrowed a new hole there. She was glad for the respite that home would provide to allow her to clear her head.

After she exited the shuttle bus that had taken her to her car in the long-term parking lot, she stood next to her dusty Impala for a few moments, barely recognizing it, another vestige of her former life. It was a car she had never liked but that had been inexpensive since they'd bought it used. She glanced around the lot at the nearby cars and spied a medley of oversized SUVs and minivans. She didn't want one of those either as they were much too big for her both in their interiors and in the amount of space they took on the road. Who needed that much room? She shook her head in annoyance at America's consumerism run rampant to such a degree that her poor car looked like the sickly kid on the playground being surrounded and intimidated by all the big, tough kids.

As she pulled out of the lot, she found herself tensing up at the thought of returning home and dealing with Sally's demands and also a house full of memories of Donald. She knew that part of her reason for her sudden departure to San Francisco followed by trips to Hawaii and Alaska was that she wasn't ready to accept that she was alone in the world. Sally would argue with her and tell her she was silly and that she still had her own children and her grandchildren, but to Georgia, she was alone. Donald, for all his faults, had been her rock and her steady company. He truly had been her other half, and she didn't want to live in their house without him.

She toyed with the idea of selling the house, but she wasn't sure she could bring herself to do that just yet. Her new widow friends from the cruise had been full of advice about the best ways to move on. Melinda had sold her home and given away all of her husband's clothing and most of his belongings and moved into a condo while Kathy had taken on boarders who she rarely saw but who gave her house a 'feeling of fullness' as she said. Shantelle, on the other hand, couldn't bear to part with any scrap of her beloved Kenny's belongings, so she kept everything as it was when he died, but she had moved herself into the spare bedroom and decorated it to her tastes. She told Georgia that she rarely entered the master bedroom, but knowing that it was the same as when he left her gave her comfort.

They had advised her to find what worked for her, so she could effectively move on because, as they all informed her, right now she was simply running away from her problems and her sorrow. Until the moment they'd said that to her she hadn't considered her trip to be an attempt to run away, but once they spelled it out for her, she saw it for what it was, and in the final night aboard the ship, she had bawled like a baby for hours.

The next morning, she'd said good-bye to the ladies through eyes puffy from crying. Shantelle, who had become quite dear to her, hugged her and assured her that it would get easier, and they all once again encouraged her to come with them to the Mediterranean the next summer. She had given them a tentative 'yes' and Shantelle had squealed in delight and hugged Georgia to her emaciated frame. If she did go to Greece with them, Georgia would insist that Shantelle eat more.

Before she knew it, the lights of her town were before her. She grunted in astonishment to find that a few new businesses had gone up and even opened on the outskirts of town during her absence. She slowed as she drove down Main Street and passed buildings that she'd known all her life but that seemed alien to her.

As she drove into her neighborhood, she began to see familiar faces and even returned a few waves directed her way. Then she turned the corner onto her street and braked the car to a halt. Two cars were sitting in her driveway. She swore under her breath. "Can't even give me a moment of peace, can they?" she grumbled as she took her foot off the brake and slowly approached her house.

As soon as she pulled into the driveway, her front door flew open and all five grandchildren came rushing out of the house. She smiled in spite of her irritation and reached to open the door, but Willow beat her to it.

"Grandma!" the children all yelled at once as they pulled her from the car and threw their arms around her. "We missed you."

"I missed you, too," she assured them as she returned their hugs and silently reprimanded herself for not thinking about the impact her disappearance had had on the children. "I have gifts for everybody," she announced and the children all rejoiced. "Help me with my bags," she told them as she opened the trunk and let them reach in to hoist the laden suitcases.

"Whoa, Grandma, what's in this thing?" her only grandson asked her as he tried to lift it with his undeveloped arms. "Did you bring us the entire state of Hawaii?"

She laughed. "Almost, dear." She watched and assisted the grandchildren carry the bags into the house where Randy suddenly appeared and helped by grabbing a bag in each hand and carrying them down the hall to her bedroom.

Sally yelled above the uproar about presents, "Go outside for a while, you guys, and after Grandma has time to rest up from her drive home, you can see what she brought you."

There were a few grumbles, but Willow stepped in and effectively corralled her younger siblings out the door and in the direction of the small park at the end of the block. Georgia watched them go and then turned to her daughter and said, "If you were concerned about my exhaustion, you could have waited a bit before coming over." She smiled at Sally to deflect the slight sting of her words.

Sally frowned at her. "I thought you'd like to see your grandchildren. It's been a while."

Georgia sank into a chair. "I know it has, honey, and I'm glad to see all of you."

Randy returned and sat down on the sofa across from his mother. "So, you had a good trip, then?"

She nodded. "I did." She paused and decided to wait out her children and see whether this was a secret ambush or a sincere welcome home gathering.

Sally sat down next to Randy and looked at her mother. 'Ambush' Georgia decided by the look on her daughter's face.

"Now what, Mom?"

Georgia sighed slightly. "Now what, Sally? What are you really asking me?"

Sally pursed her lips. "Are you staying here, or are you going to go off on more little trips."

"I don't need or appreciate your condescending tone." Georgia stood and went into the kitchen to get a drink of water. Randy followed her and told her that he had stocked a few items in her refrigerator. She thanked him and asked about Bowser.

He nodded out the window. "See for yourself." She looked into the backyard and smiled to see her old dog asleep in his favorite sunny spot by the rhododendron bush. "I brought him over with me today in case you want him back."

She turned to look at him and saw that he'd become attached to the old dog. "If you don't mind, I'd like you to keep him. I'm not staying long."

Sally gasped upon hearing this from the other room and rushed into the kitchen. "So, you are leaving again and going off on another trip."

Georgia nodded. "Yes, I am."

Sally's eyes narrowed. "Where? Back to Hawaii to see your new boyfriend?"

"Now, honey, don't be crass. It doesn't suit you. No, I'm going to New York City."

Both of her children gasped upon hearing that, and Randy spoke his alarm first. "Mom, why would you want to go there, especially alone? It's a dangerous city." He paused momentarily and eyed his mother. "You are going alone, right?"

She chuckled and patted his crossed arms. "Yes, dear. I'm going alone." She looked meaningfully at her daughter who appeared to doubt her mother's sincerity.

"I've already made all the reservations, and I leave in three weeks."

Sally sat with a thud in the nearest kitchen chair. "So soon?"

Georgia nodded. "By then the kids will be back in school, but I can spend their last couple weeks of summer vacation with them like you wanted me to."

Sally drummed her fingers on the table and shook her long bangs out of her eyes. "I don't understand why you need to go at all, Mom."

"I know you don't." She shrugged. "Maybe I don't either, but I just want to go see the world a bit before I die."

Sally harrumphed. "You're not going to die. You are in incredible health."

Georgia sat across from her sulking daughter and felt like they were reliving Sally's teenage years. "I am now, that's true, but for how much longer?" She caught her daughter's eyes. "Why don't you want me to enjoy the time I have left?"

Sally's face softened. "I do want you to enjoy it, Mom, but I don't see why you have to go gadding all over the country to do it. Why can't you stay here and enjoy yourself?"

"Because the things I want to see and do are not here," Georgia replied, stressing each word in the hopes of driving sense and understanding into her daughter.

Randy joined them at the table. "When will you be back?"

Georgia leaned back and looked squarely at each of her children. "Immediately after Thanksgiving."

"What?!" Sally practically yelled. "You're going to stay away for three months?"

Georgia nodded. "Yes. I'm going to see all the sights in New York City and then I'm going to Boston and Philadelphia, and Niagara Falls. Then I'm going back to New York for their big Thanksgiving Day parade, and then I'm coming home."

Sally had stood and was intensely pacing the kitchen from table to sink and back again. "How can you go away for that long? I just don't understand what has gotten into you, Mother, and I don't know how you can squander Dad's money that way."

A sharp intake of breath came from Randy, and Georgia slammed her fist down on the table. "You listen to me, young lady! What I do with my, repeat my, money is of no concern to you. Your father left you each a sizeable chunk in his will, and I added to it from his life insurance out of the goodness of my heart. If I choose to spend every last dime I have globetrotting the earth, then that is exactly what I will do with it, do you understand?"

Sally looked at Randy as if she expected him to speak up and agree with her, but when he didn't do anything but raise his hands in defeat, she stormed out of the kitchen. Georgia heard the front door open and slam shut and then the sound of Sally's minivan starting up.

As the roar of the engine faded into the distance, Georgia looked at her son. "I suppose you think I'm crazy, too."

Randy said, "She doesn't think you're crazy, Mom. She worries about you, that's all. Your sudden decision to go off on your trip threw us all for a loop, but we supported it. I worry about you, too. I just don't bother you incessantly like Sally does."

She smiled at him. "I shouldn't have yelled at her. I'd better call her." She started to rise, but Randy pushed her gently back into her seat.

"Let her cool off. I'm sure she's picking up the kids now, and they'll all give her hell about wanting to come back and see Grandma. She'll be back before you know it."

Georgia knew he was right, so she sank against the back of the chair and took a long look at her oldest child. "You seem different."

He raised his eyebrows at her. "I do?"

She nodded. "Yes, more relaxed, or something."

He shrugged. "Bowser has a positive effect on me. They say that dog owners are healthier and live longer lives than people without dogs."

"No, it's something else."

He avoided her eyes. "Well, I didn't want to say anything yet, but I've been talking to Mary again."

"Really?" Georgia frowned at her son. "She's divorced again, then."

"Now, Mom, don't say it like that." He leaned back and crossed his arms, and she suddenly realized that he'd lost a lot of weight in his belly area. That was the difference. Why hadn't she seen it earlier?

"I'm sorry. Tell me what has happened."

He chewed on his lip for a minute. "You know I never stopped loving her." She nodded, so he continued. "Well, I heard from a mutual friend that she and her husband were having problems and it looked like they might divorce."

"Do they have any children?" she interrupted.

He paused and looked away. She took that as a 'yes.' "I'm o.k. with that, Mom. You may not believe me, but I am."

Tears sprang to her eyes as she remembered Evan and Jerry's special bond with the boy. "I do believe it, dear. Go on."

"Well, I went out of my way to bump into her one day when she was leaving work, and we just made small talk for a few minutes. Then I asked her how things were, and she confirmed what I had heard about the divorce, so I offered to buy her lunch the next day, so she could tell me about it."

Georgia shook her head at the lengths people were willing to go for love. "How is she?"

"She's the same, really, and she told me that she's always regretted leaving me for him. We were young, and the thought of all those years ahead of us made her panic. Turns out that she left me because she knew she was pregnant with his child." He looked at his mother, who only looked back at him waiting to hear the rest of his story.

"She said she wouldn't have married him if she hadn't been pregnant, and that he's been a mean husband and has cheated on her the whole time."

Georgia snorted slightly and then apologized when Randy shot her a glare, but inside she was thinking that what goes around comes around.

"Anyway, Mom, she's free of him, and we've been seeing each other – only a couple of times, but I want to see more of her. I've met her two daughters also, and they are really sweet. The youngest is the spitting image of her," he added with a smile that confirmed for Georgia that her son had never gotten over his love for his wife even though she had deserted him for another man.

"The spitting image, huh? So, she must have curly red hair and dimples to boot."

Randy grinned. "You guessed it. Her name is Molly and the older one is Mavis."

"Nice names," Georgia said. "I'd like to meet them."

"Really?"

"Absolutely." She then proceeded to tell Randy all about Ingrid and Evan, and they shared their changing philosophies about love and relationships. Both agreed that love wasn't something you could control, and that relationships came and went, and you needed to hold on to whatever good thing came your way.

Finally, Randy said, "So, tell me about Manny."

She looked at him and shook her head slightly. "No, I don't want to tell you about any other man that isn't your father."

He laid a hand across her folded ones. "Mom, Dad is gone. I've accepted that. But you're still here, and I would never presume, like Sally might, that you aren't entitled to more love in your life. I want to hear about Manny."

"I'll probably never see him again," she said, trying to get him to forget about it.

"Oh well, I'd still like to hear about him. Humor me."

She shrugged and began to tentatively tell her son about the giant of a man she'd met on a beautiful tropical island at a luau and how he'd captured her heart a little bit and made her realize that there could in fact be love after Donald.

Chapter Twenty

"Ooooh!" Shantelle squealed as yet another giant balloon drifted by their hotel window. Georgia smiled despite the fact that her new friend had been squealing almost non-stop since the beginning of the Thanksgiving Day parade.

Once again Shantelle pointed below them at the crowd gathered along the streets outside the hotel and thanked Georgia for having the foresight to get a room in this hotel with a street-facing window overlooking not only the parade route but also a slice of Central Park. In their short stay, they'd already spent many hours looking out the large window and watching the people of New York City from six stories up.

"They look so cold," Shantelle said. She shivered despite the heated room. "I know these old bones of mine wouldn't have been able to stand out there all morning in this weather."

A light snow had been falling since late last night, and even though the roads had been cleared for the parade, a thin layer of whiteness covered the shoulders and caps of the spectators who had come out in droves despite the frigid temperatures. Georgia imagined that she would have withstood the cold if she'd been alone because she'd like an up-and-close view of the floats as well as the beautifully clad participants, but she also was thankful that she'd thought to book this room months ago from the library of the Alaskan cruise ship. It had been one of only a handful of rooms available during the Thanksgiving time, and it had cost a pretty penny, but it was worth the cost to keep Shantelle warm and happy and for them both to be able to see the entire parade in comfort.

Georgia pointed down the road where she could see a large marching band approaching. "Look. I think that is the Hawaiian band. Jerry told me to watch for them."

Shantelle craned her neck to get a better view and squealed again as she spotted another huge balloon trailing the band. "I just love these balloons. I can't imagine why it takes so many people to hold onto them, though."

Georgia smiled at her friend's gentle naiveté and rose for a better view of the street directly below them. The sidewalk was crowded from the street to the hotel's façade, and as far as she looked to the left and to the right she only could see a throng of people. She was actually glad not to be down there jostling for a vantage point from which to see the celebrities as well as the not-so-famous people passing by on the floats.

"More coffee?" she asked Shantelle as she moved to the kitchenette to pour herself another cup.

"Yes, please," Shantelle replied before squealing once more and adding, "but hurry, you're going to miss Santa."

Georgia rushed back as quickly as she could while carrying two cups of coffee. "If Santa is coming, then the parade is over."

Shantelle almost pouted. "Really? Well, it was a beautiful parade." She picked up her steaming cup and took a gentle sip. "Thanks again for inviting me here, Georgia."

"You've thanked me a million times already. I'm just so glad you agreed to it."

Shantelle shrugged. "Well, I had nothing better to do, really. My daughter is still a bit peeved with me for abandoning her, but she'll get over it. After all, she has to grow up someday; the girl *is* almost forty." They both laughed.

They sat together staring out the window, watching the crowd slowly disperse for about an hour. Georgia noticed the snowflakes were growing in size and intensity, and she felt hypnotized by their dance against the large window pane.

She'd already been told by Jerry that it was a balmy eighty-five degrees in Hawaii and by Sally that there was a blizzard in Nebraska with travel on the highways being avoided and the airport in Omaha cancelling all of its flights. She didn't know if this snowfall was going to turn into a blizzard or not, but she did have plans to fly home next week, so she hoped the weather would clear up both in New York and in Nebraska by then.

She almost hated to go home, but she'd made the promise to do so back in late August, and she wasn't one to break a promise. Besides, she was looking forward to spending Christmas with her children and their families in her house once more before making a final decision about what to do with it. Randy had already assured her that he would come over to help her put up the outside lights the way his father used to do.

Her trip to the East Coast had been everything she'd hoped it would be and more. She'd visited every conceivable landmark and tourist attraction she could think of, and she'd spent many an evening sending photos home to Sally and the kids who were compiling them all in an album for her that they planned to give her at Christmas.

The Statue of Liberty, despite it being one of the most visited sites in New York City, had been her favorite stop along the way, and the Ground Zero memorial had reduced her to tears even though she hadn't known anybody who had died on that horrible day. She'd covered as much ground of Central Park as her knees would allow in the cold air, and she'd even ventured onto the subway, but only one time.

During her month outside New York City, she'd seen the Liberty Bell and Independence Hall, but she hadn't been as taken with Philadelphia as she thought she would be, so she'd cut her visit short to take a drive north up into Maine while the foliage was turning from green to vibrant yellows, reds and oranges. She'd simply let her whims guide her and stopped for the nights in quiet local roadside inns.

However, she'd eventually begun to feel lonely, so she'd decided to give her new friend, Shantelle, a call. Upon leaving the cruise ship in Seattle, she knew that she'd made a lifelong friend in the older woman, and as soon as Shantelle answered the phone, Georgia's loneliness dissipated.

They'd chatted a while, and then Georgia had told Shantelle of her Thanksgiving week plans in New York City and how she'd always wanted to see the parade up close. Shantelle said that had been a lifelong dream of hers, too.

"Why don't you come join me?" Georgia had blurted before even thinking about it.

A moment of silence came from the other end followed by Shantelle's characteristic childish squeal. "Really? You're inviting me to come see the parade with you? In New York City?" Then Shantelle had laughed and dismissed the idea as impossible.

Suddenly, Georgia had realized how much she didn't want to be alone for the parade and how much she wanted her friend to come enjoy it with her. She had cajoled Shantelle and insisted over and over that Shantelle would not be a burden and that she did want her company. Finally, Shantelle had said she'd think about it and that Georgia should call her back in a couple of days.

A few days later, after a full day of sightseeing in Boston, she'd called Shantelle. Their conversation still made Georgia laugh thinking about it.

"Hello," Shantelle said as she answered the phone.

"Hi, it's Georgia," Georgia began, but that was about all she had a chance to say during the rest of the conversation.

"Oh, thank goodness. I thought you'd forgotten all about your offer, and I was going to feel so silly since I've already purchased my tickets and I'm all packed. I'm due to arrive the Thursday before Thanksgiving as you suggested the other night to avoid the worst of the holiday travel. Can you meet me at JFK? Or would you prefer I just get a taxi to the hotel?"

"I can meet you. I'm so glad," she started to say, but again she was cut off.

"O.K. Let me give you my flight information. Do you have a pen and paper?" Shantelle had given her the information and proceeded to thank her over and over for inviting her and telling her that she'd never been to the Big Apple before and that she couldn't wait to see Georgia again. "Just promise me that we won't visit any museums while I'm there. I want to experience the city, not the history of it."

Georgia had managed a quick "I promise" before Shantelle once again raced off in another direction. When they'd finally ended the conversation and hung up their prospective phones, Georgia had burst out laughing in her quiet hotel room.

The remainder of her solitary travels had been more enjoyable knowing that Shantelle would soon be joining her and that she could share some of the places she'd already found in New York with her friend and re-experience them with her.

Since Shantelle's arrival, they'd tromped all over the city within a ten block radius of their hotel, and they'd taken a taxi to visit other places. However, the highlight of the visit was this simple morning, sitting together in front of the window and watching the long parade pass by.

Now, Shantelle looked at her and said, "So, what are we going to do to top that?"

Georgia winked and said, "It's a surprise."

"Oh, you, just tell me."

Georgia shook her head. "No. I don't want to ruin the surprise."

"Well, what are we waiting for?" Shantelle stood. "Let me get my coat."

Georgia chuckled inside knowing she didn't really have a surprise in store for her friend, but that whatever they did, Shantelle would enjoy as much as a small child

182

opening gifts on Christmas morning, so she rose also and grabbed her new heavy coat and gloves.

As they exited the building, they saw that the street, although still busy, looked nearly deserted in comparison with the crowd of people that had only recently been there. Streamers and confetti littered the snow and made everything look like a crazily decorated bowl of vanilla ice cream.

They slid their boot-clad feet through the small drifts and kicked up fluffy snow in front of them. Then they paused as Georgia got their bearings and steered them in the direction of the large department store which hosted the annual parade. She wanted to stop by that store on this crazy day.

Before they got too far, though, she spied a line of horse drawn carriages. Deciding that she needed a 'surprise' to fulfill her promise to Shantelle, she pointed them out to the other woman who clapped her hands in delight. They waited for a break in the slow-moving congested traffic before wending their way between idling taxis and loaded-down family vehicles.

Shanelle pointed to a carriage about midway in the line. "Can we go in the one that looks like Cinderella's pumpkin?"

Inwardly Georgia groaned at the idea, but then she shrugged thinking 'why not?' Nobody here knew them, but even if they did, she and Shantelle had just as much right to ride in that carriage as some little girl did. They'd once been young and believed in fairy tales, too. Just because their princes had both grown old and deserted them permanently was no reason not to take a ride and dream about make-believe princes.

They hurried to the waiting coach and inquired the price from the rotund coachman. When he told them, both their faces showed shock at the cost, and Georgia was about to turn him down to suggest something else, when Shantelle stopped her with, "It'll be my treat."

Georgia shook her head. "Oh, no, dear. It's too expensive. Besides, it was my idea."

"No, really. I insist. I want to go for a ride, and I'll never be back here again on such a glorious day, so let's do it."

"Are you sure?"

Shantelle nodded, so they climbed into the carriage. Fortunately, the coachman had thought to bring a couple of thick blankets with which they covered themselves as much as possible. He shook the reins and clucked his tongue at his horse, and suddenly they were off.

As they passed the other carriages, the women laughed at their impulsive silliness in not choosing a carriage that actually had a roof to keep the still falling (although much more gently now) snow off their heads. Then the carriage turned into Central Park, and they forgot all about the chill. They'd entered a true Winter Wonderland, and they didn't mind that people were staring at them and even pointing. Certainly they were a conversation piece – two old ladies wrapped in blankets, their eyes as big as saucers as they oohed and aahed at everything they passed while sitting in a pumpkin-shaped carriage that was covered in strings of tiny white lights.

"If Sally could see me now, she'd die of embarrassment," Georgia said to Shantelle, and they both burst into fits of giggles. The coachman turned once or twice to look down at them and shake his head.

Suddenly, he stopped and said, "Would you ladies like to watch the ice skaters for a minute?"

"Oh, yes," Shantelle said as she started to climb down.

Georgia was more hesitant. "Will you wait for us?" She didn't want him to drive off and leave them after Shantelle had paid him such a hefty fee. When he nodded and began to dismount himself, she understood that he wanted to take a quick break himself to get some coffee from a nearby stand.

She joined Shantelle at a raised spot where they could see the entire ice rink laid out before them. It was full of families enjoying time together after the parade. They smiled as they watched a young father attempt to teach his little girl how to maintain her balance while trying to keep his own.

"I remember skating on a pond near my grandparents' farm when I was small," Georgia said.

Shantelle turned a bit to look at her. "Weren't you afraid of falling through the ice?"

Georgia thought about it. "I don't recall. Probably, but that's not what I remember now as I look back on it. We had those awful skates you had to put on with a key."

Shantelle nodded. "Oh, I remember those. Horrid things, weren't they?"

"Yes, but I still miss those days," Georgia said with a slight catch in her voice.

Shantelle patted her friend on the arm. "I know, dear. I know." The coachman appeared behind them and gently cleared his throat. Shantelle turned toward him.

"Ready to go?" He nodded and they followed him back to the coach.

As they left the park, Georgia felt the magical charm of the ride receding with the echoes of laughter coming from the skating rink, but she knew that this ride would always remain dear to her heart.

They alighted where they'd begun their journey, and Shantelle tipped the driver. As they walked away, Georgia asked, "Did you think that was necessary? After all, the ride cost so much to begin with."

"Oh, Georgia, don't be a Grinch. It's Thanksgiving and the poor man has to work while we play. He deserved it."

Georgia smiled at her sweet friend and imagined the young woman she had once been. No wonder Kenny had adored her and her caring ways. "You're absolutely right." Then she steered Shantelle in the direction of the department store. "Now, let's go see Santa."

"Oooh," Shantelle squealed, "can I sit on his lap?"

"I'm sure he'd like that, dear." Georgia grabbed Shantelle's arm, and they set off through the snow to see Santa.

Chapter Twenty-one

"Are you sure about this, Mom?" Randy asked as he leaned on his snow shovel and surveyed the progress he'd made on the driveway.

Georgia paused in her job of spreading ice salt over the spots where the snow had been cleared but where the ice from the sleet that had preceded the most recent storm still clung to the cement. She didn't want any of her Christmas guests to slip and fall on their way to the house.

"I've already told you a million times that this is what I want. If you really want to buy the house from me, I'll sell it to you." She started to scatter the pellets again.

"You know I do, but I don't want to pay less than you would have asked if you'd put it on the market." He scraped at a thicker layer of ice with the shovel.

"Randy, I am not going to make you pay what I would have asked. The amount I told you is more than fine."

He scratched at his head under his stocking cap. "Sally and Jerry will be mad."

"Now, why would they be mad? Sally and Clark have a nice house that is just the right size for their big family; this place wouldn't hold them all, and your brother is content in Hawaii."

"I mean that they will be mad that they aren't getting their fair share of the selling price." He paused and coughed slightly as his mother glared at him.

"So, I take it that you all have discussed what you were going to do with the place once I died."

He half-heartedly lifted a bit of snow and threw it on the pile. "No, but I'm sure they would have expected to share in the earnings from selling it someday."

Georgia harrumphed loudly. "I see. Well, it is still my house, right?" Randy nodded but avoided her eyes. "So, I get to say what happens to it, and if Sally and Jerry have a problem with that, they can take it up with me!"

Randy looked at his mother. "O.K., Mom. Calm down. I just don't want to rock the boat."

Georgia took a deep breath of the frigid air. "I know. I understand, and I don't want to offend any of my children, but I'd also really like to see the house go to somebody who will take good care of it, and it would be even better if I could come back to it from time to time. If you really want the house, you can buy it, dear."

Randy gazed beyond and above her, taking in the entire house slowly. He paused when his eyes reached the peak of the roof. "Remember that time when Dad fell off the roof?"

She turned and craned her neck to look up to the rooftop as well. "Don't I ever. Scared the hell out of me! First the racket of the ladder crashing in the driveway and then that horrific 'thud.' I just knew something horrible had happened."

Randy was laughing now. "Good thing the ladder sort of catapulted him into the yard. The landing only broke his leg instead of killing him."

Georgia began to giggle. "Oh my, yes. And, of course, let's not forget that it wasn't his fault for placing the ladder unevenly or trying to climb down from the roof without the assistance of anybody to hold the ladder."

"Yeah, good old Dad, nothing was ever his fault." Randy wiped a laugh tear from his eye. "He never attempted to go on the roof again, did he?"

Georgia shook her head. "Nope. The next time he wanted the antenna adjusted, he actually called the TV repairman as he should have the first time." She doubled over with laughter. "Not only was his leg broken, but he couldn't watch TV for a week, so he drove me bananas. I kept coming up with reasons to run errands to get away from him."

They both stood silently staring up at the roof. Finally, Randy said, "I miss him."

Georgia approached her son and set the bag of salt pellets on the driveway. "I do, too." She brushed some snow off his jacket. "It really would mean a lot to me knowing that you were here living where your father and I had such great memories."

"So, why don't you want to stay, then, if the memories were good?"

She blinked up at her son and considered his question. "Because, that's all they are now – memories. I want to go live what is left of my life before I become too old to enjoy it. I can't really explain what I'm feeling, but I need to leave and find my true place."

"You always told us that 'home is what you make of it.'"

She smiled. "That's right, I did." She turned to gaze at the house again. "But without all of you in it, this is just a house to me. It's not my home. I guess I need to find my real home."

Randy nodded. "Mom, I asked Mary if she could ever consider being my wife again."

Georgia inhaled quickly and covered her heart with both hands. "And?"

"She said that she could." He smiled. "She always liked this house, too, so I think I would like to make it a home for myself and Mary if she'll really have me again."

"Oh, Randy. I'm so happy for you." Georgia began to cry.

Randy put an arm around her. "Don't cry, Mom, or I won't believe you."

She patted his diminished belly. "No, really, I'm very happy." She stepped away from him, picked up the bag and started to sprinkle pellets again. "Let's get this finished before everyone shows up. I still have a couple gifts to wrap."

"Well, go inside and wrap them, then. I'll finish out here."

She handed him the bag of ice melt and gingerly walked over the slippery spots to the open garage. Turning, she said, "We'll tell the others tomorrow after we've opened all the gifts."

He seemed to consider it, but then he said, "Actually, I'd like to tell Jerry and Sally myself, individually. Then I can explain things better."

"Are you sure?"

He nodded. "Yes. I may need to smooth over Mary's re-entrance to this family a bit with Sally anyway. She's never really forgiven her for breaking my heart all those years ago."

Georgia pulled her scarf off and shook out the snow that had accumulated from the flakes blowing off

Randy's shovel. "As long as you have forgiven her, that's all that matters." She began to leave, but Randy stopped her with a question.

"What exactly are you going to do, though, Mom?"

She turned toward him and smiled secretively. "I'll save that announcement for tomorrow after the gifts." She winked at him and went inside the house that would soon belong to her son.

In the living room, she went to work wrapping the remaining gifts she'd brought back from New York City. They were all snow globes that she'd purchased for each family member. Despite knowing that snow globes were one of the most cliché souvenir purchases, she'd still fallen in love with a collection she'd found in a store near her hotel. She knew that she couldn't tote them all home in her suitcases, so she'd paid extra to ship them to her house.

Upon her return, they still hadn't arrived, and she'd worried for a day or two, but then the delivery truck had turned into her driveway, and the driver had come to her door and asked her to open her garage door since he had three larges boxes for her. After he'd left, she had opened the boxes and inspected each snow globe to be sure that none had broken in transit.

They were all intact, so then she set to work deciding which globe was right for which family member. She'd first set the one with the Statue of Liberty aside, having decided that it one was the one she was going to keep for herself.

Now, she wrapped the final one which contained a miniature version of the ice rink in Central Park and a

New York City skyline behind it. This one, she had decided, would be for Jerry because the image of the man attempting to teach his child to ice skate was firmly ingrained in her memory, and that man had reminded her of Jerry at the time. She would tell him about it when he opened the gift.

In fact, she thought up stories to go with each globe that helped to illustrate why she'd paired it with each family member. She scooted the final present beneath the tree and then rose to check on Randy's progress.

As she peered out the window, she saw that he wasn't alone. Mary and two young girls were nearby. The girls were playing in the snow in the front yard while Mary and Randy talked. She smiled as she watched her son with the only woman he had ever really loved, and then she let the curtain fall to give them their time together without her prying eyes.

She went to the kitchen to start making some hot chocolate, thinking the girls would enjoy the warm treat once they came in from the cold. As she passed her phone, she saw the message light blinking.

She pushed the button and was pleasantly shocked to hear Manny's voice. "Hi, Georgia. Sorry I missed you. I just wanted to hear your voice when I wished you Merry Christmas instead of doing it via e-mail. Maybe I'll try later. I'm, uh, really looking forward to seeing you again. O.K., uh, I'll talk to you soon. Aloha."

She smiled and then glanced around to see if anyone had snuck in and overheard the message. Seeing she was still alone, she quickly deleted the message and then gathered everything she needed to make hot chocolate. As the water heated, she heard the garage door open and the sudden pounding of boots on the mud room rug followed by Randy's voice telling the girls to not get snow everywhere.

"It's all right," she called to them. "Just slip your shoes off and come out here. I'm making you some hot chocolate."

There was a rush of activity, and two girls appeared in the doorway followed by Randy and Mary. "Mom, this is Mavis, and this is Molly," Randy said as he introduced the girls to Georgia.

She smiled at them. "Nice to meet you." Then she stepped toward Mary. "And it's so nice to see you again, Mary."

The younger woman smiled shyly. "I'm glad to be back, Georgia."

Georgia gave her a warm hug and then ushered them all to the table. As she poured the hot chocolate, she asked, "Who wants marshmallows?"

"Me!" both girls chimed at once.

"Me too," Randy said as he sat between the two girls. Then he pointed at an area in the back yard. "That's where I'm going to put the swing set."

The younger girl oohed and aahed and clapped her hands. Georgia smiled at her son and finished serving the drinks. Then she pulled out a package of cookies and sat down at the table to join them.

While she caught up with Mary a bit, Randy encouraged the girls to finish their cocoa, so he could show them around the house. As they disappeared into the living room, Georgia heard their exclamations of delight when they saw the large decorated tree, and then there were even louder shouts of joy once they learned that there were packages under the tree for them.

Mary turned toward Georgia. "You didn't have to do that," she said.

"Oh, yes, I did. You're family, too."

Mary whispered, "Thank you."

"No problem." She paused before adding, "Just one condition."

Mary looked at her warily, and Georgia returned her gaze firmly. "Don't break his heart again."

Mary swallowed. "I won't. I never should have let him get away the first time."

Georgia patted her on the shoulder as she rose to clear away the mugs. "If you hadn't, you wouldn't have your girls, so it all happened for a reason."

Mary followed her to the sink, carrying the remaining mugs. "Thanks for understanding." She looked around the kitchen. "He tells me that he's buying the house from you."

Georgia nodded. "That's right. It's time for me to move on and let a new family have the place."

"But where are you going?"

Georgia leaned closer to Mary. "It's a secret." She then winked at her. "But I'll tell you tomorrow."

Mary smiled. "So mysterious. I don't remember you being so mysterious."

Georgia looked out the window from where she'd watched the seasons pass over and over for so many years. "It's time for a little mystery in my life. What will happen next is all an unknown, and you know what?" She turned and looked at the younger woman.

Mary said, "What?"
Georgia grinned. "I like it."

Chapter Twenty-two

Georgia stared down at her dead husband's tombstone. The snow-covered mound behind it had sunk some since the funeral many months ago, but it would be a while before the ground over Donald's final resting place would be flat again.

She knelt, placing her scarf beneath her knobby knees for extra protection from the frigid ground and snow. Reaching out, she placed a gloved hand on Donald's name and then traced the lettering, brushing snow from the crevices as she went.

Her eyes strayed to her own name engraved in the left half of the large stone, and she sighed. It was an all too real reminder of her own mortality. When they'd purchased the stone and discussed what to put on it, she and her two eldest children, especially Sally, had not been in agreement. She'd wanted to simply purchase a single stone for Donald, but both Randy and Sally had been appalled at the implication that Georgia wouldn't someday rest next to their beloved father.

She had told them that the plot was already paid for, and that when she was gone, if that was where they wanted to put her, then they could do that. She'd tried to explain that she wasn't ready to see her name on a gravestone, but Sally had scoffed at her. Randy had tried to side with his mother a bit by telling Sally that they could take care of adding a stone with Georgia's name later "when the time came."

Sally had said, "But it will look ridiculous for Dad to have a single headstone. All married couples do double ones. What will people say when they see poor Dad out there with his solitary stone? It's bad enough that you ran off right after he died and then met some man; now you don't even want to claim Dad in death!"

Randy had tried to shush his sister because the mortician was looking at the three of them a bit wide-eyed. Sally's voice had reached a level of shrillness, but she turned on her brother and hissed, "Don't you 'shush' me."

Finally Georgia cut in, giving the mortician a pinched smile. "Would you give my children and me a few moments?" The man nodded, rose and left, shutting the door firmly behind him. She turned in her chair and looked sternly at Sally. "Enough." Sally opened her mouth to interject something, but Georgia raised a silencing hand, and Randy was smart enough to let his mother have her say.

Georgia stood and walked to the window. She lifted a mini-blind slat with her finger and peered out at a gray morning covering a gray parking lot where Sally's gray mini-van sat next to the mortuary's black hearse. She took a deep breath, dropped the slat and turned toward her two children.

"I loved your father, don't you ever forget that." She fingered her bracelet. "But I'm not dead. I'm standing right here very much alive."

"I know that, Mom," Sally said, "but someday you'll be gone, too, and I'd think that you'd want to be buried next to Dad." Her brows furrowed downward into a deep V over her nose. "Isn't that what you'd want?"

Georgia looked around at the small office, a room that had seen far too many family discussions concerning death, and she just wanted to leave and get as far away from there as possible. However, she also needed to make her daughter understand something.

"Honestly, Sally, I don't know." Sally gasped and then started to cry. Randy awkwardly patted his sister's arm before turning puzzled eyes on his mom.

"You don't want to be buried next to Dad, Mom?" he asked her.

Georgia shrugged. "Depends on when I die. I'm only sixty-three. My grandmother lived well into her nineties. That's more than thirty years still. Who knows where I'll be by then, or even . . ." she trailed off.

"Even what?" Randy asked.

Sally scowled and sniffed as she wiped her face free of tears. "Even if she might have a new husband, that's what she means."

Again Georgia shrugged. "A lot can happen in thirty years."

Randy nodded. "She's right about that," he said to his sister who promptly shoved his hand off her arm where it had still lingered.

Sally rose and tossed her crumpled tissue into the trash can next to the desk. "Well, even if you do run off and marry that Hawaiian gigolo or somebody else, you're still the only wife Dad ever had, and he doesn't deserve to spend eternity alone out there in the cemetery." She swept her arm in the general direction of the graveyard which actually lay a few miles from where they were standing. "And if you loved him, like you say you did," Sally almost

198

sneered at her mother, "then I'd think you'd want to come back here and keep him company."

Georgia sighed. She was tired of arguing about this with her daughter. Sally was right to a certain extent. If she did pass on soon, then she'd want to occupy the spot next to Donald, but if she lived those thirty years she was hoping to still live, then she'd want to make other plans depending on where her life took her.

Randy eyed his mother. Then, ever the level-headed one, he suggested a compromise. "How about if we go ahead and put your name on the stone, Mom, but we'll leave it completely up to you whether you ever use the plot next to Dad or not. I mean, we can always engrave your date of death on the stone whether you're actually interred there or somewhere else."

Georgia looked from her son's placid face to her daughter's pinched one. "Fine," she acquiesced. "But we're keeping it simple. Your father was a simple man. He wouldn't want some flowery or ornate headstone."

Sally nodded. "Just your names, birthdates, Dad's date of death and 'parents of Randall, Sally and Jerald.'"

Randy cleared his throat. "No. If that goes on, then it needs to say 'Randy.' I hate the name Randall." He looked at his mother who wore a slightly shocked expression. "Sorry, Mom."

She smiled. "It's O.K., and I'm sure that Jerry would rather we put 'Jerry' as well. But that's it."

Sally interrupted. "What about the grandkids? We have to put 'grandparents of Willow, Matthew . . .'"

Georgia held up a halting hand. "No. Absolutely not."

Sally pursed her lips. "Why not?"

Georgia glanced at Randy who seemed slightly uncomfortable. "Because, dear, your precious five aren't necessarily the only grandchildren we're ever going to have."

"Well, then, we could always add those names later if Randy and Jerry ever have any children of their own."

Georgia stepped closer to her daughter and leaned over her, her nostrils flaring ever so slightly. "Now, you listen to me, Sally. Jerry's Evan may not be blood, but he's a grandson to me, and Randy is fixing to remarry Mary, and those two little girls of hers will be family as well. I'm not playing this game of 'blood only makes a person family,' and I'm not having you or anyone else tinkering with your father's headstone every time another child comes along. We're keeping it simple, and that's that."

The mortician knocked lightly on the door and poked his head in. "You guys have this sorted out, or do you need a bit more time?"

Georgia raised a questioning eyebrow at her daughter. Sally turned to her brother for support, but he was also looking at her with raised eyebrows. She sighed and said, "We're ready to decide on a stone now."

The young mortician bustled into the room and opened his laptop. "That's wonderful. Let me show you some of our most popular models, and we can go from there."

Now as Georgia peered at the shiny face of the dark gray granite stone, she nodded to herself, pleased with their choice of stone and that she'd stood firm on the engravings. Quickly scanning the area, she saw she was alone except for some other visitors many rows over who wouldn't hear anything she was about to say.

Placing a hand on his name again, she said, "Well, Donald, I've come to say good-bye for a while. I'm not sure when I'll be back, but I promise to come see you every time that I do. Wish you could have stuck around to see Jerry get married. You'd love his step-son, Evan. He's a hoot and a half. And I know you had nothing good to say about Mary after she broke Randy's heart, but you need to know that they're back together, and he's about to gain two step-daughters of his own." She chuckled a little. "Guess an awful lot has happened in the year since you've been gone."

Out of the corner of her eye she caught movement, so she stopped talking and looked over to see the people she'd spied before drawing a bit closer. She waited, but they stopped again and then they moved back the way they'd come and got into an idling car. She watched them drive slowly down the lane and out of the cemetery.

"It's just you and me now, Donald, and I'm getting cold." She stood, retrieved her scarf from the ground and used it to wipe snow from her pant legs. "Before I go, though, I want to tell you something." She smirked a little. "I'm betting that Sally has already told you, though, but you still need to hear it from me." She paused and took a deep breath. "I met a man." Tears formed suddenly in her eyes as she gazed down at her husband's name.

"I didn't mean to. I wasn't looking for him. And despite what Sally might have told you about him – his name is Manny, by the way – he's not a gigolo. He's a gentleman." She used the scarf to wipe at her face before the tears froze on her cheeks. "I want you to know that I'll always love you and that I miss you, but I also don't. Miss you, that is."

She put a hand to her mouth. "That's a horrible thing to say, I know, but maybe you understand. I want to thank you for leaving me when you did and how you did. None of that horrible lingering illness wasting you away and none of that growing old and senile together until we didn't even know each other anymore."

A sob escaped her, so she paused and looked up at the sky. A lone hawk flew over; she followed its flight until it disappeared behind the tree line. "You gave me the gift of freedom when you died. I hate to put it that way, but that's exactly what it is. That's why I might not be back to visit for a long time. I'm going back to Hawaii to see Jerry and Manny. I only wish you'd gone to Hawaii with me when you were alive." She stroked the stone one last time. "Well, actually, Donald, there are so many things I wish you'd have done while you were alive. The steps of the stairway of regret are worn away with thousands of 'if onlys,' aren't they?"

Georgia stepped back from her husband's grave and glanced again at her own name engraved in the headstone next to his name. She knew that this lonely cemetery on a hill outside the town where they'd lived would never hold her remains. Donald would have to wait out eternity without her. She wrapped her scarf around her neck, nodded at Donald's name, turned and walked away.

Chapter Twenty-three

The warm, salty breeze whipped Georgia's hair around her face and continued to pull wisps of it from the up-do she'd worked so hard to create earlier this morning. Giving in to the demand of the wind, she pulled the final orchid from her hair and shook the mass free.

She looked across at Manny who was smiling at her and saw him wink before returning his attention to the bride and groom. She, too, refocused her attention onto her son and Ingrid who had just joined Jerry at the makeshift altar Johnny had created for them down the beach from his restaurant.

Once word had reached Johnny through his brother, Manny, that two of his best-loved customers were getting married, he had insisted that they not only let him cater the wedding reception but also host the wedding. Jerry had told the big Samoan that he and Ingrid were just going to hold a small ceremony with a couple of witnesses, but Johnny hadn't relented until they'd at least agreed to eat a luncheon in the restaurant after the wedding.

Then he'd said that as long as they were coming to the restaurant for lunch, they might as well have a nice short wedding on the beach nearby. Since neither Jerry nor Ingrid really cared where the wedding took place, just as long as it took place somewhere, they had finally caved in to his persistent requests to hold the wedding on his beach.

Now, Georgia and Manny were serving as the matron of honor and best man while Evan stood by holding the rings. Johnny's large family comprised the only other guests while the minister was a chaplain from the base who'd been sworn to secrecy about the upcoming nuptials as Jerry didn't want to endure any of the raunchy initiations that the servicemen liked to inflict upon men about to marry. He preferred to keep his desk free of blow-up dolls and the mound of leis that were always accompanied by the worn out joke about getting 'laid.'

Georgia gazed upon her new daughter-in-law, a woman she'd come to love dearly over the months she'd been her neighbor. Ingrid wore a simple white Hawaiian style wedding dress with a circle of flowers atop her head and nothing but sand clinging to her feet. She clutched a small bouquet of purple orchids like the one Georgia had just torn from her hair.

Jerry was also barefoot and wore a colorful Hawaiian-styled shirt and khakis rolled up at the ankle. Evan and Manny were dressed in matching floral shirts and shorts and wore purple leis around their necks.

As the chaplain finished the ceremony, Georgia stepped back and raised her camera to catch a photo of the newly married couple's first kiss. Then she passed the camera off to Johnny, so he could take some of the entire wedding party.

Johnny snapped a few and started to lower the camera to review them on the screen, but suddenly he lifted the camera to his eye again, so Georgia was about to pose again when she felt herself swept off her feet and lifted by Manny. "What in the world?" she asked as

Manny started off toward the restaurant carrying her in his arms.

He laughed and looked down into her face. "Well, since you won't marry me, I thought this might be the closest I ever get to carrying you across the threshold."

"Oh, put me down, you silly man," she said as she struggled a little. Knowing he wouldn't listen to her, she finally relaxed against him and wrapped her arms around his neck. He walked quickly and entered the restaurant ahead of everybody else. Before releasing her, he gave her neck a quick nuzzle and planted a hard kiss on her lips.

As the others entered, they discovered Georgia adjusting her dress and looking flustered yet happy. "What did we miss?" Johnny called out before disappearing into the kitchen to check on the progress of the meal.

Jerry and Ingrid approached the table that Johnny had laid out for them earlier. "How sweet," Ingrid said as she touched the carefully set silverware and noticed the name cards Johnny's wife had made using shells instead of paper.

They sat down and soon were served a meal of Johnny's special pork and mounds of mashed potatoes per special order by Evan. Then they cut the small cake that Johnny had made and his wife had decorated with purple orchids made of frosting.

Finally, they drank a toast to a life full of happiness, and they each added one special request.

Jerry said, "May I make this woman as happy as she's made me, and may I be a good step-father to Evan."

"May I be a good wife to this man and a great mother to the child we'll soon have." She placed a hand upon her slightly rounded belly and clinked juice glasses with Jerry.

Before they could drink, though, Manny interrupted them. "I'd like to make a toast." Everyone looked at him expectantly. He cleared his throat. "May I be a part of this family for the rest of my life even if it's not official." He looked meaningfully at Georgia.

Georgia rolled her eyes before saying, "May the two of you have a long life together, and may you always work together as parents."

They all raised their glasses and drank. Suddenly, Evan said, "I didn't get to say one."

Jerry smiled at his new stepson. "Go ahead, then. What would you like to say?"

Evan considered for a minute and then lifted his glass. "I want my mom to stay married this time because I like Jerry, and I hope you have another boy because I don't want a baby sister."

His mother laughed. Jerry tousled his hair. "We'll see about that, sport."

Then Evan added, "And I want Grandma Georgia to stay living in our old house. I like having her around to spend time with me while you guys are busy." Georgia smiled at him and assured him that she wasn't planning on leaving soon. Finally, Evan looked at Manny and said, "I hope you keep liking Grandma Georgia even if she won't marry you."

Manny threw his head back and laughed uproariously. Then he looked at the startled boy and said, "Don't you worry about it. Georgia's my wife in here." He pointed to his chest and grabbed Georgia's hand to raise it to his lips.

Evan frowned and looked puzzled. "So, you are married?"

Georgia shook her head. "No, dear, but I care about Manny very much."

"So, why don't you marry him?"

Ingrid tried to distract her son with another piece of cake, but Georgia waved her attempts away. "It's O.K." Then she looked seriously at Evan. "I was married for a long time to Jerry's father. He died over a year ago now, but inside I feel like I'll always be married to him. He's the father of my three kids, you see." Evan nodded, so she continued. "While I care very much for Manny, I don't know if I want to be married again. He knows that, but he keeps hounding me anyway." She looked meaningfully at Manny.

Manny shrugged. "What can I say, kid? She's a knockout."

The adults all laughed, but Evan asked, "What's a knockout?"

"I'll explain another time," Jerry assured him. "Just know that we look on Manny as a member of the family already, and he doesn't need to marry Grandma Georgia to be considered as family."

"Thanks, son," Manny said.

Jerry slowly turned his head to look at the man who had just called him 'son,' a term he hadn't heard from a male since his father had died. He swallowed and nodded slightly at Manny.

Johnny appeared at the table carrying Georgia's camera. "One more before you leave," he demanded.

They all crowded together and smiled for the camera. "Perfect," Johnny said before he returned the camera to Georgia.

Manny slapped the table, causing everyone to jump. "Well, I hope you two have as much fun on your honeymoon as Georgia and I are going to have cruising the Mediterranean with her three widow friends from Phoenix."

Jerry laughed. "I doubt it. We only have to entertain each other, but you have to keep four women company."

"Three," Georgia corrected him. "Shantelle is bringing a beau."

"Really?" Ingrid asked. "You didn't tell me that. Who is he?"

Georgia shrugged. "A widower from her neighborhood. Also a younger man," she said as she looked slyly at Manny.

"Some women have all the luck," Ingrid said as she playfully nudged Jerry who wrapped his arms around her and planted a kiss on her nose.

"Yes," Georgia said, "and Kathy and Melinda are burning with jealousy, so we'll have to be extra nice to them on the cruise."

Manny waggled his eyebrows at her. "Sorry, m'dear, but I only have eyes for you." Then he began to hum and softly sing "Georgia on My Mind."

She shoved him slightly. "Oh, you. You know what I mean."

The wedding party stepped out onto the large covered porch and looked out over the water. Evan asked if he could go play in the waves for a bit, and Ingrid said he could. They all followed him down the beach and watched him pull off his dress shirt before plunging into the shallow water in front of them.

They stood quietly for a while accepting the wind upon their faces and listening to the call of seagulls and the distant whir of traffic on the highway that hugged the coast.

Georgia thought back over her year of loss and gain. She'd lost a husband and gained a new love. She'd relinquished the only home she'd known for over forty years and gained a house in Hawaii next door to her youngest child. She'd quit her job and gained a new one on the base tutoring the children of servicemen who transferred so often that their children didn't get an adequate education. She'd left behind everything she knew in Nebraska and gained a whole new life and set of friends that shared her love of travel.

The only things she didn't have nearby were her oldest children and her other grandchildren. She missed them a lot, but she didn't regret coming to Hawaii.

Thinking of them, she finally asked, "So, who wants to break the news of your marriage to Sally?"

Jerry sucked in his breath. "Not me," he said. "I'll never hear the end of it that I didn't invite her to my wedding."

"Actually," Ingrid interrupted, "she already knows. I called her days ago."

"What?" Georgia and Jerry exclaimed at the same time.

Ingrid gazed at them like they were children. "She was perfectly fine with it and wished us well. She understood that we wanted to keep it small, and besides, they couldn't have afforded to fly the whole family here for the wedding."

"Well, well, well," Jerry said as he looked admiringly at his new wife, "look who gets to play peacemaker with my sister from now on."

"Don't be silly. She did ask, though, that we send her photos right away."

Georgia said, "I'll take care of it when I get home. I'll send the photos and then finish my packing."

Manny turned to her and offered her his arm. "We'd best be off, my dear. I'll take you home and then go take care of my own packing."

She took his arm and they walked toward his car. They turned and waved good-bye to the newlyweds who were delaying their honeymoon trip until Georgia and Manny returned from their Mediterranean cruise, so they could leave Evan with Georgia while they visited New York City. Georgia's trip there last fall and stories about the city had made them want to go see it for themselves.

As Manny pulled away from the restaurant, he tried once more to sway Georgia and said, "Maybe I'll convince you to marry me while we're on that ship and you're feeling romantic."

She looked out at the sea before it disappeared behind a hill. "Maybe," she said quietly.

He cocked an eyebrow at her and grinned. Then he started the car and gunned the engine. They went around a curve in the highway and slipped out of sight.

One More Glimpse

My daughter walked down the street
To play at her friend's house today.
I watched from the window as she
Trampled through the slush on the road,
Sliding her feet as if she were
Skating over the icier sections
Where the plow hadn't scraped low enough.
She clutched her coat around her,
Preferring that to actually zipping it up.
The breeze brushed her hair back
From her face and out of her eyes,
Allowing her to avoid the many puddles
Of melted December snow.

She walked away, and I stood alone,
Following her every movement until
She turned the corner and disappeared
Behind a house, but I waited, knowing
She would reappear, momentarily,
In the space between that house and
The next -- one more glimpse of her
Before she slipped out of sight.

All too soon, I will stand alone at
This same window hoping and
Waiting for one more glimpse of her
And wishing I could return to
This wintry day of her youth.

The following story was an Honorable Mention recipient in the Children's Fiction category of the 76th Annual Writer's Digest Writing Competition.

Darrel

"Hey, Darrel, what do you have for lunch today," Cory yelled as he charged at the big unshaven man.

Darrel instinctively pulled his Superman lunch pail to his chest, hugging it with both arms across his blue work uniform. "Mine," he said in his thick speech.

"Mine," Cory mimicked. "Mine, mine, mine."

My brother, Evan, and I watched the scene from our porch. There was nothing new about it. Cory took every chance he could to torment Darrel, the forty-year-old retarded man who still lived with his parents just down the block from us.

"He's such a jerk," I said to Evan who looked up at me, green eyes wide with a five-year-old's astonishment.

"But Megan, I thought you liked Darrel."

"Not Darrel, silly. Cory's the jerk."

"Oh, yeah." Evan turned back to the scene and stuck out his bottom lip like he always did when he was worried.

"It's all right," I said as I put my arm around his shoulders. "Why don't we go sit in the tree house until Mom gets home?"

"Okay," he agreed. We left the porch and headed toward the empty lot across the street. Evan's eyes never left Cory, our next door neighbor and all-around bully.

Cory caught sight of us leaving, and, as usual, he couldn't let us leave peacefully.

"Hey, Darrel, maybe you should go play with the other baby of the neighborhood," he said, pointing at Evan. "You two could talk baby talk together."

Darrel looked at us with confused eyes and clutched his lunch pail even more tightly to his chest. "Mine," he stated.

"Yeah, yeah. Yours," Cory said as he pushed Darrel away. He'd lost interest for the moment in the retarded man. Evan and I were his new targets.

"Where are you and baby Evan going, Megan? Going to play in your tree house? Can I come too?" Cory grinned evilly. He enjoyed harassing us, and every other kid on the block, and he wouldn't stop until he was bored with it.

"Buzz off," I said to Cory as I nudged Evan ahead of me.

"Buzz off," Darrel mimicked as best he could.

I looked back at him, startled to hear him say anything other than "Hi" or "Mine." He gave me a crooked smile, and I smiled back.

"Yeah, buzz off, Cory. Only humans belong in houses." I turned and marched off with Evan to the tree house.

"Well, only monkeys live in trees!" Cory yelled after us, his anger quickly reddening his freckled cheeks.

Reaching the tree, Evan and I picked up the ladder and placed it solidly against the thick branch into the grooves Dad had cut for us. We climbed up and sat on the rug in our tree house. It was a just a few boards nailed together to make a floor and some walls, but it was roomy. From there, we had a good view of the whole street.

"Cory's following Darrel," Evan said. "Why is he so mean?"

"I don't know, but at least he's left us alone," I answered, trying to sound relieved although inside I felt miserable for Darrel.

Cory walked backward in front of Darrel, trying to steal his lunch box. From our oak tree, we could hear Darrel saying, "Mine, mine, mine," as he dodged Cory's pudgy hands.

"What a jerk," I mumbled, wishing someone bigger and stronger than Cory would teach him a lesson about picking on people.

"Yeah, what a jerk," Evan echoed.

"Hey, Evan, look at that plane." I pointed to a crop duster flying low overhead. Evan was fascinated by planes. "It's coming right toward us. Let's lay back and watch it fly over," I suggested.

Evan's face lit up, and he immediately lay on his back. The noise of the plane got louder and louder until it sounded like a giant buzzing fly.

"There it is!" He pointed skyward as the plane flew over us.

"There it is," a high-pitched voice repeated from below. We sat up and found that our ladder had been removed.

"Cory, put it back!" I scrambled to my feet. We weren't more than fifteen feet from the ground, but looking straight down made me suddenly dizzy, so I quickly sat down next to Evan.

Cory stood below with the ladder at his feet, laughing up at us. Evan began to cry.

"How will we get down, Megan?"

"Don't worry. Mom will be home soon." I put my arm around him and looked down the street, hoping to see Mom's blue Tempo coming around the corner. "Just wait until our mom gets home, Cory!"

"Oh, I'm so scared of your mommy," Cory replied sarcastically.

Suddenly his laughs were cut short, and we heard him say, "Hey! Let go of me!"

Evan and I peeked over the edge, expecting to find Cory simply playing another joke on us. To our surprise, Darrel had wrapped his arms tightly around Cory from behind and lifted him off the ground.

"I said let go of me!" Cory tried to twist free of Darrel's arms as he attempted to kick backward against Darrel's thighs.

Very gently, as if he were a China doll, Darrel placed Cory on the ground, face down, and held him in place with one of his big feet. Then he picked up the ladder and set it against the tree.

Evan and I climbed down as fast as we could. At the bottom, we stopped to smile at Darrel.

"Thanks," we both said.

Darrel grinned. "Welcome," he managed to say in his garbled speech.

Evan picked up the lunch pail from the ground where Darrel had dropped it and returned it to him. "Yours," he said.

Darrel nodded his head and removed his foot from Cory's back. Cory rolled over, shouting revenge and spitting dirt out of his mouth. Darrel reached out a hand to help Cory up. After a moment's hesitation, Cory took it, and Darrel pulled him to his feet.

For a second, I caught a glimpse of something mischievous in Cory's eyes, but as Darrel continued to smile innocently at him, that evil look disappeared.

Cory brushed off his jeans and walked away. Darrel hugged his Superman lunch pail to his chest and headed for his job at the Center.

"Let's go home." I took Evan's hand.

"I can't wait to tell all the kids what Darrel did to Cory," Evan exclaimed, his eyes bright with the excitement of seeing the neighborhood bully bested by a retarded man.

I watched Cory's retreating figure, his shoulders hunched, head held low, hands shoved in his pockets, and I said to Evan, "No. This will just be our secret – just between you and me."

Summer Nights

Kicking the can – olly, olly, oxen free!
Clotheslining myself in the old lady's back yard
Falling and scraping my elbows and a knee --
For me, that neighborhood game was so damn hard!

Walking my friend, Kim, home two doors down
Prolonging time together just to talk more,
Keeping her safe from Rich, the bully and clown,
Who lived in the house right next door.

Searching for night crawlers with my gramps
Trawling the alley back of his house after a rain
Pulling so hard, gave my fingers cramps,
And often I'd split a stubborn worm in twain.

Sitting on my porch, backlit through the screen,
Listening to the insects play their nightly tune,
Fading light transforming all to dark from the green
Of another glorious day in the middle of June.

Hearing my mother calling for me and for Kevin, too,
Leaning out the front door, each yell of our names
Getting more adamant, our butts she would chew
When finally we'd deign to leave our night games.

Walking little Peppy around the whole block,
Tugging his leash as he stopped to sniff and pee
Marking his territory – he was quite the jock –
Nightly ritual for my Pomeranian and me.

The following story was an Honorable Mention recipient in the 2018 Lorian Hemingway Short Story Contest.

Backyards

A short story

A deep-throated growl rumbled across the patchwork of brown grass, packed dirt and various automotive pieces that comprised Old Man Lawson's backyard. Jess hadn't slunk through his backyard for the past couple of months out of respect for the dead because that's what Old Man Lawson was -- dead. From what she could remember her mother telling her shortly after the old man's funeral, his deadbeat, no-good, asshole of a son had "temporarily" moved in until all of his father's estate was settled.

Her mother had scoffed at the word "estate" just as she'd done at the word "temporarily," but Jess had caught her mother standing on the front stoop more than once gazing down the block to where the "deadbeat" was poking away at something under the hood of one of his father's numerous "piece-of-shit" cars lining the driveway and side yard of the house.

Now Jess froze as the growl became deeper and more threatening. Without turning around, she slowly moved her head and her eyes, searching for the source of the sound. She heard a sudden clanking noise off to her right just as she caught the beginning of movement. As she propelled her body to move to the left, she swiveled her head to get a look at the dog.

A whir of brown fur rushed at her, dragging a heavy chain. Jess ran for the back chain link fence, placed both hands onto the metal tube at the top, and with one thrust of her high-top clad foot, she launched herself over the fence. The middle section of fence rattled its protest as she fell to the ground with a thud into the Delaneys' backyard.

A slow clap and derisive chuckle met her as she rose from the ground, brushing the grass off her knee and rubbing her right elbow where she'd landed hard. "Watch out for Bruno, there. He's a real killer."

She shot Steve Delaney a hard glare before turning to get a good look at Bruno. The small bulldog was pacing as close to the fence as his chain would allow him to be, and he was barking at Jess. Steve walked over to the fence and gave it a solid kick to make it rattle loudly.

"Aww, shut up, you dumb dog!" he shouted as he made a threatening gesture over the fence at the animal. Bruno immediately stopped barking, snuffled a couple of times and then waddled back to the shade provided by the rickety deck. After circling a few times, he plopped himself down in the dirt and promptly fell asleep.

Jess made a disgusted noise. Then she glanced once at Steve before walking to the far back corner of the Delaneys' yard. She began to climb the fence as quietly as possible to not disturb Bruno. As she pulled herself to a standing position with the aid of some low-hanging branches on the Delaneys' apple tree, she heard Steve ask, "Why don't you use the sidewalk like a normal person?"

Looking back over her shoulder at him, she replied, "What the hell is 'normal'?" Then she jumped down into the newly spread mulch beside Mrs. Conroy's lilac bushes. She wrenched a lilac cluster from the largest bush, waved it jauntily at Steve's departing form and then tiptoed around all twenty-five of Mrs. Conroy's garden gnomes before squeezing through the perpetually agape side gate.

Thus Jess Palmetto made her way down four blocks to her best friend's house. When she arrived at the back door of the Garfield residence and knocked lightly on the patio door, she heard Amy's mother yell from the laundry room for her to come in. Knocking was simply a show of courtesy on Jess's part, a sign saying 'I'm here, so please allow me access to your wonderfully crazy home.' A knock meant 'I'm not quite family, and I know it.'

She waded through the toys strewn across the TV room, greeted Amy's mother with a quick nod, and then sauntered into Amy's bedroom. She found her friend lying spread-eagle on the floor with one arm under the bed. A lot of heavy curse words were emanating from her petite friend.

Jess flopped down onto the bed with a jolt and was rewarded with even more cursing from Amy. She then peered over the rumpled mass of bed sheets and looked into Amy's upturned scowling face. "Oops. Sorry. Didn't see you there."

Amy pulled her arm free of the bed's nether regions. She was clutching a belt which she whisked once across Jess's thigh before threading it into her belt loops. "Sure you didn't." As she cinched the belt, she asked, "So, what do you want to do?"

Jess shrugged. "You texted me, remember?"

Amy pulled her hair back into a messy ponytail and eyed Jess in the reflection of her full-length mirror. "Thought you'd have come up with a good idea while you were snooping through the neighbors' backyards."

Jess threw Milo, Amy's favorite stuffed dog, at Amy's head as she reminded her, "I don't snoop."

"Hey, that's animal cruelty, you know," Amy chided as she bent to retrieve Milo from the floor. Then she quickly tossed Milo at Jess's head. "And we both know that you do, in fact, snoop."

Jess propped her chin on Milo's soft back. "At least I don't steal any of the stuff."

Amy applied a quick touch of mascara to her lashes. "You ever see stuff worth stealing?" She paused to consider her reflection before adding another layer of mascara to her naturally sparse eyelashes.

"Sometimes," Jess answered. "But I get into enough trouble just walking through their yards. Imagine what'd happen if I actually took something."

Amy raised her eyebrows and recapped the mascara. Then she sat down on the floor and began to pull on her shoes. "Did that old lady on Prescott call your mom again?"

"Naw, it was some new babysitter at the Hitchensons'. Apparently I scared the 'beejezus' out of her. If she'd been doing her job, she would have been out

221

back playing with Mike and Patty instead of sitting inside." Jess suddenly laughed. "I can still hear her frantic little squeal when she finally noticed me in the sandbox playing with the kids *she* was supposed to be watching."

Amy stood and tugged once to make sure her ponytail was secure. "Were you wearing your hoodie?" She smiled knowingly at Jess.

"You know I was." Jess grinned up at her friend. "And I had the hood up with my back to the house."

Amy shook her head. "Yeah, you probably gave that poor girl a heart attack. Anyone we know?"

Jess shrugged. "I don't know. I heard the scream and got the hell out of there."

Throwing a light jacket on, Amy grabbed her small bag where she kept her phone, driver's license and debit card. Then she searched her cluttered dresser top for her keys and grabbed a handful of loose coins as well. "Shall we?"

"You haven't said where we're going," Jess reminded her.

Amy paused to consider. "Who cares. Let's just get out of here for a few hours."

The girls walked through the kitchen and grabbed two sodas from the refrigerator. Amy's mother spied them just before they reached the front door and asked them where they were going. "To the mall," Amy quickly replied without breaking her stride.

"I want you home by four," her mother called after them.

"Four-thirty!" Amy called back as she strode to her well-used Jeep.

The girls jumped into the vehicle and set their sodas in the cup holders. Jess took one quick look at Amy's house and saw her mother peering out at them from her front office window. She gave a weak wave as Amy threw the Jeep into gear and pulled away from the curb.

Before she could open her mouth, Amy said, "I know, I know. I should appreciate my mother more because she actually gives a shit about me, blah, blah, blah, blah, blah." Amy swerved to avoid a pothole.

Jess grabbed her soda and opened it. "I didn't say a thing." She took a long swig of the cool beverage.

"You didn't have to. I know you were thinking it." She turned the Jeep onto the main thoroughfare and eased into the heavier traffic.

As Amy drove, Jess found herself peering down alleys and wondering what lay down each. Suddenly, Amy flicked on her blinker and pulled into one. Jess looked with surprise at her friend. "Where are we going?"

"Matt's place." Amy eased her Jeep into a small space left between cars already crowding the backyard of a beat up two-story house.

"Matt?" Jess asked. Amy gave her a knowing look and then flipped down her visor to check her face once more in the small mirror behind it. "Not the Matt who got sent to juvie a couple years ago!" Amy simply cocked an eyebrow at her. "What the hell, Amy? Why are we here?"

Amy opened her door and jumped out. "Come on. It'll be fun."

Jess watched her friend take a few steps toward the house and then pause to beckon for Jess to join her. She

223

opened her door and slid out onto the brown grass. "All right, but just for a little bit."

Amy nodded and then squeezed between a parked pickup truck and the side of the unused tilting garage. As they approached the back door, they could hear music coming from the open windows. It suddenly spilled out louder as the warped door opened and a guy stepped out.

"You came!" he yelled, his arms wide as if he hoped for a hug from them. "We were just about to bring the party out here." He turned to yell inside. "Hey, bring that cooler out here, will ya?"

As Matt stepped down from the cement back steps, Jess eyed him warily and wondered how her friend had become messed up with the kid who'd been expelled and sent away after repeatedly punching Mr. Shilousky, the science teacher, just because Mr. Shilousky had given him a failing grade on the mid-term. She'd heard whispered comments, though, that Mr. Shilousky had actually owed Matt money for some drugs. Either way, she didn't feel comfortable being around Matt.

Other people started coming out of the house. Somebody turned the music up inside the house so it could be heard better outside, and somebody else offered Jess a beer which she politely refused. She noticed, though, that Amy quickly accepted and began drinking the beer that was offered to her. She stepped close to her friend and said, "Your mom's going to smell that on you, you know."

Amy peered mischievously over her can at Jess. "Don't be a party pooper," Amy chided her as she wiped a trace of beer off her upper lip.

A voice behind Jess added, "Yeah, don't be a party pooper."

224

Jess turned to see Steve Delaney sneering down at her. "Aw, hell no," Jess said. She looked at Amy. "I'm not staying."

Amy grabbed her arm. "Aw, come on. We just got here. Just for a little bit."

Jess tugged her arm free and shot a steely look over her shoulder at Steve. "No, Amy. Let's go."

Amy's sweet-looking pout turned into a scowl. "I want to stay." Her eyes strayed from Jess's face to where Matt stood leaning against the bent clothesline pole. His gaze was fixed on Amy, and he winked at her.

Jess said, "Stay if you want. I'll walk." She began to move away.

Amy rushed after her. "Please don't go. There are plenty of other people here you can talk to. You don't have to talk to Steve."

Jess looked once more to where Steve was. He was staring at her, openly mocking her with his eyes. He cocked his beer can at her and took a swig before sauntering over to confer with Matt. "No, Amy. I'm not staying. Are you coming with me, or do I have to walk home?"

Amy looked from Jess's face to Matt and then back to Jess. Then she took a step backwards, set her mouth firmly and said, "I guess you'll have to walk." She set her chin and added, "You like walking anyway."

Jess shrugged. "Fine by me, but the next time you just want to 'hang out,' text somebody else." She stomped off before Amy could reply.

As Jess moved beyond the jumble of parked cars in Matt's backyard and into the alleyway, she began to worry that she'd made a mistake. The backyards that butted up to the alley were all unkempt and full of broken toys, beat up garbage bins and rusted patio furniture. She hurried past an open garage where two old men sat smoking and stumbled out onto the side street.

She looked back once to see if, perhaps, Amy had come to her senses and was even now starting her Jeep. A faint rumble of music and voices coming from Matt's house reached her ears, but no car engines joined the noise. Squaring her shoulders, Jess peered ahead and saw that she could maneuver quite a few blocks simply by sticking with the alleyway.

Unfamiliar with this neighborhood yet uncomfortable with the scrutiny that comes with walking down sidewalks in front of houses, she decided to give the next alley a shot. She crossed the street and entered the shade of a bunch of mature trees that hung over the alley.

She stepped around a few potholes, surprised to find water in three of them. There hadn't been any rain for a few weeks. The sound of water gushing from a spigot caught her attention as did the little boy filling a small bucket from it. Walking backward away from him and his puddles, she watched with merriment as he proceeded to fill up an empty pothole before heading back to his house for more water.

Jess slid her sneakers over the gravel in the alley and found a larger rock to kick. She passed a set of lavender colored sheets on a line, a yard with two bright yellow bird baths, another which was completely engulfed by the weeping willow tree whose branches kissed the lawn, and a man mumbling obscenities as he attempted to wrangle an unwieldy grill from its storage spot in the garage.

Kicking her rock across another side street, she passed into the alley of the next block. Here the yards were noticeably more well-tended. A multi-colored large umbrella stood open over a glass patio table, bushes were planted neatly against the property lines, a few houses had small lights along the paved walkways from their garages to their back steps, hoses were neatly coiled or wrapped around holders mounted to the siding, and the garages had doors which actually closed.

Jess stopped kicking her rock, picked it up and pocketed it. Then she began to walk more slowly, peering into each backyard to catch a glimpse of how their owners lived. This was why she walked through backyards more and more and further and further from her own house. The front of a house was simply the facade it showed the world; the backyard, though, told the real story.

The hammock hanging between two trees and over a small patch of dandelions showed that the person who lived there was laid back while the neatly trimmed and weed-free grass of the next house made Jess wonder if the two neighbors didn't occasionally bicker.

How the people treated their dogs told Jess even more than how they treated their yards. One home had a sturdy fence with a noticeable doggy door cut into the back door while at another yard she stood long considering setting free a dog who was chained and seemingly without a water bowl. Just as she was about to open the gate to enter the yard, the dog, a German Shepherd, leapt to its feet and lunged at her, barking furiously. A man stepped into view from the side of the house and yelled at the big dog as Jess quickly slipped into the shadows beside his garage.

Jess continued down two more blocks through the alley before she turned east to start working her way home. She hurried across the street and down one block before the neighborhood became like her own, one of houses with garages facing the streets that had no need for alleys. She wandered down the side of the first house and then jumped the fence into its backyard.

Most yards were enclosed with chain link fencing, but some had upgraded to higher and sturdier wooden fences. Those were more difficult to climb, and sometimes Jess cut herself or got a splinter in her butt, but she usually managed to get over almost any fence. Her uncle Frank who was well-traveled had told her that in other parts of the world the people put broken glass or even barbed wire at the tops of their fences. As she jumped down from one particularly high fence, she was glad that that custom hadn't found its way into her part of the world, at least yet.

Even though, she tired from climbing fences, she most enjoyed the backyards that were fenced. She liked the divisions and that each was a little self-contained microcosm. On one block, she passed through an expanse of three unfenced yards, and she felt momentarily exposed and vulnerable.

Before entering the backyards of her own block, she took a quick peek into Mrs. Johnson's backyard through the space between two slats of the tall fence. She had never entered Mrs. Johnson's backyard. It was a garden oasis whose sanctity she had no plans to defile with her presence. Mrs. Johnson was well over eighty, but every day she went out and tended to her rose bushes and her numerous bird feeders. Even now Jess saw that Mrs.

Johnson was bent double trimming a tiny bit off a profuse rose bush.

Smiling, she turned to the backyard that abutted her own, leapt the fence and skirted the yard via the shadows, keeping herself as invisible as possible from the family she could see milling around inside. She hadn't really met them yet even though they'd moved in five months ago, but she knew a lot about them, and she envied the three kids their intact family. Pausing briefly, she saw the father grab plates and set them on the table. She pulled her phone slightly out of her pocket and glanced down at the screen to check the time.

"Shit." It was already six o'clock. That was one drawback of taking the backyard way home -- it always took her far longer than if she were to use the sidewalks like 'normal' people did. Then she shrugged. It wasn't as if her mother would be missing her or that there was a supper waiting on the table for her.

That kind of normalcy had stopped immediately after her father's and younger brother's death in a car wreck six months ago. Jess slowly eased herself over the fence and into her own rundown backyard. The love and care had gone out of the yard just as it had gone out of her life.

The daylight was only beginning to fade from the sky, but Jess knew from her mother's slumped shape at the kitchen table that the nightly drinking was already in full swing. She lowered herself onto her partly broken swing and watched her completely broken mother, the glass barrier of the sliding door the only tangible thing separating her from the woman inside.

Jess pushed off and allowed herself to lightly swing, the chains on the swingset groaning rustily in protest. Something poked her leg sharply through the cloth of her jeans. She stopped swinging, stood and dug her hand into her pocket. Pulling out the rock she'd been kicking earlier, she hefted it once and then threw it with all her might against the glass door.

It made a dangerously loud thud but simply ricocheted off the glass and onto the broken concrete patio beside the low deck. Inside, her mother stirred, rose unsteadily and walked to the sliding door. She cupped her hands and placed her face between them, peering out into the yard.

Jess stood, staring back at her mother, daring her to come outside and join her.

Her mother slowly lowered her hands and reached for the door handle, but then she paused and let her arms drop to her sides. Jess saw a small cloud form on the glass in front of her mother's mouth, and then her mother turned away, retrieved her glass from the table and disappeared from view.

Around Jess, insects began their evening serenade. Jess sighed. "Next time, I'll bring a bigger rock," she told the backyard chorus. A momentary hush fell over the tiny singers, but as Jess turned her gaze from the kitchen to the stars she could now see in the darkening sky, a litany of song swelled around her.

"Good night, Dad." A star seemed to wink at her. "And good night to you, too, little bro." Jess remained that way for some time, staring up into the evening sky, momentarily at peace, the dark backyard a protective cocoon around her.

Driveway NBA

Dribble, dribble, fake a move,
Shift and run -- dribbling still
-- sudden stop, feet planted.
One fluid motion of arms, hands
And ball rushing upward.
Release, follow through,
Perfect arc.
       Silence . . . .
Swish!
       "Oh, yeah!"
A celebratory jerk backward
Of fist and elbow, waist high.

The crowd of one -- mom on the porch
-- cheers enthusiastically, knowing
That no pro game her son dreams
Of playing in can ever match
This one on the driveway.

Quitter

A novella

Jeff was a quitter. He always had been -- at least as far back as he could remember. Well, maybe not that far back but certainly as far back as it really mattered, and he knew exactly when he had started down the quitting path. Now, here he was thirty years later, still a quitter, with the ultimate irony in front of him -- he knew how to quit everything, but he couldn't quit quitting.

A week ago after quitting the latest in a string of jobs, he'd made a decision. He needed to start over. That decision had brought him back to the small Nebraska town where he'd spent most of his formative years and where the quitting bug had hit him full force in the middle of his junior year of high school. He'd decided that the only way he could quit quitting was to go back and undo his first one.

No one at his old school remembered him because all the staff from his high school years had moved on, retired, or died, but the basketball coach had been surprisingly open to Jeff's offer to help out with the team. The coach was nearing the end of a long career of coaching in numerous schools, and, like most old coaches, he was tired. Having someone volunteer to help, free of charge, seemed like a blessing from above. Of course, Jeff hadn't explained his ulterior motive for wanting to help, and the coach hadn't asked.

The first day he showed up for practice, Jeff hung around the sidelines, unsure of what to do. Finally, a ball bounced his way, and he picked it up. A player yelled, "Yo, dude, throw me the ball." At that, the coach turned and saw him lurking by the bleachers. He gestured for Jeff to come join him. Jeff threw the ball to the player, shoved his hands into his pockets and strolled over to Coach Sands. The coach handed him a roster and a whistle.

"The boys are wearing their practice jerseys, but the numbers are the same as their game jerseys. Get to know their names, and if you catch one of them doing something wrong, blow the whistle and make him do it right."

For a moment, Jeff was overcome by the urge to run out of there. He wanted to quit before he'd even started. What did he really know about basketball, after all? He'd quit the team in high school and hadn't played since. In fact, he seldom watched it on television, preferring reality TV instead where people didn't quit; they were voted out. As he stood looking out at the small sea of boys scrimmaging on the two courts, his eyes fell on one who was erratically dribbling the ball and doing so much traveling that he ought to be holding a suitcase rather than a basketball.

Before he could give more thought to abandoning his newly acquired position, Jeff heard a whistle and realized it was his own. He whistled again and strode purposefully onto the court toward the traveler. The boys had all stopped and were looking quizzically at him. Jeff wrenched the ball from the boy's grasp.

Quickly he checked his roster for a name to go with number ten. Matt Westerfield. "Who taught you how to dribble, Matt? You're traveling all over the place."

Matt glared at him. A few other boys snickered while the rest remained mute and looked shocked. One, who seemed to be a friend of Matt's, asked, "Who are you, mister?"

Jeff looked around the gym and saw that all action had stopped and the boys were looking at him. "I'm Jeff Brown, and I'm here to help your coach."

Matt stepped toward him and said, "Coach doesn't need any help, especially from you." He slapped the ball out of Jeff's grasp and began to dribble it away.

Out of the corner of his eye, Jeff saw the coach raise his whistle. Jeff waved a hand in his direction and then deftly knocked the ball out of Matt's hands. Stepping in front of the boy, he looked him squarely in the eyes and said, "Give me ten laps." A gasp went up around him along with some agreeing noises.

Matt narrowed his eyes. "Do you know who I am?"

Jeff nodded. "You're a punk kid who thinks he's more important than the team. Now, give me fifteen laps."

"Fifteen? You just said ten."

"That was before you talked back to me. Now you owe me twenty. Keep it up, and you'll be running all night."

Matt looked toward Coach Sands. "He's not going to help you," Jeff said. "Get to running."

Instead of running, Matt took a step toward Jeff and lowered his voice. "You'll be sorry." Then he stepped back and peeled off his practice jersey. "I quit," he said for all to hear. Then, he threw his jersey in Jeff's face.

Calmly, Jeff caught the jersey before it fell to the floor. "Use your head, kid, not your gut. Run the laps, and then we'll work on your dribbling technique."

Matt scoffed, spit on the floor, turned and walked away. The other boys watched him go, shook their heads, and before Jeff knew it, he was surrounded by all the players wanting to know who he was and if he knew who he had just kicked off the team.

"I didn't kick him off," Jeff replied. "And, personally, I don't care who he is. To me, he's just a quitter, and I don't have time in my life anymore for quitters."

Coach Sands blew his whistle and ordered the boys into some basic drill work. Jeff sidled over to him and sheepishly asked, "So, who is that kid, and what sort of problems have I caused you?"

Coach Sands peered at Jeff over his glasses with a slight twinkle in his eyes. "Matt is the superintendent's son, and I'd say you just bought us a whole peck of problems."

Jeff cursed under his breath. "I'm sorry. I certainly didn't expect that sort of reaction from him. He was traveling all over, so I wanted to help him do it right."

The coach interrupted him. "You can't help someone who doesn't want to be helped." Then he looked Jeff squarely in the face. "But I expect you already know that, don't you?"

Jeff blinked in surprise. The coach chuckled. "People in small towns have long memories. I did a little checking, and it turns out my neighbor was on your high school team – the one you quit. Name's Dave."

Jeff smiled in chagrin. "Dave Wilson. Yeah, I'm sure he remembers me. How is he these days?"

"Ornery, a bit alcoholic and twice divorced. Other than that, he's a nice guy."

Jeff laughed. "I'll have to visit him sometime. Tell him how much I appreciate him spilling my beans."

The coach said, "The truth was due to come out sometime."

Jeff nodded. "Anyway, I'm sorry.

"Not as sorry as you may be tomorrow when we meet with the superintendent."

Jeff gulped. "Meet with him? Do we have to?"

Coach Sands' lips twitched in amusement. "Her."

"Excuse me."

"Her. The super is a woman -- a rather mean one, at that. She's not going to be very happy with us for kicking her son off the team."

"We didn't kick him off. He quit."

"I know, but that's the way Matt is going to tell it, so that's what she'll believe happened until we set her straight. I reckon I'll get a phone call from her tonight. Good thing I got that caller ID thing." He laughed and slapped Jeff on the back. "Don't look so downtrodden. This'll be fun. Things were boring around here until you showed up."

Before Jeff could reply, the coach blew his whistle and gathered the players around him. He introduced Jeff and told them that they were to listen to him during practices.

"Yeah, because if we don't, we'll end up like Matt," one of the players grumbled.

"Only if you're a quitter," Coach quickly replied. "Are you quitters?"

"No," the team answered.

"You don't sound too convincing! I'll ask you one more time. Are you quitters?"

"No!" the team answered in unison and with fervor.

"Good, now hit the showers, and I'll see you tomorrow."

Jeff began to walk away, but the coach called after him. "I'll see you tomorrow, too, won't I?"

Jeff turned and looked the older man in the eyes. He read doubt in their blue depths. How easy it would be just to walk away from this. Chalk it up to a bad idea gone sour. He took a deep breath. "Sure, Coach, I'll be here. You can bet on it."

The eyes warmed a bit. "You can call me Ron."

"All right, Ron. I'll see you tomorrow. In fact, I'll be here early, so we can meet with Mrs. Westerfield."

"O.K. Let's say 3:00, and be sure to call her Doctor Westerfield. None of that Missus stuff." He winked at Jeff.

"Got it. See you then." Jeff walked out of the gym into the chilly autumn evening. He stood for a long while in front of the school breathing in the crisp air and watching the boys exit the gym through a side door and get into their cars.

"Everything changes, and nothing changes," he mumbled to himself, remembering when he and his friends did the same thing in the same parking lot. The cars were larger back then, the lot was unpaved, and the boys had different hairstyles and no visible tattoos, but other than that, nothing else was different with the picture.

Shoving his hands in his pockets, Jeff walked down the steps and began to stroll toward Main Street. He was hungry, and he thought it was time to re-acquaint himself with his hometown.

Fifteen minutes later, he entered the first local café he came upon, a place simply called "Monica's." Most of the customers looked at him when he stepped inside, perhaps because he brought a gust of cold air with him, but many continued to watch him as he made his way to a booth at the back of the small restaurant. He nodded politely at a few but didn't make eye contact with any.

He slid into the booth with his back toward as many of the curious stares as possible. A teenaged waitress appeared with a glass of water and a beaten-up menu. He thanked her and then turned his attention to the list of nightly specials paper-clipped to the laminated menu. When she returned, he ordered a Reuben sandwich and a cup of tomato soup. With nothing else to look at and feeling eyes upon him, he turned slightly in his seat and glanced at the nearest patrons.

They were a family of five, a farm family by the looks of their coveralls and well-worn caps. The father peered at him over his coffee cup. Jeff noticed that the man's eyes looked familiar. Suddenly the man lowered his cup, and Jeff smiled.

The two men rose simultaneously and reached out to grasp each other's hands in a firm shake. The second man boomed for all the café to hear, "Jeff Brown, you old son of a gun, what brings you back to town after all these years?"

"Hey, Butch. You're looking good. Thought I'd come back and see if you were still chasing all the ladies, but it looks like you found one and settled down." He smiled at Butch's wife. "I pity you, ma'am, having to put up with this crazy guy."

"You and everybody else in town," she replied in a half-serious tone.

Butch quickly introduced Jeff to his family. He and his wife, Tina, had been married for twenty-three years, and they had two sons and a daughter. Then, he invited Jeff to join them at their table. Jeff saw that they were nearly finished, though, so he politely declined the invitation.

"I don't want to keep you from anything."

"Heck, the chores can wait a bit. I haven't seen you since the year after graduation. Where have you been hiding?"

"Here and there," Jeff answered vaguely. "Why don't we get together another night soon, and we'll catch up?"

Butch grinned. "I'd like that. I go to The Watering Hole every Saturday night." Behind Butch, Jeff saw Tina roll her eyes. "Why don't you meet me there around 9:00?"

"I can't believe that old place is still open. Sure, I'll be there. You coming, too, Tina?"

She guffawed a bit too loudly. Then, quieter, she said, "No, Saturday night is my time with friends, and I already have plans. I'm not a drinker, Jeff. I leave that to

Butch." She rose. "Come on, kids, get your stuff together, so we can get going."

"Nice to meet you," Jeff called after her. She smiled in return. Then to Butch he said, "Nice family you have there."

"Yeah, I did all right." He shrugged into his coat. "What about you? You got a family?"

Jeff shook his head. "I had a wife once. Now she has a family with a different man."

Butch looked uncomfortable. He searched his pockets for enough change to leave an adequate tip, cleared his throat and then said, "Well, I'll see you Saturday, then."

Jeff nodded. "Yeah, Saturday."

Butch turned to go and then quickly turned back and stepped nearer to Jeff. "Hey, did you happen to see the name of this place when you entered?"

Jeff said, "Yes, why?"

Butch's eyes danced. "Know anyone named Monica?"

Jeff's eyes widened and then narrowed. "Not that Monica."

His old friend grinned broadly. Then he slapped Jeff on the back. "She's cooking tonight, and when she knows that a new customer is out here, she serves that person herself. Man, why didn't I think of this earlier? I would have insisted you join us just so I could see the fireworks that are likely to go off in here."

Jeff tried to peer into the kitchen, but he couldn't see enough of it to get a glimpse of anyone working back there. He swallowed. "What's she like now? Does she still look the same? Is she married?"

Butch laughed. "I'll leave you to find that out on your own. I gotta go. The family is in the truck, and my wife hates to wait. You can tell me all about this on Saturday." Then he looked around. "Heck, if you make a big enough scene tonight, I'll hear about it tomorrow. Some of the best local gossipers are here tonight."

With that, Butch turned and walked toward the door, nodding to people as he went. Jeff considered following him out, but as he turned to his booth to retrieve his jacket, he saw her coming from the kitchen carrying his supper. He quickly sat and made a big show of unwrapping his silverware in the hopes she would just set down his food and leave. No such luck.

She placed his food in front of him, wiped her hands on her apron and then remained standing next to the table. He tried to glance up at her without revealing too much of his face.

"Hi, I'm Monica. I own this place," was as far as she got with her introduction before she gasped in recognition. Then she plopped down in the seat across from him and leaned back against the cushion.

He took a sip of water and studied her over the rim of the plastic glass. Time had treated her well for the most part. She was still pretty even though the red in her hair probably came from a bottle now, and she still had a temper from the appearance of her blazing green eyes. Cat eyes. Those eyes used to melt his heart, but now they were about to put it into cardiac arrest.

"Hey, Monica, how are you?" he finally squeaked out. He tried to take another sip of his water but spilled most of it onto his shirt.

"Better than you, by the look of things," she replied with an edge in her voice. "What are you doing here, Jeff?"

He tried to use a bit of sarcasm. "Eating. Isn't this a restaurant?"

"Cut the shit," she said abruptly. "You know what I mean."

He sighed. "I've come back to settle some scores."

"With whom? Not me, I hope, because that score can't be settled."

He shook his head sadly. "No, I'm sure it can't. Anyway, the score I need to settle is with myself first. I hadn't planned to see you."

She laughed bitingly. "Thanks. So glad I still mean nothing to you after all these years." She rose.

He tried to grab her hand, but she was too fast for him. "Monica, that's not what I meant. I really didn't think you'd be living here. I thought you'd moved to Oregon."

She stepped away from the table and gave him a withering look. "Enjoy your meal, sir, but after tonight might I suggest you take your business elsewhere. There's a steakhouse, a pizza joint and two other cafes in town that would appreciate your money. I don't want it. The meal's on the house." She turned and walked away without looking back at Jeff even once.

A silence remained in the dining area to Jeff's supreme discomfort. He ate his soup as quickly as possible. Then he wrapped his sandwich in his napkin, rose and placed a twenty on the table. As he left the café, whispered conversations began all around him, and by the time he reached the door, the room was abuzz with talk.

Outside, he breathed in the night air and decided not to wait until Saturday night to visit The Watering Hole.

The next morning, Jeff awoke in his hotel room and blinked blearily at the bedside clock. It was already after ten. Cursing himself for drinking too much and staying up too late playing pool with guys who were more than happy to take his money on foolish bets he knew he couldn't win, he pulled the covers off and saw he was still dressed from last night. He continued to berate himself as he stripped and stepped into a cool shower to knock the rest of the alcohol out of his system. He shaved as best he could with an unsteady hand that hadn't yet sobered up, and he found his nicest shirt and only pair of slacks to try for a good impression while he got his ass chewed by the dragon lady superintendent.

Then he drove down to the corner gas station for an extra large cup of coffee and a newspaper. He drank the coffee while he read up on local news. The paper was mostly filled with articles about school events, and in reading about the most recent basketball game, he was happy to note that Matt Westerfield had only scored two points while contributing eight turnovers. This, he felt, might be a useful piece of information when he met with Matt's angry mother later.

Leaving the gas station, he realized he didn't have anything to do until his three o'clock rendezvous with Ron Sands and Doctor Westerfield. He got into his car and reopened the newspaper. This time he turned to the help wanted ads. There weren't many as this was a small town, but he read what was there.

He immediately disregarded the ad for a dishwasher at Monica's. He had a feeling that she'd rather hire the devil himself than Jeff Brown, ex-lover and breaker of her heart. After her ad, he read one for a mechanic at the tractor dealership, another for a bus driver for the school, and, the only one he took any serious consideration of, a carpenter with a general contracting outfit. It was the same crew he had worked for during his summers when he was in high school. Perhaps the man who now ran it was the son of his old boss. They had the same last name -- Peters.

Starting his car, he vowed to check into the job that evening after basketball practice. He pulled out of the parking lot and headed downtown. He slowly drove down the streets, revisiting his old haunts and discovering new buildings and homes in places that had been fields when he'd lived here. The town was essentially the same as it had been thirty years ago, though, and soon he found himself parked in front of what had been his childhood home.

His parents had moved to Florida a few years after his graduation. He'd had no other family here to bring him back for visits, so seeing the house now brought a flood of memories to the surface. He noticed a curtain move slightly in a window upstairs and surmised that the current owner was probably watching him and wondering why he was sitting in a beat-up old car in front of the house.

Slowly Jeff pulled away from the curb, promising to come by another time and meet the people now living in his old house. He wanted to know if they'd kept the window trim where he'd carved his name in his bedroom or if they'd replaced it with something new and unscarred.

He drove around the block and peered between houses into his former backyard where he saw a new deck had been installed along with a sliding glass door where a well-used wooden screen door used to hang.

Full of nostalgia now, he looked at his watch and realized he should get to the school. When he pulled into the faculty lot, he saw that the superintendent had a special spot, and that spot contained a very large Harley. He stepped out of his car and approached the bike. It was fully loaded and painted a bright yellow. The chrome shone in the sunlight, and Jeff noticed that this bike was made for only one to ride.

"I am so screwed," he muttered to himself. Then, kicking a wayward stone as he walked, he shuffled toward the school. He entered the gym and looked around for Coach Sands. Unable to locate him, he asked a passing student where to find the main office.

The girl looked him up and down a bit suspiciously before pointing. "Go down that hall. Take the first left and then just go straight. You'll find it." He knew he would since it was in the same location as it had been when he was a student here, but he'd wanted to look like a visitor rather than an uncertain assistant coach.

She hurried off before he could thank her. He stuffed his hands in his pockets and began the walk of shame. As he rounded the first corner, trophy cases and large photos greeted him. He slowed to view some of them. Most of the memorabilia was from recent years, but he did find a large faded photo of the state qualifying basketball team from his sophomore year, and there in the back row, a photo of a much younger and much happier Jeff Brown.

He shook his head and walked away. When he got to the office, the secretary greeted him warmly. He asked where he could find Coach Sands and she pointed to a closed door only a few feet away from them. He stepped toward it and read the nameplate which said Dr. Westerfield, Superintendent of Schools.

"Are you Mr. Brown?" the secretary inquired.

He turned and smiled weakly. "Guilty," he quipped, trying for funny but failing miserably.

Her warm smile iced over a bit. "She's expecting you. I'll let her know you are here." She picked up the phone and announced him. As she replaced the receiver, she said, "You can go in." Then, as he turned away, she added, "Good luck."

Jeff took a deep breath, knocked lightly and then turned the knob. As he entered the spacious room, he nodded at Coach Sands, who was sitting comfortably in a large, padded chair. Jeff saw that the chair reserved for him was noticeably less accommodating. He stepped forward and held out his hand. "Doctor Westerfield, I'm Jeff Brown."

The woman did not shake his outstretched hand. She scowled up at him from her seated position behind her massive desk. "I know who you are, Mr. Brown. Please, sit down."

He did as ordered, glancing sideways at Ron. The other man winked quickly at him and then turned his attention to the superintendent.

"I was just telling Dr. Westerfield that I support what you did yesterday at practice, and that Matt quit. He wasn't tossed off the team as he reported to his mother."

She sighed and leaned back in her chair. "Matt can be a bit dramatic at times, so I never believed for a minute that you had kicked him off, but I also couldn't believe that he would just up and quit. He loves basketball."

"Obviously not, or he wouldn't have quit." Jeff realized that he had spoken only when the woman's eyes snapped to his face.

She steepled her fingers on her desk and leveled her gaze upon him. "Perhaps not, Mr. Brown, but why don't you tell me what happened yesterday."

Jeff quickly recapped the experience, emphasizing that he had only wanted to help her son learn to dribble the ball correctly.

"And why hadn't Coach Sands done that before?" she asked, shifting only her eyes to the other man's face.

The coach cleared his throat. "Well, Dr. Westerfield, I've tried. Matt is just one of those boys who doesn't take instruction real well. Thinks he knows how to do everything already. Even likes to tell other kids how to do stuff that they can do better than him." He stopped talking when he saw the superintendent's eyes narrow. He quickly exchanged a worried glance with Jeff.

Rather than be angry, though, she sighed and leaned back in her chair, resting her arms on the padded sides. "I know how my son is. He wasn't always that way, though, and I guess I've been guilty of still seeing the sweet little boy I remember so fondly in him when I should have been paying more attention to the bratty side that everyone else sees."

Coach Sands interrupted, "Now, he's not a brat. I didn't mean to imply that."

She raised a hand to stop him. "Please, it's all right. I just want you to know that this side of him only appeared eight years ago when his father left us." She glanced at the two men, and Jeff saw her tough exterior harden even more for a brief moment and then begin to slip away. She looked right at Coach Sands as she said, "Everyone here believes that I am a widow, as you well know." He nodded. She continued, "So, I'd appreciate it if you'd let them keep thinking that." He nodded again, and she looked expectantly at Jeff.

Jeff nodded a bit too emphatically and added, "Yeah, no problem. I'm new here; I don't want to cause problems."

The other two looked sharply at him and then at each other and then, surprisingly, they broke out laughing. Coach said, "Jeff, you causing problems is why we're here in the first place."

Jeff felt himself redden a bit. "Oh, yeah, I guess you're right. But I didn't mean to cause problems."

Dr. Westerfield smiled. "No, I'm sure you didn't. Now, back to my son." She paused and looked at a framed photo on her desk. Then she turned it toward the two men. "This is my family." Seeing the men's eyes widen and their mouths turn down in surprise, she grinned. "You thought Matt was my only, didn't you, Coach?"

The coach nodded. "You're just full of secrets, aren't you, Dr. Westerfield?"

"Sometimes it's easier that way."

Jeff looked from the photo to the woman. He had to admit that he was surprised that a take-no-prisoners sort of woman like her would have so many kids. Finally, he blurted, "You have eight kids?"

She laughed. "Oh, no. I have five, all boys. Three of them are married; one of them enjoys playing the field like his father." The men squirmed a bit in their chairs. "And then, there's Matt. He was . . . an unexpected add-on. There's eight years difference between him and Brian, the one who's not married."

"Where do your boys live?"

"The three oldest all live in and around Phoenix. That's where we lived when we were still one, big happy family. Brian, at the moment, works as a comedian on a cruise ship, so he lives there. I don't see or hear from him much, but he's happy." She turned the photo to look at each of her boys. "Matt misses him, though. Eight years is a big difference, but they were very close growing up. Then," she paused to steel herself, "after Brian went off to college, my husband announced that he was leaving me for a woman he'd been having an affair with for ten years. He said he'd wanted to wait until the boys were grown and gone, but that he simply couldn't wait eight more years. Within a month of Brian's departure, Matt's father walked completely out of our lives."

Jeff said, "I'm sorry I came down on him yesterday."

The stern look returned to her face. "Mr. Brown, I'm not telling you this so you'll feel sorry for me or for Matt. I just want you to know that he wasn't always like this, and I didn't raise him to be this way. I don't want him to be a quitter, but the biggest male role model of his childhood quit on him, and since then, I've been too busy proving to myself and to him that I'm strong and can take care of everything. Perhaps I can take care of everything in this school, but I haven't done quite right by my son. Now, what are you two going to do to help me with that?"

The men looked at each other. Coach Sands began, "Well, we can't just let him back on."

She interrupted. "I realize that, but what if he made it up to you somehow? Could you let him back on in some sort of a probationary way?"

Jeff nodded. "I think that could be arranged. Actually, I have a better idea." As the other two waited to hear his idea, he paused to think it through before he said, "First, he owes me those laps. Then, he has to spend the next week of practice one-on-one with me only. No scrimmaging with the others, no talking with the others, no drill work with them, either. He is going to learn to dribble correctly, and I am going to personally see to that."

"Sounds good, so far, Jeff, but our next game is tomorrow night."

"He sits that one out and the one after that, and he doesn't get to suit up, either. He just sits on the bench and cheers on the rest of the team. Then, he gets to play, but only in two quarters. After that, we'll see if his attitude and his technique have improved enough to let him play for more."

He waited for their reactions. The coach and the superintendent exchanged approving glances. Then she said, "I like it, and you have my support. I'll corner my son and get him to practice today." She rose, and the men stood. "You men had best get to practice. You don't want to be late."

They laughed and shook her hand. This time, she willingly and warmly took Jeff's outstretched hand and even held it for a moment as she said, "Thank you, Mr. Brown, for knocking my son down a notch, but I hope you realize that this isn't going to be easy."

As she released his hand, Jeff smiled. "Nothing worth doing ever is, ma'am." She smiled back at him, and Jeff noticed that she was actually a pretty woman -- a bit older than him, worn around the edges by life, but pretty, nevertheless.

A few minutes after practice had begun, Jeff felt a presence behind him. He turned to find a sullen Matt Westerfield standing there toeing the baseline. "Hey," he said, quietly, as to not cause more friction between the two of them.

Matt didn't look up. "Hey," he parroted. Then he looked out of the corner of his eyes, and Jeff followed their direction. He saw Dr. Westerfield standing in the doorway, her arms crossed over her chest. She nodded ever so slightly at him, and he returned it with a bigger nod.

"My mom says I have to apologize to you."

"Is that so?"

"Yeah."

Jeff waited. "Is that your idea of an apology?"

Matt shrugged and began to gnaw at a jagged fingernail.

Jeff turned away from him. "Let me know when you're ready to offer a real apology." He made a show of studying the boys on the court, but his ears were peeled for any sound from the boy behind him, and he could see the superintendent still waiting in the doorway. He didn't want to let her down, but he wanted Matt to own up to his mistake like a man.

Finally, he heard a soft "I'm sorry." He pretended not to hear it. The boy coughed. Jeff ignored it. Then, he felt a light tap on his shoulder, so he turned around and looked with raised eyebrows at Matt.

Matt took a deep breath. "I'm sorry," he said in a louder voice than before, but he continued to avoid Jeff's eyes.

"Look at a person when you apologize." Jeff noticed the slight flicker of annoyance cross Matt's face.

He licked his lips, squared his shoulders, looked Jeff straight in the eyes and said, "I'm sorry, Mr. Brown."

Jeff held his gaze a moment, judging the boy's character by what he saw in his eyes. It was enough to convince him that he and Matt would be able to work together because what he saw in the boy's eyes was the same thing he'd seen in his own eyes every day for close to thirty years -- regret.

Jeff nodded and held out his hand. Matt blinked a bit in surprise and then grasped it firmly in his own. As they shook, Jeff said, "I accept your apology, Matt. Now, I'd suggest you get to running. You owe me twenty laps, and I'm adding five more for your taking so long to apologize. I hope you don't have a problem with that."

Matt slowly shook his head. "No, no problem. Mind if I stretch a bit first?"

"Go to it, but I'll be counting those laps, and when you're done, we're working on dribbling technique. Yours is shoddy, to say the least."

Matt moved off and began to stretch. Jeff looked to the doorway and gave a small O.K. sign to the superintendent who nodded in return before moving off into the hallway.

As Matt ran his laps, Coach Sands did what he could to keep the other players from gawking too much or attempting to interact with the runner. One boy, Nathan, who was a friend of Matt's, couldn't quite grasp the message until he was ordered to run lines for not listening to his coach. The other boys snickered, but a withering look from their coach shut them up fast. No kid likes to run lines, especially as punishment.

Jeff stood in the very corner of the court, so Matt was forced to turn that corner right behind him, and as he rounded it for the first time, Jeff said, "Let's hear you count them off."

"One," Matt mumbled.

"Louder the next time around," Jeff called after him. He watched the young man run and saw how with each lap his chin came up just a bit more until by the time he was on his twentieth, he was winded but not sullen anymore.

"Twenty-one," he said loudly as he passed Jeff. Jeff stepped to the ball rack and grabbed two, and then he walked over to Coach Sands.

"Mind if I take him into the hallway? I think it would be better if we could work alone today, at least."

The coach nodded. "Fine by me." He gestured toward the team. "So, how do they look?"

Jeff cringed and tried to be evasive. "They've got potential."

Ron Sands laughed. "Yeah, they're pretty crappy." He sobered quickly. "It's my fault, really. I should have retired from coaching and teaching years ago. My heart's not in it anymore -- at least, the way it should be. I love the game, you know, and I love the kids. They're great. But I just don't care enough anymore to get after them like I should." He shrugged. "I'll probably hang it up after this year."

"Now, don't say that. You're a good coach, and now you have me to help you unlock that potential that is in there somewhere." He pointed vaguely toward the boys just as one of them shot from the three-point line and put up a beautiful air ball. The two men laughed.

Seeing that Matt had finished his laps and was walking back and forth near the baseline to cool off, Jeff excused himself. He tossed a ball at Matt. "Come with me." Matt followed him into the hallway and stopped at the water fountain for a drink.

Jeff turned to face the young man. "Let's see you dribble the ball."

Matt looked long and hard at the ball between his hands, sighed deeply and then pushed the ball to the floor. As it bounced and spun up toward him, his right hand came down flat on top and smacked it back to the floor. Before he got a chance to touch it again, Jeff reached out and began to dribble it.

"Like this," he coached. "Gently, actually. Let your hand conform to the shape of the ball, and then just let your fingers push it." He handed the ball back to Matt and then started to bounce his own ball. "Match your bounces to mine."

Matt watched the older man's technique for a minute, and then started to imitate it. His movements were a bit wooden, but Jeff noticed a difference right away.

"That's much better," Jeff encouraged him. "Now, let's try to incorporate some walking with that. Realize I said walking not traveling."

Matt mumbled something, and when Jeff asked him to repeat it, he said, "I don't know what traveling is."

Jeff was astonished. "How can you not know that?"

"Well, it isn't that I don't know what it is. I just don't know when I'm doing it."

"All right, we'll take it slowly." Jeff could see a few tears welling up in Matt's eyes, and he was sorry he'd come down so hard on him the day before. Just because he'd made mistakes in his life didn't give him the right to assume that this kid would, too. However, he had quit the team, and Jeff definitely recognized that negative quality when he saw it, so he decided all this had been for the best, and he really wanted to help this kid improve.

Gently and repeatedly, he explained and demonstrated proper and incorrect technique when it came to moving and dribbling at the same time, and within an hour, he was pleased with Matt's improvement. Tomorrow he planned to put him through a variety of drills on the court one-on-one with him before the basketball game began.

They walked back to the gym and watched the rest of the team practice a bit. Jeff made Matt identify who was traveling and who wasn't. He correctly spotted most of them.

Before he left for the night, Matt said, "Thanks for the second chance, Coach Brown."

"No problem. See you tomorrow." He smiled as Matt walked away. He'd just been called Coach for the first time ever, and it felt good.

The next evening, Jeff nervously took his position on the sideline as the assistant coach of the basketball team. He was aware of many questioning eyes upon him, as there weren't a lot of people who already knew that Coach Sands had taken on an assistant. After tonight, the whole town would know. He took a few calming breaths, and tried to tune out the crowd in the bleachers, the noise of the pep band and the pounding of his heart. He took up a position which he hoped would let people think he was relaxed and in charge; he crossed his arms over his chest and stood off to the side a little while he studied the opposing players as they warmed up. Eventually, he found that he was actually studying their movements and had become less conscious of the crowd of people.

The buzzer sounded, starting lineups were announced, and the game began. He made himself useful by recording stats, and he had Matt help him. Between the two of them, they kept a sound record of attempted shots, turnovers, baskets made and from where and by whom. The coach already had statisticians, but Jeff wanted to feel like he was contributing, and he hoped to catch things that the regular stats weren't getting; plus, he wanted Matt to do this to focus better on the game and hopefully play better when he returned to the court.

A couple of times during the game, Matt leaned toward him and said, "He just traveled." Each time he did that, Jeff said, "Good eye." He felt the bond between them growing as the game progressed.

At half time, Coach Sands went over their weaknesses and their good points with the boys in the locker room, and then he turned to Jeff. "Anything you'd care to add?"

Jeff was taken by surprise. He swallowed and cleared his throat, searching for something to say. Then Matt said, "Tell them to stop bounce-passing the ball."

Jeff nodded. "That's right. Every time you do that at the top of the key, they steal it. They know when you're going to do it, too, because you always fake right and then bounce left, usually to Diego." He was talking to Seth, the point guard. Seth eyed him a bit warily and looked at the coach.

Coach Sands nodded and chewed on his lip. "You're right; they do take it away a lot when he bounce-passes it. Every time, did you say?"

Matt checked their stats. "Yeah. Every time. He hasn't completed a single pass that way tonight."

The coach's eyebrows shot up. "Well, then, that's enough bounce-passing for now. Understood, Seth?"

Seth didn't look too happy about being singled out, but he nodded. "Got it," he said, still looking disdainfully at Jeff.

The team returned to the court and warmed up for the second half. Coach Sands joined Jeff and Matt. "Let me look at those stats." They handed them over to him. He studied them for a bit, and then he smiled. "Keep it up." He looked at Jeff. "Maybe it wasn't such a bad idea to take you on after all." He winked and returned to his coaching duties.

The rest of the game passed in a blur for Jeff who simply concentrated on recording as much information as possible about the players' actions. When he heard the final buzzer and looked up at the score, he was disappointed to see that the team had lost by ten points.

Matt saw his face. "Don't worry. We rarely win. Losing by only ten is pretty good for us."

Jeff laughed. "Is that so? Well, we're going to have to do something about that." He remained in his chair on the sidelines for a while, studying the stats they'd recorded. He was aware of the crowd thinning out, the players leaving to shower, the coach thanking the officials and other post-game activity, but he didn't look up until he realized someone was standing in front of him.

When he did, he wished he hadn't because Monica was standing with her hand on her hip, glaring down at him. "Hey," he croaked.

"My son tells me that you have a problem with his passes."

Jeff shifted his eyes to the boy standing awkwardly by the bleachers. When Seth caught his eyes, he quickly turned away. Jeff shook his head. Just his luck. "Seth is your son?"

"Like you didn't know that. It's not enough that you walked out of my life without even a goodbye, but now you come back to town and think you have the right to tell my son how to play basketball. That's a laugh, Jeff. You, the guy who quit this team when it needed you most, coming here to coach."

She was getting very loud, and her face was flushed. He stood and reached for her arm. "Monica, just calm down."

She jerked her arm away before he could even touch her. "Don't touch me," she hissed. "And don't

258

single out my son for unwanted criticism in the locker room." Then she actually took a step toward him. "So help me, Jeff, if you do anything -- anything -- to hurt my son, it will be the last thing you ever do." With that, she turned and stormed off. Seth glanced uncertainly at Jeff before following his mother out of the gym.

Coach Sands sidled over to Jeff. "None of my business, I suppose, but what was that all about?"

Still looking at the air where she had been, Jeff answered, "Unfinished business."

"Looks like you'd better finish it," the coach said. As he walked away, he chuckled. "Wouldn't want to be in your shoes when you do, though."

Jeff gathered his papers, folded them and shoved them into his pocket. Then he grabbed his jacket and trotted off in the direction of Monica's departure. He pushed open the school doors and scanned the parking lot for a glimpse of her. In the glow of an SUV's interior dome light, he caught sight of her red hair just before the light clicked off. Then the engine revved, and she backed out of her parking spot.

When she took her eyes off the rearview mirror and put her vehicle into drive, she had to quickly hit the brakes because Jeff was standing directly in front of her Explorer. Over the space of the car's hood, they looked at each other.

Jeff's eyes shifted to the passenger seat, and he was relieved to see that it was empty. Then, without taking his eyes off her, he slowly walked to the passenger door and stood patiently waiting for her to react. She glared at him, and her hands tightly clenched the steering wheel.

Finally, she pushed a button, and her side window rolled down an inch.

"What?" was all she said to him.

"We need to talk."

She stared ahead of her vehicle for a long moment until a driver who'd been idling behind her tapped on his horn. "Fine," she blurted. "Get in."

He opened the door and crawled inside. Immediately, he was overcome by the scent of her, a scent that hadn't changed in all the years since he'd seen her, a scent that was stronger than all the odors of family life that also inhabited the car. He breathed it in, and it was like all the years of separation melted away and they were the teenagers they'd once been, in love and bursting with raw hormones. He had to bite his tongue to keep from suggesting a drive out to their favorite make-out spot.

She drove out of the parking lot and asked, "Where to?"

"I don't really know. I'm staying at the hotel."

She shot him an evil glance. "Don't even think about it."

Too late, he thought, but he said, "Just to talk. Where do you suggest?"

She considered it for a moment, and then she said, "My place."

"Your husband won't mind?" He mentally kicked himself.

"I doubt it. Course, we could take a spin out to the cemetery first and you can ask him for yourself, if you'd like." She turned onto Main Street.

"Monica, I'm sorry. I didn't know. I just assumed that . . ." he babbled a bit longer, hoping she'd interrupt him, but she appeared to take some joy out of his discomfort. Then she pulled into an alley and stopped the vehicle. "Where are we?" he asked.

"At my place," she said as she got out. She found a key and opened a door.

Jeff followed her and when a light came on, he realized what she meant by her place. They were in the kitchen of her café.

"I'm not open on game nights. Folks here know that." She turned toward him and leaned against the counter. "Care for anything to drink?"

He shook his head. He leaned against an adjacent counter, and they contemplated each other for a while. Finally he sighed and said, "I never meant to hurt you, Monica."

"What a cliché, Jeff. After all these years, that's the best you can offer?"

He spread his hands in surrender. "I don't know what else to say, but, no, I guess I owe you more than that."

She fidgeted with the trays, making the stack straighter, and then she offered, "Would you like a sandwich?"

He couldn't resist. "I thought I was barred from eating in this establishment, ma'am."

She shot him a glare, but her gaze quickly changed and she smiled a little. "I'll let it slide for tonight." She opened the large refrigerator and hauled out thinly sliced ham, lettuce, mayonnaise, and tomatoes. He reached to help her and their hands met; then their eyes met and held.

Monica turned away and plopped the sandwich fixings onto the counter. Grabbing bread and a butter knife, she began to put the sandwiches together. Without looking at him, she asked, "So?"

He cleared his throat. "So, what do you want to know?"

"Why don't you start with why you didn't come back to college after the Christmas break? Then, you can tell me why you didn't call me to let me know where you were. Then, you can tell me how someone just walks out on another person and disappears without so much as a 'good-bye' or an 'I'll see you in twenty-eight years.'" At that she turned, gesturing madly with the butter knife, and mayonnaise flew off the end of it and hit Jeff in the chest.

He looked down at the white blob on his shirt and then at her with a wry grin and raised eyebrows. She laughed and threw a towel at him.

He took the plate of sandwiches from her and walked into the dark dining area. She followed him, carrying two cold colas and a bag of chips. They sat and let their eyes adjust to the dim light filtering in from the streetlights on Main.

Jeff took a bite of his sandwich and a large gulp of his soda. "I don't really know what came over me, but when I went to Florida to visit my parents in their new retirement condo, I suddenly found myself wondering 'what was the point of college?' I mean, why was I studying for a business major when I didn't really have any interest in business? Then, it was like my entire life just rushed past me, and I saw myself working in some office, doing some job that I didn't like, married to you with three kids, slaving away to give you and them a good life, and then, what? We work, we retire, we die. I panicked." He looked across the table at the woman who should have been his wife for all those years, and that old feeling called regret came boiling up from his insides. "I know now how badly I screwed up, but then I was a scared kid who hadn't ever succeeded at anything, and I couldn't imagine how I could possibly succeed at a career, at a stable married life, and at us."

"Why did you never call? You just disappeared from my life. I only knew you were still alive because other people told me they had heard you were living in California!" It was dark, but Jeff could tell her cheeks were flushed with anger.

"Yeah, I stayed in Florida for a while, and the days turned into weeks, and those became months, and before I realized it, half a year had gone by, and I just couldn't face you. It was easier to try to forget you."

"Easier for you maybe." Her voice choked, and Jeff handed her a napkin to wipe her tears. "Now you reappear here, and you're coaching my son? This is all too surreal for me to handle."

"Like I said before. I didn't know you lived here. I would have approached this differently if I had."

"Why are you here, anyway?"

He took a deep breath and stared at his half-eaten sandwich. "I guess to make amends with myself." Then he looked at her. "And to, hopefully, make some with you, too, if that is possible."

She sipped her soda. "We'll see."

They ate in silence for a bit. Finally he asked, "So, what brought you back here?"

"Well, after I lived in Oregon for a few years, I came home for a much overdue visit."

He interrupted, "So, I heard right, then. You had moved to Oregon with another guy."

She leveled a gaze at him. "What was I supposed to do? Hang around Lincoln, pining after you in the hopes you'd reappear one day as suddenly as you disappeared? I waited that whole semester for word from you, you know."

"I'm sorry. I wasn't judging, just clarifying."

She nodded but kept her eyes narrowed. "Yeah, I went out there with a guy I met in my speech class. He had pizzazz."

Jeff chuckled. "Pizzazz?"

She smiled slightly. "Yeah, he was a charmer. He could really captivate his audience when he talked, and he worked his spell on me, convinced me to drop out after my sophomore year and go with him out west. He had a plan to go work for some former frat brother in his computer business. I never really did understand what they did, but I followed." She paused and looked down. "I was trying to escape my broken heart, but it was a stupid way to go about it. I should have finished my degree."

He reached across and laid a hand on hers on the tabletop. "Me too."

She gently extracted her hand and laid it in her lap. "I did attend culinary classes in Portland, and I worked at a very nice restaurant. But I never really loved Alex, and he didn't love me enough, either, to keep from straying, so I left him. Shortly after that, I came home to see my parents and my sister, and after a few weeks, it was just easier to not go back."

"You've lived here ever since?"

She nodded. "I started out as a waitress at the steakhouse, and once they knew I could cook, I started cooking there full-time. That's where I met my husband."

Monica paused to take a drink and realized her soda can was empty. Jeff rose to get her another. She called after him, "There's some wine in the refrigerator."

He called back in a muffled voice. "Got any candles?"

"Yeah, I'll get one." She went to the counter where the cash register was and gathered a scented jar candle and lit it. They both returned to the table at the same time and stood for a moment gazing at each other in the candlelight.

Then they sat, and he poured them each a glass of Chardonnay. "So, tell me about your husband." He heard her sniffle slightly and saw her reach to wipe a tear from her eye.

"His name was Bobby. Well, everyone called him Bob, except for me. To me, he was always Bobby. He came in one night with some friends. Turns out he was kind of new to the area. He'd been hired to sell feed and such to area farmers and ranchers, and he'd struck up a friendship with some of the local men. He liked the food and made a comment to one of the guys who told him that the lady who cooked it was good-looking and he should meet her, so they asked the hostess to get me. I came out, and I'm sure I looked a mess in my apron and tied-back hair, and I went over to the table and visited with them for a minute. Nothing more, just a minute, but when I got done in the kitchen that night, he was sitting in the lounge waiting for me to pass by. His friends had left, and he invited me to join him for a drink. I did, and we ended up closing the bar down that night. The next night after I got

265

off work, he was there again, and the following night, we went to a movie. From there, it evolved into a true relationship and eventually marriage. We'd celebrated our twentieth anniversary only a month before he died." She paused to clear more tears from her eyes.

"How'd he die?" Jeff scratched at a mark on the table.

"He was helping one of his clients put some extra feed in the loft of his barn, and he missed the top step of the ladder, fell and broke his neck. It was instantaneous the doctor said. As if that somehow made it easier for me to take."

Jeff once again reached across to take her hand, and this time she didn't remove it. "I'm glad you found someone like Bobby, Monica. I always hoped you were somewhere living a good life."

"I was. He's been gone for five years now. Those years haven't been so great, but I have Seth."

"He's your only child, then?"

She nodded. "Before he died, we were toying with the idea of having one more, but we felt like we were getting too old." She laughed wryly. "If we'd only known, I think we would have had two or three more. I would have insisted."

She stopped talking and they let the silence engulf them. They finished their wine, and she looked at her watch. "I need to get home. Seth was going to a friend's for a while, but he should be home by now. He's probably wondering where I am." She stood. "I'll drive you back to your car."

They left the café and got into her vehicle. As they drove away, he quietly said, "I was married, too."

266

She glanced sharply his way for a second, but she didn't say anything.

"Her name was Sarah, and I never should have married her. She was too good a person for the likes of me, and after not even a year of marriage, I'd managed to screw things up so badly that we got divorced. Last I heard she was remarried and had four kids. I'm glad. She deserved better than me."

"Don't you think you are being just a little hard on yourself?"

"No," he muttered, "I was an ass. To her, and especially to you."

She pulled into the faculty parking lot and stopped by the only remaining car. "Well, here you are."

"Yeah, here I am," he said as he looked intently at her.

"Goodnight, Jeff."

He opened the door. "Can I see you again?"

She took a deep breath. "We'll see. I can't answer that right now. I have Seth to consider, you know."

He nodded. "Thanks for the sandwich and the wine and the conversation." Jeff stepped out and shut the door. Then he stood and watched her drive away, and he remained watching until her taillights disappeared around the corner two blocks away. He got in his car and started it, but he didn't drive off right away; he couldn't see through the tears welling up in his eyes. Instead, he sat and listened to a love song on the radio and cursed himself for wasting so much of his life. As he dried his face, he made a promise to himself to not waste the rest of it.

Two weeks later, Jeff was installing some cabinetry in a spec house that Ralph Peters was building. Ralph had remembered Jeff even though he wasn't his former boss's son but rather his nephew. He said his uncle had spoken highly of Jeff as a hard worker once and had been surprised and disappointed when Jeff had quit the basketball team. He'd hired Jeff even though Jeff didn't have a lot of carpentry experience past high school. Ralph had told him that anyone his uncle had trusted could be counted on to do a good job. Jeff was sorry to hear that his former boss had died a couple of years ago, but Ralph had a warm and kidding personality that reminded him a lot of his uncle. Since being hired, he'd put in long hours on this house in addition to the assistant coaching he was still doing for free.

Every now and then he was hit with that old urge to up and quit and hurry out of town before he turned into one of the locals he saw each morning sitting in the convenience store booths sharing gossip over cups of coffee. While he didn't mind living in his hometown and working at his former school and with his old construction crew, he wasn't ready to make any of it permanent, but he was forced to admit that it wasn't all bad.

His relationship with Matt Westerfield had grown by leaps and bounds since he'd taken the boy under his wing and showed him proper basketball techniques, and Matt's mother had even offered to take him shopping for a motorcycle of his own after he'd mentioned in passing that he liked her bike.

Then there was Monica. They certainly weren't dating, but she wasn't freezing him out either. He ate at her café almost every night, except game nights, of course, and he often stayed until closing time, so he could help her prepare for the next day's business. He sensed her mistrust, and he knew he deserved it, but he also could tell she was happy to have him around because he'd catch her every now and then peeking out of the kitchen to see if he was seated at the table he'd claimed for himself – the same table where they'd eaten their sandwiches after his first game of coaching.

Seth was the one he hadn't yet won over, not on the court and definitely not when it came to his mother. Hostility flowed off Seth like water meant to drown Jeff. For the most part, Jeff left him alone, but a few times in practice he'd had to discipline Seth for blatantly ignoring his commands during ball-handling drills. He hated doing it, knowing that with each line he ran, Seth hated Jeff more, but he couldn't have Seth showing him disrespect in front of the other players.

Seth was the true leader of the team, and the other boys sensed his dislike of Jeff, but most of them knew it was because Jeff liked Seth's mom, so they didn't give it a lot of thought. Jeff knew, though, that if Seth really wanted to get him, he'd only have to tell the other players to go hard on him, and then his time coaching would be over. Once you lose the respect of teenagers, it's nearly impossible to regain it. Jeff wanted to avoid that because the one thing he was enjoying more than he ever could have imagined was coaching high school basketball.

So, he trod lightly where Seth was concerned and hoped for the best. Between working his ass off to help coach the team and attempting to smooth things over with Monica, he was certain that Seth would come around eventually.

He was scared, though. Jeff admitted this to himself. After numerous failed jobs, a failed marriage and nothing of substance to show for himself at the age of forty-eight, he worried that it was too late to try.

He was spending too much time in The Watering Hole with his old friend, Butch, he knew, but old habits die hard. After the first few nights catching up on old times, though, Jeff and Butch didn't have much to say to each other, so Jeff had taken to drinking his two beers in silence while watching the news on the wall-mounted TV and then walking through the cold air to his motel room. Every time he entered the small room, he'd tell himself it was time to look for a more permanent place.

But permanence scared him. After all, he wasn't entirely sure where he was going from here. Was he hoping to settle down in the town he'd left behind all those years ago? Or was it best that he just finish out the coaching season and then hit the road, like he was accustomed to doing? Wouldn't that just be him quitting again?

His boss yelled at him to grab the boxes of tiles and meet him in the bathroom, so they could get started on the shower before Jeff had to leave for the game. Jeff glanced at his watch and was surprised to see it was almost three. He only had another half hour of work before he needed to shower and dress and meet Coach Sands for their ritual pre-game meeting before the first game of the conference tournament.

It was an away game, and they had to drive about forty miles, so they'd leave about five o'clock. This would be his second away game since taking on his coaching role, and he was actually looking forward to the bus ride.

Back in high school, he'd hated riding the bus because of the uncomfortable seats, the bouncing, the yelling and the windows that never quite closed to keep out the frigid air; but now, he found he enjoyed everything that he had once despised.

He helped his boss get started in the bathroom, and then he clocked out for the day. Back at his motel room, he grinned to find that Glenda, the general manager who lived in the attached house, had washed and pressed his only presentable long sleeve shirt and black slacks. He'd helped her move her heavy refrigerator the other day so she could get behind it and clean it – something that hadn't been done in fifteen years, she'd told him – and he knew this was her way of repaying him. He was very grateful because he hadn't had time to wash them himself and was just planning to wear them wrinkled. He moved them from the bed to the table, and as he did that, he noticed a new black tie lying on the table.

Jeff felt a lump form in his throat at Glenda's kindness. He wasn't accustomed to somebody taking care of him, but Glenda had been mothering him up since he arrived and announced he was going to stay a spell while he helped coach the school's basketball team. He suspected that she had a crush on Coach Sands, and an even bigger suspicion that the feeling was mutual, but the coach was such a dyed-in-the-wool bachelor that Jeff doubted he even knew what to do when a woman was attracted to him.

After struggling a bit with the tie, as he hadn't worn one in longer than he could remember, Jeff ran a comb through his wet hair and noticed he needed a haircut. Something to think about tomorrow, he decided as he rushed out the door carrying the playbook he'd been perfecting ever since the coach had given it to him. He wanted to run a couple of ideas by the old man on the bus ride.

Jeff was more than a little surprised at his own interest and excitement in coaching. He'd initially volunteered for the position as his own form of penance to make up for his mistakes, but now he was really enjoying the role of coach to the boys. Every time one of them called him "Coach" he got a small tingle across his shoulders and a surge of heat in his chest. More than once he'd had to stop himself from tearing up.

By the time he climbed onto the bus, most of the team was there waiting for him. Coach Sands was in his customary front seat behind the driver, cap pulled low, taking a quick snooze, lulled by the rumble of the idling bus. Jeff hated to wake him, so he did a head count and found that all the boys except Seth were accounted for.

That irritated him more than he wanted to admit. He doubted it was a personal slight against him, but he couldn't help wondering if Seth was deliberately being tardy to annoy him. He asked the others if they knew what was keeping Seth, but most of them weren't even listening to him as they had their earphones already in place and their music pumping loudly in order to psych themselves up for the game.

Just as he leaned down to shout into a player's ears, he saw Seth's car pull into the lot. As he waited for Seth to saunter over to the bus, he double-checked his head count, and then he met Seth at the top of the bus stairs.

"You're five minutes late." He spoke quietly, so as not to bring unwanted attention to their conversation.

Seth pushed past him. "Big deal. It's not like you're going to leave without me." He walked to the back of the bus where a seat had been left empty for him and threw his bag toward the wall before sliding in next to it.

Jeff took one step after him, his face burning red in anger, but he felt a hand on his leg and looked down to see Coach Sands motioning for him to sit down. He turned to sit just as the bus lurched forward, throwing him against the back of his seat.

The coach leaned across the aisle. "This isn't the time or the place for a showdown of testosterone. Save it for practice tomorrow. Seth's just trying to show off for the boys, but we'll have the last laugh when he has to run extra."

Jeff nodded, and then he shook his head in frustration. Why did the kid have to make it so hard for him, both on the court and with his mother? He knew that Seth was acting out toward him because he wanted him to stay away from Monica, and he understood that, but he couldn't stand for him disrespecting him as a coach. He'd have to remedy the situation if he hoped to make this work.

Once they arrived at the gymnasium, the usual routine kicked in, and Jeff forgot about the altercation on the bus, for the time being. He showed Coach Sands his ideas, and the coach seemed to like them, and he promised to let Jeff try them out in practice.

During the pre-game pep talk, Coach Sands reminded them to work together and to watch out for the opposing team's main scorer, a wily ball-stealing short kid who was a killer at the three-point line. They huddled up, yelled "Let's win," and ran onto the court for their twenty minute warm-up period.

Jeff took his spot on the bench and began preparing his stat taking sheets. Suddenly, he felt a tap on his shoulder, so he turned around.

"Just thought I'd say hello," Monica said, "and good luck."

He swallowed. "Thanks. Hello to you, too. I'm glad you came to the game."

"Oh, I never miss Seth's games. In fact, I'm going to miss coming to them next year."

Jeff nodded stupidly. Until that moment, he hadn't even realized that Seth was a senior. In fact, he hadn't paid a lot of attention at all to what grades any of the boys were in. To cover for his ignorance, he said, "Well, you can always come watch me on the sidelines next year."

She raised her eyebrows at him. "You're coming back? To coach?"

He nodded. "I've been thinking about it."

"Really?" She lowered her head and pondered him through half-closed eyes. "Well, I'll let you get back to work." She stepped up onto the next row of bleachers and began to move away.

Jeff called after her. "If we win tonight, will you go to a movie with me?"

She turned but kept walking backward along the empty, narrow bench. "I'll think about it. You have to win first." She smiled and turned away.

He watched her make her way to the very top of the bleachers where she sat next to a couple of team parents. They began to chat, but Jeff saw her look his way once before she turned her attention to the woman sitting beside her. He grinned and went back to work.

At half time, the team was down by twelve points. Jeff followed them to the locker room, where Coach Sands was waiting for everyone to sit down. The coach paused, and then he looked at Jeff.

"Any suggestions garnered from all that writing you've been doing?"

Jeff blinked. He quickly opened his binder and began scanning his notes. He hated it when the coach put him on the spot like this, but he did have a couple of ideas and proof to back them up.

"First of all, Seth, you're still telegraphing your passes, but we'll work on that more in practice tomorrow." He glanced Seth's way and saw the boy shooting daggers at him with his eyes, but he chose to ignore it for now. "However, it mostly happens when they put the press on you, Seth, so we have to get them off you."

"No shit," Seth mumbled, and a couple of his friends snickered.

Jeff slammed his binder shut. "Do you want my help, or not?" He looked at each boy in turn and saw that most of them really wanted to hear what he had to say.

Matt spoke up. "Go ahead, Coach."

There was that special term again. Jeff shook off his anger and set his binder on a bench. As he talked, he grew more animated, using his whole body to show them what he wanted. "Matt is our most consistent under the basket, but he's not getting the ball. Now, Seth, I know you've got an arm because I've seen it in practice. As soon as they start to press, I want you to lob that ball down court to Matt or to anyone near him. Matt is going to hustle his ass down there and be ready for that pass. Once you get a couple by them that way, they will pull back on the press, and then you'll be able to dribble it down court and pass to one of our outside shooters. Nathan is also strong down low, so once they start teaming up on Matt, then get it to Nathan. When they go after Nathan, then pass it to Matt."

He explained a few more ideas, and was ready to launch into some others, but the coach interrupted him and told them it was time to head back out for the second half. As the boys ran onto the court for a few minutes of shooting time, Coach Sands came up beside him.

"Pretty impressive."

"Really?" Jeff looked at the older man to see if he was joking.

"Really. That's what these boys need. Your enthusiasm." He nodded toward the court. "Look. You can tell they are pumped up and ready to play."

Jeff watched the team. They did look more energized than normal. He grinned. Maybe he was cut out for this coaching thing after all.

The second half began, and Jeff decided to spend it watching intently rather than recording information. He passed his binder off to one of the team managers, a boy of twelve, who'd been helping Jeff do stats.

When the other team started to press Seth, he saw the boy shoot a glance his way before looking down court to where Matt was getting into position. Seth faked left and then he stepped right and launched the ball toward Matt. Jeff heard a gasp coming from the vicinity where Monica was sitting, but his gaze was fixated on the ball.

He watched it arc nicely through the air right over a defender's outstretched fingers. As it lost momentum, Matt stepped forward and reached for the ball. He grabbed it just before a member of the other team rushed in to intercept it. Matt pivoted, and for one awful moment, Jeff was certain he was going to take off without dribbling, but those hours together had paid off for Matt. He bounced the ball and took two beautiful steps toward the basket before leaping into a perfect lay-up.

Jeff watched the ball bounce off the backboard and fall through the hoop. He jumped out of his seat and raised both of his fists in triumph. Matt looked his way and shot him a thumbs-up. Jeff then sought out Seth and yelled, "Good pass, Seth!"

Seth raised his chin in acknowledgement, but he wouldn't look at Jeff. "Oh well," Jeff said to Coach Sands, "one victory at a time."

The coach leaned toward him. "What did you say? Sorry, I didn't catch it."

Jeff patted him on the back. "Nothing."

The coach turned back to the game. "The boys are fired up now." They watched Nathan steal the ball and head down court for an easy lay-up. The crowd of parents behind them cheered.

Jeff watched in astonishment as the team who had looked ready to give up at half time ran circles around the bewildered other team. They still missed shots and had a few turnovers, but for the second half of the game, it was as if a completely different set of boys had emerged from the locker room.

At each timeout, he'd give them pep talks and remind them about simple passing mistakes to avoid. He also did everything he could to praise Seth without being too obvious. Jeff knew he was the one player he most needed to win over in order to have the full respect of the team. Once he caught Seth nodding along with his suggestion, but it was a fleeting nod before Seth returned to his glacier mode.

At the final timeout, they were down by one point, and they only had ten seconds left. They had possession, and Jeff and the coach didn't want to allow any time for the other team to score. Jeff was worried that the other team would try to foul them, knowing that their free throw percentage was pretty low, so he made a daring suggestion.

"Let's put in Dillon." Everybody looked at him, including Dillon, the freshman bench warmer. "Hear me out. Dillon is the most consistent free throw shooter in practice on this team." He watched as they all nodded, looks of understanding beginning to spread. "Seth will throw the ball to Dillon. He's sure to draw a foul. As long as he makes one of his shots, we tie this up and then work like hell to hold them, so we can go into overtime. If they don't foul him immediately, then he needs to pass it back to Seth, so Seth can try for an outside shot or get it to Matt down low. Agreed?'

Coach Sands said, "It's worth a try. Dillon, check in. Nathan, you played a great game, but take a seat, kid."

Jeff watched Dillon, by rights a varsity team member but one with no varsity playing experience as of yet, hustle to check in and then join his teammates on the court. He heard a rumble pass through the parents' section behind him, but he didn't dare turn to gauge their faces.

Seth took the ball out, and Dillon scrambled to get open. As soon as he was, Seth passed him the ball, and just as Jeff had hoped, the other team's big center charged at the small freshman and slapped his arm. The referee called a foul, and Dillon hurried to the free throw line.

Jeff prayed that all those solitary free throws he'd watched the boy do both before and after regular practice would pay off now. Dillon took his first shot, and just like Jeff had seen his shots do hundreds of times before, this one sliced cleanly through the hoop. The team went wild beside him on the bench, and it took all his reserve to not leap off the bench and give a big old 'whoop.'

A hush fell upon the gym as Dillon bounced the ball. Jeff glanced at the clock. There were still eight seconds remaining. That was plenty of time for the other team to score, and his team didn't dare foul since the opposing boys all had proved capable at the free throw line. He watched Dillon bring the ball up past his face and push it toward the basket, his hand curving into the follow-through position.

This time, the ball hit the rim and ping-ponged off each side before coming down on the outside of the net. The parents groaned, but Jeff stood, knowing what was about to happen. Matt leaped and grabbed the ball right before the opposing player got it, and he continued going straight up into a perfect two-handed lay-up. The ball fell neatly through the hoop.

This time, Jeff yelled, and then he called to his players to play a tough defense but not to foul. The other team brought the ball down, and their point guard dribbled right around Dillon. Jeff grimaced, and was afraid to watch as the boy side-stepped and drove in for a lay-up.

The ball circled the rim and fell off. The boy who had shot it managed to grab his own rebound, and Jeff swore under his breath. The boy had to circle to the outside. He looked for somebody to pass to, saw the clock was at one second, so he threw up a Hail Mary. The shot fell short.

Suddenly Jeff was engulfed in boys throwing themselves upon him, hugging and yelling. He patted them all on the backs, and then he joined the line to shake the other team's hands. When the players and coach of the opposing team reached him at the end of the line, they all said, "Good game, Coach." Jeff beamed.

He returned to the bench to grab his binder and to help the boys gather up water bottles and towels. Many parents took the opportunity to talk to him and introduce themselves. Dillon's father was especially jubilant, and he thanked Jeff repeatedly for putting his son in the game.

Monica waited until everyone else moved away from Jeff, and then she approached him. "Congratulations, Jeff."

He smiled. "Thanks." He saw that Coach Sands and the boys had all moved off to gather their gear from the locker room.

"How's it feel?"

Jeff thought about it. "Nothing in my life has even come close to this." He looked down and pretended to straighten his papers while he blinked back the tears that had started to form.

"You did a great job. I was watching you."

He looked at her. "You were?" A mischievous smile tweaked his lips.

She laughed. "Yeah, I was. I never would have believed it if I hadn't seen it with my own eyes, but you are a natural fit for this."

Jeff heard one of the boys yell to him that they were heading out to the bus. He waved in acknowledgement.

Monica said, "Looks like you have to go." She took a step away. "We'll talk later." She turned toward him as she backed away. "After the movie."

"Movie?" Then he grinned as he remembered. "That's right. We won, so I get to take you to a movie."

"You know where to find me," she said, and then she melded into the crowd leaving the gym.

"That I do," Jeff said to himself.

When the basketball season ended, the team had become known as the team to watch out for in the second half of play. This was due to Jeff's innate ability to gauge their weaknesses against each team in the first half of play. In the locker room, everyone listened attentively to his suggestions, and then they implemented them in the second half. More times than not, Jeff's team would come away with a win.

They'd won their first game of district action, but the second team they'd played had simply been too good, so before Jeff was ready for it, his volunteer assistant coaching came to an abrupt end.

He could tell he was despondent about it and that he missed coaching by the way he snapped at his co-workers on job sites. He'd also taken to hanging around The Watering Hole too many nights after work because he didn't know what to do with himself now that he didn't need to go to the school for practices.

The only bright spot in his life was Monica, who had gone on a couple of dates with him. She'd made it clear, though, that she was going to take it slow with him because she wasn't going to let history repeat itself where he was concerned. She had let him kiss her, though, so he was okay with slow as long as her lips were part of the package. The slower the kiss, the better, he thought.

That old feeling, though, had descended upon him. The one that urged him to get the hell out of town and go do something more interesting with his life. The one that told him he wasn't all that great of a coach, and that construction wasn't his future. The one that told him to run now before he actually did hurt Monica again.

He'd called his parents, and he'd been surprised to hear his father's voice. The strong, deep-toned voice of his father from his youth had been replaced by the voice of an old man. His father had also seemed confused about who he was talking to, so his mother had taken the phone.

She'd told him that his father had had a slight stroke a few months back. When he'd asked her why she hadn't told him, she reminded him that they hadn't known where he was. Chagrined, he'd apologized for not letting them know he'd returned to his hometown.

His mother had been surprised to hear this, and her shock had only grown when he told her what he'd been doing.

"Coaching?" she'd said.

"Yeah, coaching. I was actually good at it, Mom." He heard the defensive tone creep into his voice, but he couldn't help it. He was tired of people not believing in him, especially his own parents.

"That's wonderful, Jeffy. So, are you going to come see us anytime soon?"

He could hear the doubt in her question. It had been ten years since he'd gone to visit them and almost a year since he'd last spoken to them. He understood her doubt. He took a deep breath. "That's why I called, Mom. I want to come see you very soon."

"Really?" The excitement in his mother's voice flowed from the telephone into Jeff's ear. "Oh, Jeffy, that would mean the world to us." He heard her start to cry.

"Mom, don't cry. I promise I'll be there. When would be good for you?"

"Oh, anytime, dear. We're not going anywhere." She tried to chuckle, but it fell short.

Jeff heard her set the phone down and then a muffled sound of her blowing her nose. When she picked the phone up again, he said, "Mom, I'll be there in a week. Plan on it."

"I can't wait to see you again. Do you remember how to get here?"

"Yes, Mom. Don't worry about me. Just take care of yourself and Dad, all right?"

"I will, Jeffy. Do you need me to pick you up at the airport?"

"No, I'm going to drive. I'll get a car. Don't worry about me. I'll call you when I'm a few hours out."

"O.K., dear. See you soon."

"Bye, Mom." He heard her hang up the phone. "I love you," he said into dead air.

His boss looked at him askance. "Let me get this straight. You want a few weeks off even though they'll have to be unpaid days since you haven't worked here long enough to earn any vacation time, and you want me to co-sign for you, so you can get a new car, so you can drive to Florida to see your parents."

Jeff nodded and tried to smile. His boss continued to regard him with a scowl. "I promise that when I come back I'll work all the extra hours you want me to to make up for this."

Doug Peters shook his head and took a swig of his lukewarm ice tea that he always carried in his thermos. "I hate to say this, Jeff, but I'm more than a bit worried that you won't come back. More than one person in this town has told me I was a fool to hire you, that you're nothing but a quitter." He paused to look Jeff squarely in the face.

Jeff sighed. "I deserve that criticism. I've earned that reputation, I admit it, but, Doug, I came back here to start over. I want to change. Actually, I need to change."

His boss nodded as he contemplated his employee. "I don't mind letting you have the time off. If you don't come back, well, it's no hair off my back, but I'm not sure about co-signing. Why don't you just fly?"

Jeff swallowed and looked at the toe of his boot. "I want to see the countryside and the road, and I want to be alone with my thoughts to really think about my life and the mess I've made of it."

"Why do you need a new car? Yours seems all right to me." He gestured toward an older model Buick parked at the curb.

"It would make it, I'm sure, but in all my life I've never owned a new car. That one was actually given to me by my parents the last time I visited them." He looked at his boss and decided that he wanted people to know that he meant to change and to change for good. "Doug, I'm almost forty-nine years old. I've never owned anything of my own – not a car, not a home, nothing. I think it's about time I grew up and proved to myself and the world that I'm not a quitter."

"What kind of car do you have in mind?"

Jeff felt a load being lifted. "Actually, I was looking at a small pickup truck the other day."

"A truck? Why didn't you say so before?" Doug slapped him on the back. "Get in. You can show me the truck, and then I'll make up my mind."

Jeff climbed into the work truck. He felt certain that his boss was going to help him on his road to independence.

The day before his departure for Florida, Jeff drove his new black Ford to Monica's. He parked it out front and climbed out in full view of the local gossip group seated at their usual table in front of the large window. He even smiled and waved at them as he entered. Then he went to his booth toward the back.

He ordered and asked the waitress to send Monica out when she had a minute. The customers were few, so he figured he wouldn't have to wait long. He sipped his water and twisted his napkin to squelch his nervousness.

Monica slid into the seat across from him. She took out the bobby pins she wore to keep her hair back while she cooked. "Hey there," she said.

"Hey, yourself. How's business tonight?"

She looked around the sparsely populated room. "You can see for yourself."

He laughed half-heartedly. He saw the puzzled look on her face, so he cut right to the chase. "I wanted to let you know that I'm going away for a few weeks."

She narrowed her eyes. "Away?"

"To Florida, to see my parents."

She shut her eyes and breathed deeply. Then she started to leave. "No surprise there," she started to say before Jeff grabbed her wrist. She waited half on, half off the booth seat.

"I'm coming back," he assured her.

She smirked. "Gee, where have I heard that before?" She wrenched her hand free of his grasp and stood.

"Monica, I swear, I'm coming back. Look, I bought a new truck." He pointed, and she turned her head.

"Pretty," she said. "What does a new truck have to do with anything?"

He didn't know how to explain that it finally meant he was ready to make a commitment. "It just shows that I'll be back because my boss co-signed the loan, and I don't want to let him down." He could tell by the look that crossed her face that he'd just said the wrong thing.

"I see. You don't want to let your boss down. A man you've known all of three months. But you'd gladly let down the woman you were supposed to marry, the woman you said you loved, the woman you'd known for years." She put her hands on the table and leaned in toward him, so the others wouldn't hear. "Do I have that straight?"

"That's not what I meant."

"Save it, Jeff. Have fun in Florida. Give your parents my best." She walked off and then turned for one parting shot. "I'll see you when you get back. Oh wait, I guess I won't see you."

He watched her walk into the kitchen and then a few moments later, he heard the back door open and slam shut. He looked toward the table of locals. They raised their coffee mugs in a salute to him before resuming their chatter.

When his waitress returned with his food, he asked her to put it in a box to go. He then paid, and left a note for Monica promising to come back in a few weeks. He said he'd been personally invited by Seth to attend his graduation and that he didn't plan to miss that. He could only hope that Monica would believe him and be happy to see him when he returned because she was the main reason he wanted to come back.

Two weeks later, Jeff strolled along the beach near his parents' retirement complex. His father drifted between moments of supreme lucidity to moments of utter confusion. He was attempting to convince his mother to hire a part-time nurse to help her out. He knew, though, that she'd need some financial help from him to pull it off.

He thought that with a lot of extra hours he could make enough to pay for his truck, rent a small apartment and send his mom some money each month. He'd suggested they move back to their hometown to be closer to him, but she wouldn't even hear of it. She made it very clear to him that they were happy in Florida and that their lives were there now.

He regretted not being there for them enough over the years, and he'd apologized numerous times to both his parents. They assured him that everything was all right and that they'd always believed he'd find his way eventually. His father, in one of his good moments, had quipped, "Sometimes you have to leave home to come home."

Jeff thought about that as he walked. Was he finally home? Right back where he started? He threw a shell back out to sea and watched the gulls dance upon the water searching for their next meal.

Suddenly, he turned and headed toward his parents' home. He was ready to tell them good-bye. He wanted to get home himself.

As he drove into town a few days later, Jeff passed the main cemetery. On a whim, he slowed his truck and signaled his turn into the second entrance, the one that led to the newer graves. He drove slowly along the gravel path, craning his neck to read the names on the tombstones. When he found what he was looking for, he stopped, got out of the truck and removed his cap.

Approaching Monica's husband's gravesite, he noted the metal sign poking out of the ground with a farm silhouette cut into it along with the word "Dad." He paused, not entirely sure why he had stopped.

He read the engraving on the headstone, and noticed that in death Monica's Bobby would always be known as Robert. He decided to use what the man was familiar with in life.

"Hello, Bob," he started before looking around to be sure he was alone. "You don't know me. Well, you might have heard of me from Monica, none of it good, I'm sure. I'm Jeff, the one who left her without saying goodbye. Lucky for you I did. You were smart enough to see what I couldn't back then."

He knelt before the large stone and placed a hand upon it. "I'm sorry I never got to meet you. Everyone says you were a great guy. You probably would have decked me, though, knowing what I'd done to your wife back then. I want you to know, though, that I've changed and that I've come back to stay. I still love Monica, and I hope to win her over. I think she's starting to like me again.

"You've got a great son, there. He looks like you in the pictures I've seen of you at the café. He didn't like me much at first, but he came around. He's even invited me to his graduation, so that's something. He was one of the best basketball players on our team. Says he's going to study biology in college. Not quite sure what he's going to do with it, but I'm sure he'll figure it out.

"I've been offered the head coaching job, and I plan to take it. You're the first to know." He stood and placed his cap back on his head. "Well, Bob, I'm sorry you can't be here to see your family and the fine man your son is becoming, but I just wanted to stop and let you know that I aim to be there for them. I hope that's all right with you." He tipped his cap. "Be seeing you."

As the spring breeze blew through the young trees of the cemetery, Jeff got in his truck and headed into town.

Author's Note

This book is dedicated to the memory of my best
...d, Amy Marie Vojtech Beran. We met during the first
.ester of our freshman year at the University of Nebraska –
.coln way back in the fall of 1986. Not only did we live on
: same dorm floor, but we also happened to be enrolled in the
.ne Spanish class, so we got to know each other well while
.alking to and from class.

Thank goodness for small coincidences like that which
.ecome life-changing pivotal moments in our lives. For thirty-
.wo years I was blessed with her as my friend, and for some
odd reason she chose to remain my friend even though we were
very different. She was taken from me, and from everyone who
loved her, much too soon when she was only aged fifty years,
five months and twelve days; and I spent my fiftieth birthday
giving her eulogy at her memorial service.

Cancer may have killed her body, but it can never take
the countless wonderful memories I have of her, and her joyful
spirit lives on in everyone who was fortunate enough to have
known her.

She and I graduated from the same college, we got
married the same summer (her marriage lasted while mine did
not), we had our first children (sons) only months apart and we
each ended up with two children (she, two boys; me, a boy and
a girl), we lived far apart yet we got together regularly, we spent
many 4th of July celebrations together, and we cheered and
encouraged one another with our endeavors.

Amy was my biggest literary fan and supporter. When
I published my first novel, *The Clearwater House*, she
immediately bought multiple copies to give to family and
friends, and she talked up the book and my other writings
whenever she could.

After she was diagnosed with stage-four cancer, I sent her a little pick-me-up note in the mail every day because I believe in the power of words and because Amy loved self-help and motivational books. I hoped and prayed that those words of encouragement and love would work the miracle that medicine couldn't. They didn't, but they did cheer her immensely, so they served an important purpose.

In one of my very last notes to her, I promised that I would dedicate my next book to her. I'm not sure if she really heard my promise or not because by the time my note arrived at her house in Texas she was already unconscious and only days away from her death. When I'd mailed it from my home in Nebraska, she'd still been lucid, but the end came fairly swiftly, and I'd put off telling her of my plan because I hadn't really known how bad she'd become until it was too late. However, her sister read the note to her, and she believes that Amy heard my promise. I hope she did.

This book is a collection of what I consider to be my sweeter stories and poems because Amy was the sweetest and kindest person I've ever known. If you've enjoyed them even a little, I've fulfilled my final promise to my best friend; I hope you've felt at least a tiny bit of the love I had for her emanating from these pages.

Thank you for reading this book, and, Amy, wherever you are, thank you for being my friend.